Change of Heart

Judith Keim

BOOKS BY JUDITH KEIM

THE HARTWELL WOMEN SERIES:

The Talking Tree – 1
Sweet Talk – 2
Straight Talk – 3
Baby Talk – 4
The Hartwell Women – Boxed Set

THE BEACH HOUSE HOTEL SERIES:

Breakfast at The Beach House Hotel – 1
Lunch at The Beach House Hotel – 2
Dinner at The Beach House Hotel – 3
Christmas at The Beach House Hotel – 4
Margaritas at The Beach House Hotel – 5 (2021)
Dessert at The Beach House Hotel – 6 (2022)

THE FAT FRIDAYS GROUP:

Fat Fridays – 1
Sassy Saturdays – 2
Secret Sundays – 3

SALTY KEY INN BOOKS:

Finding Me – 1
Finding My Way – 2
Finding Love – 3
Finding Family – 4

CHANDLER HILL INN BOOKS:

Going Home – 1
Coming Home – 2
Home at Last – 3

SEASHELL COTTAGE BOOKS:

A Christmas Star
Change of Heart
A Summer of Surprises
A Road Trip to Remember
The Beach Babes – (2022)

DESERT SAGE INN BOOKS:

The Desert Flowers – Rose – 1
The Desert Flowers – Lily – 2 (Fall 2021)
The Desert Flowers – Willow – 3 (2022)
The Desert Flowers – Mistletoe & Holly – 4 (2022)

Winning BIG – a little love story for all ages

For more information: **http://amzn.to/2jamIaF**

PRAISE FOR JUDITH KEIM'S NOVELS

THE BEACH HOUSE HOTEL SERIES

"Love the characters in this series. This series was my first introduction to Judith Keim. She is now one of my favorites. Looking forward to reading more of her books."

BREAKFAST AT THE BEACH HOUSE HOTEL is an easy, delightful read that offers romance, family relationships, and strong women learning to be stronger. Real life situations filter through the pages. Enjoy!"

LUNCH AT THE BEACH HOUSE HOTEL – "This series is such a joy to read. You feel you are actually living with them. Can't wait to read the latest one."

DINNER AT THE BEACH HOUSE HOTEL – "A Terrific Read! As usual, Judith Keim did it again. Enjoyed immensely. Continue writing such pleasantly reading books for all of us readers."

CHRISTMAS AT THE BEACH HOUSE HOTEL – "Not Just Another Christmas Novel. This is book number four in the series and my introduction to Judith Keim's writing. I wasn't disappointed. The characters are dimensional and engaging. The plot is well crafted and advances at a pleasing pace. The Florida location is interesting and warming. It was a delight to read a romance novel with mature female protagonists. Ann and Rhoda have life experiences that enrich the story. It's a clever book about friends and extended family. Buy copies for your book group pals and enjoy this seasonal read."

THE HARTWELL WOMEN SERIES – Books 1 – 4

"This was an EXCELLENT series. When I discovered Judith Keim, I read all of her books back to back. I thoroughly enjoyed the women Keim has written about. They are believable and you want to just jump into their lives and be their friends! I can't wait for any upcoming books!"

"I fell into Judith Keim's Hartwell Women series and have read & enjoyed all of her books in every series. Each centers around a strong & interesting woman character and their family interaction. Good reads that leave you wanting more."

THE FAT FRIDAYS GROUP – Books 1 – 3

"Excellent story line for each character, and an insightful representation of situations which deal with some of the contemporary issues women are faced with today."

"I love this author's books. Her characters and their lives are realistic. The power of women's friendships is a common and beautiful theme that is threaded throughout this story."

THE SALTY KEY INN SERIES

FINDING ME – *"I thoroughly enjoyed the first book in this series and cannot wait for the others! The characters are endearing with the same struggles we all encounter. The setting makes me feel like I am a guest at The Salty Key Inn...relaxed, happy & light-hearted! The men are yummy and the women strong. You can't get better than that! Happy Reading!"*

FINDING MY WAY- *"Loved the family dynamics as well as uncertain emotions of dating and falling in love.*

Appreciated the morals and strength of parenting throughout. Just couldn't put this book down."

<u>*FINDING LOVE*</u> – *"I waited for this book because the first two was such good reads. This one didn't disappoint.... Judith Keim always puts substance into her books. This book was no different, I learned about PTSD, accepting oneself, there is always going to be problems but stick it out and make it work. Just the way life is. In some ways a lot like my life. Judith is right, it needs another book and I will definitely be reading it. Hope you choose to read this series, you will get so much out of it."*

<u>*FINDING FAMILY*</u> – *"Completing this series is like eating the last chip. Love Judith's writing, and her female characters are always smart, strong, vulnerable to life and love experiences."*

"This was a refreshing book. Bringing the heart and soul of the family to us."

CHANDLER HILL INN SERIES

<u>*GOING HOME*</u> – *"I absolutely could not put this book down. Started at night and read late into the middle of the night. As a child of the '60s, the Vietnam war was front and center so this resonated with me. All the characters in the book were so well developed that the reader felt like they were friends of the family."*

"I was completely immersed in this book, with the beautiful descriptive writing, and the authors' way of bringing her characters to life. I felt like I was right inside her story."

COMING HOME – *"Coming Home is a winner. The characters are well-developed, nuanced and likable. Enjoyed the vineyard setting, learning about wine growing and seeing the challenges Cami faces in running and growing a business. I look forward to the next book in this series!"*

"Coming Home was such a wonderful story. The author has a gift for getting the reader right to the heart of things."

HOME AT LAST – *"In this wonderful conclusion, to a heartfelt and emotional trilogy set in Oregon's stunning wine country, Judith Keim has tied up the Chandler Hill series with the perfect bow."*

"Overall, this is truly a wonderful addition to the Chandler Hill Inn series. Judith Keim definitely knows how to perfectly weave together a beautiful and heartfelt story."

"The storyline has some beautiful scenes along with family drama. Judith Keim has created characters with interactions that are believable and some of the subjects the story deals with are poignant."

SEASHELL COTTAGE BOOKS

A CHRISTMAS STAR – *"Love, laughter, sadness, great food, and hope for the future, all in one book. It doesn't get any better than this stunning read."*

"A Christmas Star is a heartwarming Christmas story featuring endearing characters. So many Christmas books are set in snowbound places...it was a nice change to read a Christmas story that takes place on a warm sandy beach!" Susan Peterson

CHANGE OF HEART – *"CHANGE OF HEART is the summer read we've all been waiting for. Judith Keim is a master at creating fascinating characters that are simply irresistible. Her stories leave you with a big smile on your face and a heart bursting with love."*

~Kellie Coates Gilbert, author of the popular Sun Valley Series

A SUMMER OF SURPRISES – *"The story is filled with a roller coaster of emotions and self-discovery. Finding love again and rebuilding family relationships."*

"Ms. Keim uses this book as an amazing platform to show that with hard emotional work, belief in yourself and love, the scars of abuse can be conquered. It in no way preaches, it's a lovely story with a happy ending."

"The character development was excellent. I felt I knew these people my whole life. The story development was very well thought out I was drawn [in] from the beginning."

DESERT SAGE INN BOOKS

THE DESERT FLOWERS – ROSE – *"The Desert Flowers - Rose, is the first book in the new series by Judith Keim. I always look forward to new books by Judith Keim, and this one is definitely a wonderful way to begin The Desert Sage Inn Series!"*

"In this first of a series, we see each woman come into her own and view new beginnings even as they must take this tearful journey as they slowly lose a dear friend. This is a very well written book with well-developed and likable main characters. It was interesting and enlightening as the first

portion of this saga unfolded. I very much enjoyed this book and I do recommend it"

"Judith Keim is one of those authors that you can always depend on to give you a great story with fantastic characters. I'm excited to know that she is writing a new series and after reading book 1 in the series, I can't wait to read the rest of the books."!

Change of Heart

A Seashell Cottage Book

Judith Keim

Wild Quail Publishing

Change of Heart is a work of fiction. Names, characters, places, public or private institutions, corporations, towns, and incidents are the product of the author's imagination or are used fictitiously. Any resemblance to actual events, locales, or persons, living or dead, is coincidental.

wildquail.pub@gmail.com

[www.judithkeim.com,](www.judithkeim.com)

Published in the United States of America by:

Wild Quail Publishing
PO Box 171332
Boise, ID 83717-1332

ISBN# 978-1-7327494-3-6

Dedication

This book is dedicated to my husband, Peter, who has never had a change of heart about our being together. Thanks for all these wonderful years! Love you!

CHAPTER ONE

Emerson "Em" Jordan closed her eyes as the sound of the music enveloped her in a cloud of happiness. She was taking part in her sister's wedding at a resort along the Gulf Coast of Florida, but in her mind, it might as well be her own celebration. The dreamy man holding her hadn't proposed yet, but she was pretty sure he soon would. She'd dropped all kinds of hints about a Valentine engagement and a wedding a year later on Valentine's Day. It had been a dream of hers from the time she was a girl.

In a burst of noise, the image of dancing disappeared. Em sat bolt upright in bed and stared out her bedroom window. Through the glass she saw a colorful display of fireworks, and then she heard another loud bang.

Em lowered her head into her hands and sobbed as she recalled what had happened earlier that evening. The Fourth of July picnic turned into a disaster when her boyfriend, Jared King, had announced he needed to talk to her about something important. When she saw his serious expression and how he was shuffling his feet, a nervous habit of his, her stomach did a somersault. She'd watched her family and friends head out to walk the four blocks to the town park to watch the fireworks and wished she could run after them.

As he studied her, Jared took a deep breath and let it out slowly. " Like I said, we need to talk. I can't do this any longer. I love you, Em, I do, but I'm not in love with you. It's time to call it quits."

She lifted a hand to her cheek as if he'd slapped her and

reeled away from him. "You're breaking up with me? Like this?"

He sighed. "It's not working. And it's not going to."

Shocked, she stared at him wide eyed, certain she was about to throw up. She staggered over to one of the picnic tables set up in her parents' backyard and plopped down on the bench beside it. Bending over, Em put her head between her legs hoping to stop the world around her from spinning.

"Are you all right?" Jared asked, standing a safe distance from her.

Anger straightened her. "I'm not all right, Jared King! You just broke my heart! I'm not sure I'll ever be all right again!"

"I'm sorry, Em. I really am." He'd simply turned and walked away, leaving her to clutch her body, too weak to run after him, her dreams scattered around her like crushed blossoms.

For the next few weeks, Em managed to continue working at the family's flower shop, but, in truth, she barely functioned. Jagged edges of her broken heart kept poking her insides, taking away her breath, stealing the cheerfulness she usually wore like a comfortable, old sweater to protect her. Not even the sweet smell of freesia in the flower shop could chase away the pain of Jared's words. It was a good thing that Jared lived in New York City, an hour away. She couldn't bear to see him. She returned to her task of putting together a basket of summer wild flowers. She loved making things look as natural as possible, and woven baskets were good containers for the colorful blooms.

"How are you coming with the Williams order?" her grandmother, Julia Jordan, asked as she entered the work area.

"Almost done," Em said, standing back to appraise the placement of flowers.

"Looks wonderful, sweetheart." After the death of her husband many years ago, her grandmother had opened the flower shop she'd named Rainbow's End in their small, upstate town of Ellenton, New York. In her mid-seventies, Julia was still an attractive woman with gray hair cut in a bob, sparkling eyes, and a face that reflected beauty enhanced by her inner peace. Em smiled. Of all the people in the family, her grandmother understood her best. Two optimists who came together. Didn't the name of her flower shop say it all?

Later, as Em was putting together a bouquet for a husband to send as a surprise to his wife, she couldn't hold back the question that had been gnawing at her insides. "Gran, Jared told me he loved me, but he wasn't in love with me." It still hurt to say the words.

Her grandmother's blue-eyed gaze, so like her own, rested on her thoughtfully. "He wasn't the right man. Don't worry. You have time."

"But, Gran, I'll be thirty-two next spring! And every man I meet ends up being wrong for me. First, there was Garrett. He turned out to be gay, for heaven's sake."

Gran clucked her tongue. "The opera singer in New York was the hardest for me to imagine your marrying. Imagine him already married to a concert pianist on tour!"

"Yeah, that was another bad time. He'd told me he was lonely. I thought it was because he was living so far away from family. I didn't imagine him having a wife. Neither he nor news releases ever mentioned it."

Gran placed a hand on Em's shoulder. "I'm so glad you agreed to come back to Ellenton to live. The trouble with you, Emerson, is you want to believe only the best in everybody in every aspect of your life. That makes you a special person, but one who is bound to get hurt."

"I know everyone teases me about being a Pollyanna, but I'd prefer to live happily rather than face doom and gloom all the time."

Gran drew her into a hug. "Maybe it's time for you to have a change of heart, become a little more careful, more realistic. Nothing too drastic, mind you."

Em laid the red rose in her hand on the workbench. "Are you saying it's time for me to grow up?"

"In a way," she said kindly, brushing Em's long, blond hair away from her face. "You and I, we're two of a kind. We dream of what could be without seeing things as they really are. Who knew my husband would die at a young age, leaving me with a young son to raise and no money?"

"I'm glad you decided to open a flower shop. I love it." Em drew a shaky breath. "But, Gran, I hope you understand I can't go through Valentine's Day working here. That's when Jared was supposed to propose to me."

"No worries. I already figured that out. Besides, my neighbor, Marilyn, needs to find a job. I promised I'd hire her on a part-time basis, thinking if she worked out, I'd bring her on board full-time before the holidays. That will give you a chance to start thinking about opening the landscape design business you've been talking about."

Relief sprinted through Em. She'd never want to hurt her grandmother, but no way, no how could she endure making beautiful bouquets, lovely nosegays, or single-rose love letters of her own design for others during the romantic time of Valentine's Day.

As fall hurried through September and October toward the holidays, depression hit Em hard. She had no intention of dating anyone, but still, holidays were no time to be alone. She was struggling to find something to make her feel more positive about her life.

"Why don't you go away for Valentine's Day?" her sister, Elena, suggested. "I have the perfect place for you. Remember the house Mom and Dad thought of renting for my wedding? Seashell Cottage? Maybe that's something you could do. Get a friend to share the cost, then go and have fun! I'll text you the number for the rental agency."

Em felt like magically flying through space to Philadelphia to give her sister a hug. "That's perfect! I'll look them up on the web and give them a call. Thank you, sis. That would be a wonderful break for me—a break I really need. I'm pretty sure I can talk Kat into going with me. She's single again and is as depressed as I am."

They chatted for a few minutes longer, and then Em clicked off the call and hurried over to the computer in the flower shop. She found the website easily, and before she could stop to think about it, she called the rental office.

"Palm Rentals and Realty," a cheerful voice answered. When Em queried her about Seashell Cottage, the woman at the end of the line said, "Funny you should call. The young, married couple who were going to rent it cancelled yesterday. It seems she's pregnant and won't be able to travel at that time. Any chance you could take all ten days they had? It's the only free time we have for the winter."

"I think so. Let me speak to my friend, and I'll confirm that with you by the end of the day."

Em clicked off the call and immediately called Kat.

"Whassup?" said Kat.

"I've got the perfect plan for Valentine's Day," said Em, unable to hold back her excitement. "I want you to go to Florida with me for ten days. Go to the website for Seashell

Cottage and tell me what you think. We could share the cost, have a great getaway, and forget our dating troubles."

A customer walked into the flower shop. "I've got to go. Call me back ASAP."

With a new spring in her step, Em went to the front of the store and took down the information for an anniversary bouquet. The older, gray-haired gentleman dictating what he wanted was adorable. Wearing jeans and a bright-blue flannel shirt that matched his eyes, he seemed full of life as he spoke.

"Where do you want this delivered?" Em asked him.

The man gave her the address of the St. Mark's Rehabilitation Center. "This isn't for my wife. I promised an old, deceased friend that I'd take care of this for him for as long as his wife lived."

"You mean before he died he asked you to do this for him?" Em's eyes filled with tears. It was such a romantic gesture.

"Yes. I live in the next town, but each year I come and place the order for him."

"I've been working here for only a few months, but that is the sweetest thing I've ever heard," gushed Em, blinking rapidly to stave off fresh tears.

Just then, her grandmother entered the store carrying a small pile of mail. She waved at the gentleman. "Well, Michael, nice to see you. That time of year again?"

"Hi, Julia. It's good to see you." He exchanged smiles with Em's grandmother.

"I was sorry to learn about Angie's death," Julia told him. "How are you doing?"

He shook his head. "After a year of mourning, I think I'm finally ready to accept she's gone. In fact, I was hoping I could convince you to go to dinner with me. May I call you?"

"I'd like that, Michael. Thank you." A rosy hue filled Gran's cheeks.

Observing them, Em's heart filled. Was this a love story in the making? From the looks they were giving each other, it might be. She could already see how perfect the two of them would be together.

Michael shuffled his feet. "Well, I guess I'd better go. I'm meeting a bunch of guys for coffee. We do this once a week."

"That sounds very nice," said Julia. "Sort of like my group of women meeting for wine and talk every week."

They stood facing one another. Em wondered if they realized the smiles stretched across their faces were telling a story of their own.

Michael turned to go and then turned back. "I'll call you later today, Julia."

"That will be fine. I'll wait for your call."

After he left the shop, Em faced her grandmother. "I think he likes you, Gran. *Really* likes you, if you know what I mean."

Her grandmother shook her head. "That's what I meant the other day, Emerson. You take a moment and weave it into a romantic fairy tale. A bit more realism will keep you from getting hurt. Michael is a lovely man, as was his wife, Angie. We'll go out to dinner and enjoy ourselves, but that's it. I have no intention of falling in love at my age. Why would I want to change my life? I have all the freedom I want without getting entangled with someone else."

Em let out a sigh. "Okay. I won't mention it again."

"That's my darling granddaughter," Julia said, patting her on the shoulder, a little sign of encouragement. "Now let's see what else is happening here."

She bustled away toward the back of the shop, leaving Em to wonder why her grandmother wasn't the least bit romantic. Maybe, as you got as old as her grandmother, dating, marriage, and everything that went with them just weren't important anymore.

Em was cutting the thorns off the stem of a yellow rose when Kat returned her phone call.

"What do you think?" Em whispered a silent prayer for a positive response.

"I'm in. I can pay my share. The place is fantastic, and I have leftover vacation from this year that I can apply to next year and not miss out on my normal number of vacation days. I've already checked out bikinis online. I found a black one that even I think is dangerous."

Em laughed. Kat had a beautiful, tall, lean body and liked to show it off. This easy acceptance of herself was part of the fun of being with her.

"I'm so happy you'll do this. Knowing I won't have to cope with Valentine's Day will help me get through Thanksgiving and the Christmas holidays."

"Yeah, I know what you mean. I've gone out a couple of times since Dave suddenly decided we weren't a couple, but I'm sick and tired of the dating scene here in the city."

"Come on out to the country for a weekend," said Em. "It'll give you a change of pace."

"I might do that," said Kat. "A change will do me good. I'd better go. Boss man is coming."

Em clicked off the call. Her previous boss didn't condone use of cell phones during work hours. In his early sixties, he didn't understand younger people's use of social media or the need to even occasionally, not frequently, check one's cell for updates and social news.

As Em called the realty company, excitement poured through her like a balm to heal her wounds. "We'll take it for the full ten days." She smiled as she uttered the words, already feeling better about the future. Maybe Gran was right, she thought. She didn't need a man to make her happy. She had girlfriends like Kat.

###

The week leading up to Thanksgiving began the blur of long days preparing fall flower arrangements for individual customers and business clients as far away as New York City who depended on Rainbow's End to decorate their offices. It hadn't been easy for Gran to build such a strong business, but she had a way of appealing to people with a sense of honesty that most liked.

Thanksgiving was spent at her parents' house, with Elena, her husband, Andrew, and their dachshund, Daisy, a nice addition to the usual presence of her parents and Gran.

After the Thanksgiving meal, Elena and Em were happy to do the dishes for an opportunity to talk privately.

"I want to thank you again for the suggestion of renting Seashell Cottage in February," Em told her sister. "It's made such a big difference to me to have that to look forward to."

"Have you heard anything from Jared?" Elena asked, giving her a worried look.

"Not one word," said Em, as she stacked dishes beside the sink. "It's just as well. I've decided to follow Gran's idea and not worry about finding a man. As she says, she has a lot of freedom, and she wants to keep it that way. Me, too. I'm done with dating."

Elena finished rinsing a large serving platter and studied her. "That doesn't sound like you, Em. You've always wanted to be married, have a big, fancy wedding, and a lot of kids. As a young girl, you had more dolls than anyone else, declaring them your family."

"I know, but Gran says I have to be more realistic, that I always fantasize about things. Better for me to change, stop looking at relationships through pretty rose-colored glasses, and protect my heart."

Elena frowned at her. "She's telling you that because you two are so alike. Gran's heart got broken, but that doesn't mean yours will be broken again."

Em held up her hand to stop her. "I don't want to talk about it. Right now, I have to get through Christmas and New Year's, then I can relax and think about my trip to Florida."

"Okay. I won't say another word, but I do worry about you. How are things going here?"

"I love working in the flower shop. And I've been thinking about going into the landscape design business. That's another reason for not rushing into a new relationship."

"Your own business? Like you always talked about before you got into marketing?" Elena asked. "That's a great idea. You're so creative! I wish I had your talent."

"Ha! You're like Dad. All business. What would Andrew have done without your support to get him through medical school?"

"Yeah, but accounting is boring to some people," sighed Elena.

"Jared wasn't boring," said Em, and stopped. "Come to think of it, sometimes he was. Especially when he discussed some of the work he was doing for clients. Not actual names, of course, but numbers and details that seemed very complicated and, yes, downright dull."

Em smiled at her sister. "But you're not boring. In fact, you're bright and beautiful." Two years older than she, Elena was a pretty down-to-earth person who exuded a lot of warmth along with a quick, eager brain. She had the Jordan strong nose, and a hint of pink in her blond tresses, making them a strawberry-blond that nicely offset her green eyes.

Elena hugged Em. "Thanks. I need to hear things like that, especially now that I'm starting to show my pregnancy and am feeling quite heavy."

"Remember, if it's a girl, you promised I could be her godmother."

"That's a deal. But I think Andrew is hoping it's a boy."

"I can't wait to become an aunt," said Em.

"Oh, Em," said Elena, turning to her as she wiped a pot dry with a kitchen towel, "you have no idea how wonderful you are. When a guy really falls for you, it's going to be hard and for forever."

"I hope so. I love it when I see how some people are with one another. Let me tell you about a friend of Gran's. It's the sweetest story ever." Em slid the pot Elena handed her into its proper place in the cupboard and poured herself a cup of hot decaf from the coffee maker.

Sitting opposite her sister at the kitchen table, she told the story of Michael Leaman, the act he did for a deceased friend, and how blushed Gran's cheeks had become when he'd asked her to go to dinner with him.

"Did she go?"

"Yes, but she hasn't said a word about it since, and I've put off asking her about it, hoping she'll mention it on her own. Of course, we're so busy at the flower shop at this time of year, we never seem to take a break together."

"How is it working out for you having to live with Mom and Dad?" said Elena. "We haven't had the chance to really talk about it. Quick phone calls and texts don't compare to a heart-to-heart talk, like now."

"I'm glad it's temporary. After I come back from Florida, the new townhouses by the river should be completed. I've put a deposit down on one of them."

"Ah, here are my girls," said their mother, taking a seat at the kitchen table.

Though not related, Donna Jordan with her prematurely gray hair and bright-blue eyes looked remarkably like her mother-in-law—tall, slim, and with aristocratic facial features that she'd passed on to her daughters. Their father had, apparently, taken a ribbing for the likeness when he'd first brought Donna to meet his mother. But neither of the women complained; they'd hit it off at the beginning, though after a while, Donna extricated herself from the flower shop and went back to school for her teaching degree. Word was, they liked each other better that way.

Talk continued about the upcoming holidays. Elena and Andrew would spend time in Philadelphia with his parents instead of coming to Ellenton. Though her mother tried to be fair about it, Em knew how deeply disappointed her mother was about the arrangements. She liked her daughters around her.

Gran entered the kitchen and joined them. "My favorite part of the holiday. Being with all my girls."

Elena patted the empty chair beside her. "Sit right here, Gran."

Em gazed around the table at the others, and her heart filled. People called her unrealistically optimistic, but why wouldn't she be when she was lucky enough to be part of a family like hers?

The lights blinked off and on again.

"Looks like the storm that's been forecast for this afternoon is coming in," said Gran.

A shiver crossed Em's shoulders. Life could be so unpredictable.

CHAPTER TWO

With Elena and Andrew visiting Elena's in-laws for Christmas, the holiday seemed empty. Even Daisy was missed, though the dachshund was a bundle of energy, sometimes causing distress to Walter, the tabby cat Em's mother had adopted as a bedraggled kitten.

"Are you sure you don't want to come with us to the Davis's New Year's Eve party?" her mother asked. "You might run into some of your old friends."

"I'm positive." Em suppressed a shudder thinking of all the questions she'd be asked about why she'd left New York and if she was about to be engaged to the man whom she'd brought home for the Fourth of July celebration.

After her parents left, Em sat alone in the family room. The fire glowed a pretty orange in the fireplace and seeped a welcome warmth into the cool room. Curled up on the couch, she clicked on the television eager to see another Christmas movie. When she realized it was nearing the end of the story, she pressed the mute button and turned away from the screen. This film would, no doubt, be shown another time, and she didn't want to ruin it by seeing the end.

Fighting loneliness, she got up, went into her bedroom, and stared at the summery clothes inside her closet. The trip to Florida would be good for her.

On a whim, she called Kat. When she heard Kat's request to leave a message, she was pleased to think of her out partying. Kat was someone who'd always find a good time.

Em returned to the couch, wrapped a blanket around

herself, and settled down to watch other people's lives unfold on the television screen.

After the holiday rush was over, putting the flower shop back into order took time. Em didn't mind. Each day spent doing that brought her closer to February and her vacation.

One evening, she was finishing up for the day, exhausted from training Marilyn on year-end procedures as Gran had directed, when her cell phone rang. She checked caller ID. *Kat.*

"Hey, girl! I haven't heard from you in forever!" cried Em. "Did you get my messages?"

"Yes, I got them," said Kat, her voice unusually quiet, reserved.

"So, where were you? Why didn't you answer my calls or my texts? Is everything all right?"

"Yes and no," Kat said.

"So, give me the good news first," said Em. She didn't understand why some people always wanted the bad news first.

"Okay," Kat said, letting out a long, slow breath. "The good news is I'm dating a wonderful guy. He's even talked marriage and a future together."

"What? How long has this been going on?" squealed Em, thrilled for her friend.

"Since New Year's Eve," Kat replied quietly. "We were invited to the same party. We got to talking and suddenly everything clicked."

"If that's the good news, what's the bad news?" Em asked, as a knot of suspicion began to unravel inside her.

"It's Jared." After a long stretch of silence, Kat said, "I'm so sorry. I didn't mean for it to happen, but as it turns out, we're perfect for each other. We mesh, you know?"

Em gripped the edge of the table and hung on as the room began to spin. It had to be a bad dream. A nightmare.

"I'm sorry, but I'm cancelling the trip to Florida with you," continued Kat. "Don't worry, I'll pay any fees myself. I feel so bad about this, but it's way too late. I can't turn my back on Jared. I love him."

"He's already talked with you about the future?" croaked Em, her voice high and tight.

"Yes," Kat said.

On legs gone weak, Em gingerly made her way to a sink, wet a cloth with cold water, and lifted it to her forehead. "I see."

"I don't want you to worry about Seashell Cottage. I'm going to pay all cancellation fees. That's only fair."

Only fair? The whole scenario was horribly, impossibly unfair. Couldn't Kat see that?"

Em set down the cloth and forced herself to stand erect. "I'm not cancelling the trip to Florida. The idea of staying at Seashell Cottage has kept me going for months."

"Who are you going to get to stay with you?" Kat asked.

"That really isn't your concern," Em said, forcing a firmness to her voice that she wasn't easily capable of at the moment.

Kat sighed. "I suppose you hate me. I wouldn't blame you if you did. I would've told you before now, but it happened so fast I wasn't sure it would last. Now, I know it will, because he says he feels the same way about me as I do about him."

"Look, Kat. I've got to go," she said, unable to tolerate another minute of Kat's exuberance about the man who'd broken her heart.

"I'm sorry. So very sorry," Kat said, and clicked off the call.

Em lowered herself to the floor, unable to stop the tears

trailing down her cheeks.

Later, after she felt as if there were no tears left inside, Em lifted her phone and called her sister.

After Em had done her best to get the details out without a few more rounds of tears, Elena said, “I’m so sorry. That stinks. I can’t believe Kat would ever do something like that to you. You were best friends, weren’t you?”

“Not really. We were city friends who shared an apartment with others,” Em answered truthfully. “And office friends.”

“Still, that hurts,” Elena said. “What are you going to do about the cottage? How can you afford to pay for it yourself?”

“I can’t, but I couldn’t let Kat know that. Besides, like I told her, the idea of this vacation has kept me going through the lonely holidays, and I can’t, I won’t stay in town for Valentine’s Day. What am I going to do? Do you know of anyone who would have the time and money to share the cottage with me?”

“Not offhand, but let me think about it. Soldier on. Things are bound to get better.”

“I know, because they can’t get worse,” Em sniffed, stemming another flow of tears.

CHAPTER THREE

Uncertainty filled the following days. Em had no idea how she could pull off the vacation she'd wanted and now needed more than ever. Working in the flower shop helped to divert her attention. The varied colors, textures, and aromas of the flowers and plants inside the store calmed the waves of betrayal that sometimes washed over her, questioning her judgment of character. What bothered her most was Jared's willingness to discuss marriage so quickly with Kat. She'd waited in vain for months for him to propose.

Gran came up to her one day and squeezed her shoulder. "Things are meant to be," she said quietly. "Whenever a window closes, a door opens. Even when you can't imagine it, your life will improve. I don't want you to worry about that vacation you planned. Something will work out. I wish I could pay for it myself, but I can't."

Just when Em thought she couldn't produce another tear, her eyes filled. "That's so sweet, Gran, but I could never let you do that, anyway. It just wouldn't feel right." She hugged her. "I love you so much!"

Gran smiled as she hugged Em back. "Love you too. Now let's get that order ready for the country club."

Em was putting the finishing touches on the flower arrangement for the entry hall at the country club when her cell rang. *Elena.*

"Hi, sis. What's up?"

"I'm calling because I think I've found the perfect person to share your time at the Seashell Cottage. You're definitely not looking for any romance in the future, right?"

"Are you kidding? No, no, and no. Why?"

"Do you remember Devin Gerard, the best man at my wedding?"

"Vaguely. I was so wrapped up in Jared that I hardly paid attention to him. We had the obligatory dance at the wedding, but I was watching Jared the whole time."

"Okay. That's a good thing. Apparently, Devin's ex-girlfriend had no interest in his profession and complained about it all the time. They broke up a year ago, and he has no intention of letting any woman destroy what he's worked so hard for. He's just come back from six months in Costa Rica, and he's exhausted. When I suggested a vacation at Seashell Cottage, he was intrigued—until he heard he'd be sharing the cottage with you."

"What? Really?" She frowned. "If he feels that way, why would I want to share the cottage with him?"

"Because he's a decent guy who doesn't play around. Frankly, I think you need this vacation. It's a beautiful spot and you've looked forward to this break for a long time. The last few months have been horrible for you, and it's beginning to show."

"What do you mean?"

"I mean the whole loving, kind, happy-go-lucky attitude that makes you so special is fading away, and I want to see it restored. The cottage is big enough the two of you won't be in each other's way, neither one of you is interested in the other, and you both need this time."

Suspicion forced Em to pause. "Are you sure you're not doing this to set me up?"

"Em, after all you and Devin have been through, I wouldn't do that to you, nor would I do it to him. I love you both and definitely don't want to see either one of you hurt again."

"What's wrong with him? Why hasn't he been married by now?"

Elena clucked her tongue. "See? This new attitude of yours is what I'm talking about. There's nothing wrong with him except he's married to his work. It's important to him and to the people he's serving."

"Yeah? What does he do?" Em knew she sounded mistrustful, but she couldn't help herself. Trusting men had become an issue with her.

"He like Andrew, is a doctor. He's been working to establish clinics for children in under-developed countries and to improve overall health care for them and their families."

Em let out a soft sigh. "Okay, that's nice. I didn't mean to sound so suspicious."

"It's going to be all right, Em. Like I said, he has no interest in forming any relationship with anyone because he's using this rest period to prepare for another trip out of the country, and he wants time to rethink his career. I know you well enough to believe when you find the right man, you'd want him to stick around, not be traveling all over the world."

"True." Em let out a sigh of relief. Sharing the cottage with him might not be such a bad idea after all.

"So, will you do it?"

"Yes," Em said, with a quiet determination to make this work.

As the day of departure to Florida grew closer, Em's excitement grew. She worked energetically to make sure Marilyn could take over for her in the flower shop while she was gone. Though Gran would never want to admit it, the days of doing most of the work herself were gone. In her seventies now, it was time for her to slow down.

To save money, she decided to drive to Florida instead of flying and having to rent a car. Besides, she loved her little VW convertible and thought it would be perfect in Florida.

The day before she was to leave, she received a letter from Kat, wishing her a nice vacation and telling her once more how sorry she was about falling in love with Jared. Em read it and then crumpled it up. She was sorry too. Sorry she'd allowed herself to believe she'd found someone with whom to spend the rest of her life. She made a vow never to let that happen to her again. One major heartbreak was one too many.

That night, she loaded the car so she could make an early morning getaway. The roads were clear, but a snowstorm was forecast for the northeast, and she hoped to beat it.

She locked the car, and after saying goodnight to her parents, slipped into bed. Her clothes were laid out on a chair for the next day. All she needed was a good night's rest. She closed her eyes and told herself to go to sleep.

After tossing and turning for hours, Em got up, quietly dressed, and, on tiptoe, left the house.

Outside, all was still as big snowflakes drifted down, white dots of concern in the early morning light.

She unlocked her car and slid behind the wheel, grateful for the early start. She'd get onto I-87, connect with I-95 and then shoot down the coast as fast as she could in an attempt to stay clear of the snow heading Ellenton's way. The smell of snow was in the air, that particular aroma that skiers and kids loved.

As she made her through the town and outlying areas, she felt as if she were on an adventure. Many of the houses and buildings were dark, block-like shapes sitting alongside the road like sentinels protecting her way. Lights in other houses waking up seem to wink at her, telling her she had a chance to beat the storm.

She pressed on until she reached the interstate. Here, activity was in full gear. Large trucks roared past, sure of the way, as if they'd traveled the highway many times before. She entered the highway and followed a moving van until she was more comfortable on the road. Snowflakes swirled around the wheels of her car as she drove, stirred up enough to be unable to settle on the surface. Em knew time and wetter flakes would change that and kept on going.

Em drove past New York City and through New Jersey before she dared to stop. Then she relished hot coffee and a big breakfast at the service area she found along the way. She gazed at the other travelers in the dining area, wondering where they'd come from and where they were going. This time of year, she wasn't the only traveler heading south to warmer weather.

The farther south she got, the more excited she became. She stopped in South Carolina for the night, thrilled to be able to move around comfortably without her winter parka.

The next morning, eager to be on her way, Em got up at dawn, quickly ate the breakfast the motel provided and took off. The hours on the road gave her time to think about her life. If she was going to be alone, the idea of opening a business of her own was appealing. She could start slow with a landscape design company by providing advice to some of Gran's customers. She'd done that in the past, and they'd liked her ideas. And, if she liked it doing it, she could, perhaps, expand to other services working with other companies. She'd need the money. Living at home had made her realize that though she liked small-town living, she wanted to be in her own space. The offer she'd put in on a new townhouse under construction had been accepted. She was waiting to hear when she could move in. If luck was with her, it would be right after she returned, as she'd been promised.

By the time Em reached Florida, she was excited about her plans—plans that didn't depend on anyone else to make them right. She sighed at the thought of how much time and energy she'd invested in dreams of weddings and starting a family of her own. So what if most of her college friends and acquaintances were married? Marriage wasn't for everyone. Certainly, not for her, she told herself, trying to believe it.

Comfortable with the idea that she wouldn't pursue any relationship, Em felt her body relax. There was no need to worry anymore about the future. She had a plan, and it was a good one.

Em pulled into the driveway of the Seashell Cottage, and sighed happily. It was as lovely as its pictures.

She got out of the car and took a moment to stretch. Then, in a rush of joy, she ran toward the beach. The sound of the waves hitting the sand and pulling away in a rhythmic pattern was music to her ears. In sneakers, she walked out onto the sand, feeling it shift beneath her feet, until she reached the hard-packed sand at the water's edge. Inhaling the salty tang of the air, she laughed, a sound of pure excitement! Every mile of driving was worth it to stand there now.

Em studied her surroundings. Farther down the beach, people were sitting on the sand in beach chairs or lying on towels. Little sandpipers moved in a bunch, scurrying along the lacy edges of the Gulf water like a horde of shoppers on bargain day. Seagulls, terns, and other birds made lazy circles in the sky, their white wings forming a pretty pattern against the blue of the sky. Em clasped her hands together and closed her eyes, thankful for this opportunity. When she opened them, she laughed out loud at the pelicans skimming the surface of the water searching for food, looking like participants in an air show.

Feeling as if she could take wing herself, Em hurried to her car eager to unpack and get settled in the house. The rental agency had given her the code for the lockbox containing the key to the house. She took the information out of her purse and went to the front door, punched in the numbers, retrieved the key, unlocked and opened the door, and stepped inside.

Her gaze swept the interior with admiration. The two couches in the living area were covered in a tropical-green fabric. Hibiscus-pink pillows sat on the couches and brightened the room. Their color was duplicated in the handwoven rug that lay atop the off-white tile floor. Two overstuffed chairs carried out the theme in a floral pattern of green and pink.

Em went to investigate the rest of the house and discovered a bedroom suite off to one side of the entry hall. She walked inside and was pleased to find a small office area, plenty of closet space, and a large bathroom with both a shower and a huge soaking tub. A large window in the bedroom gave her a clear view of the beach. The fading color of the sky outside the window was duplicated in the quilted blue bedspread on the king bed. Loving the feel of the room, she immediately claimed it as hers.

After returning to the open living area, she searched the hall on the other side and found two additional, roomy, nicely decorated bedrooms each with an en-suite bathroom.

From there, she entered the large, modern kitchen and discovered, as advertised, it contained everything anyone would need to cook.

"Kat, you don't know what you're missing," she said to the empty room, and then grinned at the sound of her voice echoing against the walls. It might be foolish to talk to herself this way, thought Em, but it felt good.

She went out to her car to gather more of her things. As she reached for a suitcase in the backseat, she heard a car drive up beside her. She turned as a gentleman studied her through the window of his car and nodded a greeting.

Curious, she waited for him to get out of his black BMW. He'd been at the wedding, but as she'd told Elena, she hadn't paid him much attention.

He climbed out of the car and faced her. "Em, glad to see you again. I'm Devin."

Em swallowed hard. *Whoa!* The man she recalled from the wedding looked nothing like this. This one was as buff as you could find. Tall, muscular, dark-haired, and with features capable of modeling for GQ, he was what her Gran would call a dreamboat.

"Hi, Devin. My sister told me you're here for a rest. That's good, because I am too," she blurted, too unsettled by his appearance to stop herself. "I'm here for total relaxation. The goal is to do my own thing with no worries about anyone else."

He pushed up his sunglasses to the top of his head and grinned. His green eyes sparkled with intensity. "Sounds good to me. It's been a while since I've been able to do something like this."

Flustered by the way his gaze had roamed over her, Em grabbed her two suitcases and a bag of snacks she'd purchased along the way and headed to the house. She'd return for the rest.

Without looking back, she carried her things to the bedroom. When she realized Devin didn't know the layout of the house, she set her things down and went to greet him at the door.

"Hope you don't mind. I've chosen the beach-side bedroom. There are two other bedroom suites off to the right."

"Whatever you choose will be fine." He glanced around. "Compared to what I'm used to, this is pure luxury." He walked past her carrying a small black suitcase and a computer case.

Em returned to her car for the canvas bag of shoes she'd brought, picked up the straw hat that lay on the backseat and locked her car. For better or worse, she had her stuff.

Inside, she worked in her bedroom unpacking her suitcases, laying things in drawers or hanging them in the closet. Unsure what to pack, she'd brought more than she'd probably need, she admitted to herself, thinking of the lone suitcase Devin had carried inside.

The late afternoon sun felt warm through the window. She decided to put on one of the swimsuits she'd brought. On her first day in Florida, she was going to hit the beach. It was number one on the mental list she'd drawn up of the things she intended to do during her stay.

Dressed in a raspberry-red bikini, she stood in front of the mirror. She couldn't help thinking of the difference between Kat and her. Unlike Kat, her body tended toward curvy. It hadn't bothered her in the past, but now self-doubt crept in. She tucked her streaked wheat-colored hair behind her ears. Her facial features were pleasing. Not a stunner, she knew she was appealing, with an easy smile and thick-lashed, blue eyes that spoke of kindness.

She turned away, chiding herself for even caring about it now. She was not out to impress anyone, least of all, Devin Gerard.

She sprayed on suntan lotion and then grabbed a towel from her closet and headed out to the beach.

As she stepped onto the sand, she was surprised to see Devin sprawled on a towel nearby. She glanced at him and quickly looked away, vowing to break old patterns. No matter what he or any other male looked like, she was not out to make friends with him. *Co-exist and that's it,* she reminded herself.

At a distance from him, she dropped her towel on the beach and headed out for a walk. After sitting in the car for two very long days, it felt good to stretch her legs. She moved smoothly, quickly along the shore absorbing the sights and sounds of beach life like sweet treats on her tongue. Knowing of the cold and ice back home, she reveled in her surroundings.

She walked for a mile or so and turned around. She was surprised to see Devin jogging toward her. She stopped and braced herself for conversation, but as he neared, he kept his pace and moved beyond her.

She continued her walk both disappointed and relieved he seemed as eager as she to spend time alone. It was just as well. Elena had warned her he had no interest in women at this point in his life, and she'd promised Em that she had made that point clear to Devin as well regarding her.

So be it, thought Em, picking up her towel and returning to the cottage. Tonight, she decided, she'd go out to eat, maybe discover a nice, inexpensive place. She'd heard all about "early bird specials". She'd see what everyone was talking about. Alone.

CHAPTER FOUR

Billy Bud's Bar was as funky as the name. Em walked into a large, wood-paneled room whose walls were covered with fish nets, plastic anchors, shells, and other maritime items. At six o'clock, the place was filled with people of all ages.

Em found an empty seat at the bar.

The young bartender slid a plastic-covered menu over to her. "You here for Happy Hour and Early Bird Specials?"

"I guess." She glanced at the menu. The Early Bird Specials were on one side of the menu; the Happy Hour cocktail and wine selections on the other.

"What can I get you?" the bartender asked, giving her an appreciative look. "We've got great draft beer or maybe you want one of our special tropical drinks."

"I'll go for a tropical drink," Em said.

"How about Sex on the Beach?" the bartender said, wiggling his eyebrows at her.

Em couldn't stop the heat that raced to her cheeks. She knew it was a cocktail, but still ...

The bartender noticed and laughed. "Sex on the Beach is one of my favorites to make—vodka, peach schnapps, grapefruit juice, and cranberry juice. I make them special."

Laughing, Em said, "Okay. I'll try one."

While she was waiting for her drink and perusing the menu, a guy came up beside her. He leaned close and eyed her. "You here alone?"

She turned. "Yes. That's how I like it."

He shrugged. "Hey! I'm just asking."

Em didn't even look as he drifted away. This was her time alone.

Her drink came. After taking a sip, she gave a thumbs up to the bartender and ordered a grouper sandwich. It sounded tropical.

An older couple sat down next to her. "Great evening, huh?" said the gray-haired man, smiling at her. His wife leaned forward and waved to her. "Hi, I'm Alice, and this is Herb."

"I'm Em," she said to be polite.

Not to be dismissed, the couple began talking to her, and soon she found herself listening to all the trials of owning two places—one in Florida and one in Ohio.

Time flew as she ate her sandwich and conversed with them. By the time she was through with her meal, every mile of the trip south was pulling at her eyelids.

She paid her bill, got to her feet, and left the bar satisfied that dining out would be no problem. Especially if she went out early. Clearly, if Kat had come to Florida with her, it would be a different story. But she didn't feel the need to party.

Back at the cottage, both Devin and his car were gone.

Em made her way to her bedroom, changed into her favorite nightshirt, the one with the New York Yankees on it, and crawled into bed.

Tomorrow was another day of freedom, of finding herself.

Sunlight played hide and seek with her fluttering eyelids, teasing her until she opened her eyes wide and gazed around the room. It took her a few seconds to realize she was in Florida, not New York. Em heard the sound of someone in the kitchen and remembered she was living with a man with no expectations of anything beyond a brief friendship. He'd spoken to her as if he was meeting her for the first time and then disappeared. She had no idea when Devin had returned to the house last night.

She checked her watch. Eight o'clock. She scrambled out of bed before she realized she wasn't on any time schedule. After slipping on the terry robe provided in each guest suite, she padded into the kitchen.

Devin looked up at her and smiled. "Good morning. I've made coffee. Help yourself to it." In workout shorts and a T-shirt, he looked hot as hell.

"Thanks," she said, doing her best not to stare at him. "I'm going grocery shopping this morning and will replace what you've used."

He shook his head. "No need to do that. We're each doing our own thing. Right?"

"Right," she quickly agreed as she poured herself a cup of coffee. She didn't dare suggest they pool their money and buy things together. He was making it clear he was going to remain independent.

Em carried her cup of coffee out to the porch and took a seat in one of the rocking chairs. Though the air was cool, it held the promise of warmth to come. The sun shone on the water making the crests of the waves shimmer with brightness. The rhythmic sound of the water rolling into shore and pulling away was relaxing, pulling a sigh of happiness out of her.

She heard the sound of the door sliding open behind her and glanced at Devin as he took a seat beside her.

"Ahhh, this is nice," he said. "With all the work I've been doing lately, I've forgotten to give myself time to relax. That's one of the reasons I agreed to come here. I remember this area of Florida from being part of your sister's wedding party."

"I haven't been back here and, like you, I realize how much I've needed this."

"Weren't you working in New York City?" he said.

"You remember that?" she said, surprised.

"We were part of the same wedding party, so, yeah, I remembered that. You were with some guy with glasses who couldn't dance."

She opened her mouth to protest and closed it. A bubble of laughter began to boil within her and before she could stop herself, it came out in gales of laughter. *My God! Devin was right! Jared couldn't dance very well. She'd been so lovestruck she hadn't minded.*

"What so funny?" Devin asked, his eyes filled with questions.

Still chuckling, Em said, "You're right. Jared was a horrible dancer. I realize that now."

"Hmmm," he responded. "I take it the two of you are no longer together. Is that why you're living in Ellenton?"

Em took her time to answer. She felt like a teenager who'd had a bad night at the senior prom. But it was so much more than that. After Jared had ended their relationship, she'd had moments when she'd thought her entire life was over.

"I left New York City for Ellenton after my grandmother asked for my help running her flower shop. She never liked the idea of my living in the city, and by then, I was ready to leave."

"Do you like it?" Devin asked, studying her.

She instinctively knew it wasn't a simple question. "I love working with flowers. I might open my own landscape design business one day. I'm thinking about it, anyway." She studied him. "So, what exactly are you doing? You're a doctor, right?"

"Yes. I'm a pediatrician." His green eyes darkened, became sad. She waited for him to say more. "Guess I'd better get going. I've signed up for the gym." He stood and indicated the plantings around the house. "The landscaping here needs a little sprucing up."

Em returned his smile. "Yes, I've noticed. I thought I'd go to the library and do a little research on tropical plants. That might help me decide if it's something I really want to do."

He gave her a little salute. "See you later."

Watching Devin walk away, Em filled with curiosity. She couldn't help wondering what had made Devin so sad.

She stayed on the porch until he drove away. Then she went inside to see what she could find out about him online. Her sister had asked her not to research him before making the trip, but now that Em had met Devin, she wanted to know more about him.

His resume was impressive. Medical degree from the Perelman School of Medicine at the University of Pennsylvania, internship and residency at the Hospital of the University of Pennsylvania. She knew from one of her high school classmates how excellent the pediatric program was at that university. In fact, her friend had called it number one in the country.

She moved on to other information about him until she came to the last entry—the mention of the work he'd recently completed in Costa Rica helping to run a medical clinic for children and families.

Working with poor and suffering people, trying to make a difference in their lives must be rewarding, she thought, remembering the sadness that had momentarily washed over his features.

After taking a shower and putting on shorts and a long-sleeved shirt, Em went into the kitchen to survey supplies. As she worked on a grocery list, the ten-day vacation didn't seem very long.

She traveled to a nearby Publix supermarket and took her time planning what and how much to buy. It seemed silly not to share some items with Devin, but Em knew it was best that way. She was already on a slippery slope thinking that Devin was a very nice, very handsome man. *Step back,* she reminded herself.

At home, she carefully placed all of her refrigerated items on one shelf so Devin would know what was hers and did the same with the cupboard space. Then she grabbed a bottle of water and left for the local library.

A couple of hours later, she returned to the cottage with a few books she'd found at a bookstore. Hungry, she headed into the kitchen.

Dirty dishes were neatly stacked in the sink, indicating Devin had been there. She made herself a small turkey and tomato sandwich on rye and grabbed another water.

Eating at the kitchen table gave her a chance to get a closer look at her surroundings. The townhouse she'd bought offered a modern kitchen with dark wood cabinets and stainless-steel appliances. Compared to them, this kitchen with its white-painted cupboards seemed much more hospitable, or maybe it was the warm atmosphere.

Em rinsed and put her dishes in the dishwasher and then walked outside with one of the reference books she'd bought. She'd been warned by one of the clerks at the book store that growing things in this area was easy, maybe too easy, because of the constant maintenance required to tame the fast-growing plants. She knelt on the grass and began to pull weeds between the plants she was studying when she saw the shadow of a man standing behind her. She whipped around, and was surprised to see a light-brown-skinned man wearing a straw hat staring down at her. From beneath the hat, dark hair was highlighted by gray strands.

"Sorry to frighten you." His smile accented his white teeth and brought a twinkle to his dark eyes. "What are you doing with my garden?"

"Your garden?" She rose to her feet and faced him. "You're the owner?"

He grinned. "No, the gardener. I was sick last week, but yes, I've been hired to take care of the plantings and lawn here."

"Oh, I hope you don't mind what I've done, but I'm trying to learn about plants in this area." She held out her hand. "I'm Emerson Jordan, visiting from upstate New York. I'm thinking of opening a landscape design business and want to know about growing things here."

'I'm Benito Santana." His grin was full of mischief. "Are you offering to help me?"

"Not exactly. Well, maybe, for a while," Em said, charmed by him.

He looked from her to the work she'd done weeding and trimming a small area. "Okay, you can ask questions while you continue. Deal?"

"Deal," Em said firmly. She was becoming excited about the idea of working with different plants outdoors.

Benito held up a finger. "Hold on. I'll be right back. I have to get Nina and some of my equipment."

"Can I help?" she asked.

"Yes, that would be a good beginning." He led her to an older-model, blue truck hauling a white, enclosed trailer behind. Across the sides of the trailer were the words "Benito's Landscape Services" in blue. Benito went to the passenger side of the truck and lifted out a little girl who was still sleeping. Em judged her to be about three or four. He spoke softly to her. "Nina, we're here. Time to wake up."

The girl's eyes fluttered open and she stared in surprise at Em. Soft dark curls sprang out from her head and, like the wings of butterflies, swayed in the gentle onshore breeze. Observing her, Em thought she'd rarely seen a prettier child.

She moved forward. "Hi, Nina. I'm Em."

The little girl nestled her head against Benito's broad shoulder.

"My granddaughter is sometimes shy," he said, patting Nina's back. He spoke in Spanish to Nina, and after she nodded, he set her down on the ground.

"Does she always travel with you?" Em asked.

"Only on days my daughter works the night shift. My daughter can't afford day care for her. Otherwise, she's at home with us."

"I can keep an eye on her for you while you talk to me about the plants and show me how to handle them," Em offered. "In the cottage, I found a drawer of things for kids to do. Later, if you and she are comfortable with it, she can play inside."

"Yes, that would be good, very kind." He spoke to Nina once more in Spanish. She stared up at Em with dark eyes that assessed her and then a smile crossed Nina's face, exposing little white teeth that gleamed against her darker skin.

Em's breath caught. As lovely as she was now, Nina was already showing signs of one day becoming a stunning young woman.

Benito walked Em and Nina around the perimeter of the house, pointing out different plants and talking about their care. At one point, he grabbed Em's hand and pulled her away.

"What is it?" she asked.

He pointed to what looked like a mound of sand. "Fire ants. Never disturb them. They sting like crazy."

They had just returned to the front of the house when Devin returned to the cottage. He was still in gym shorts and a T-shirt that showed off his body and clearly demonstrated how effective his workouts were.

"Hello," Devin said to Benito and Em before turning to Nina. "And who is this?" He knelt before Nina and spoke to her in Spanish.

Her face glowing from the attention, she reached out and patted his cheek. Laughing, he stood and faced Benito. Amidst the Spanish they spoke, Em caught only a few words.

After he and Benito finished conversing, Devin gave her an appraising look. "Benito tells me you're going to watch Nina. She wants to go down by the water. Do you mind if I join the two of you? Late afternoon is a great time to enjoy the beach."

"Not a problem," Em said. "Are you just coming back from the gym?"

He chuckled. "No, I've been visiting some friends. They're staying at the Salty Key Inn."

Nina walked over to him, grabbed hold of his hand, and then took hold of Em's hand.

"Looks like she ready to go," said Benito, giving Nina an indulgent smile.

"Okay, let's do it," said Em. The three of them crossed the lawn and stepped onto the beach.

Em took off her sandals and wiggled her toes in the warm grains of sand, loving the feel of them on her skin.

Nina sat down and tried to pull off her sandals. Em knelt to help her and laughed when Nina mimicked her, wiggling her toes and sighing with pleasure.

"She sure doesn't miss a trick," said Devin, smiling at them both.

"Yes, she's not only smart, but gorgeous."

As if she'd understood Em, Nina looked up at her and grinned.

Em ruffled Nina's curls. "Come on, let's take a look at the

water." She offered her hand.

"*Agua!*" cried Nina, pulling out of Em's grip and running toward the waves lapping at the foamy shoreline like a milky-whiskered kitten.

"Wait!" cried Em, running after the little girl.

Giggling, Nina kept on running.

Devin moved past Em in easy strides, caught up to Nina, swept her up into his arms, and swung her around.

Nina's shrieks of laughter made Em's eyes grow misty. This was a scene she'd imagined many times—her with a husband and a child. Em took a deep breath, wondering why her imagination always seemed to carry her away from reality. Wasn't that how she'd gotten hurt in the past?

As Em approached them, Devin looked at her and grinned. "She's fast. We'll have to keep a careful eye on her."

"Yes. I would hate for anything to go wrong when I'm responsible."

He frowned. "As I recall you have only your sister Elena. Right?"

"Yep. Just the two of us."

"Nice. I'm an only child but grew up in a neighborhood with a lot of kids."

"Is that why you're so comfortable around them?"

"Yeah, I guess so. A lot of the other mothers took me in and fed me meals when my mother worked late, and in return, I helped them out."

"And now?"

"Now, I love being able to do what I can to make a better life for kids who don't have it easy."

Observing the way earnestness had softened his handsome features and how the rays of sun highlighted the planes of his body, she held her breath.

The magical moment melted away as he left her side to help

Nina pick up shells. She watched him go.

"C'mon! Help us," Devin called to her.

Em trotted over to them and began hunting for a perfect shell among the piles of shells that lined the beach, battered beauties crushed by wave action. Nature could be harsh, but she also produced some miracles. She lifted a perfect tulip shell to show Devin.

Nina saw it and ran over to her. "Mine!" she said in clear English.

Devin and Em looked at each other and laughed.

"Yes, this can be yours," Em said, handing the shell to Nina.

Nina clutched the shell to her chest. "*Gracias!*"

Em exchanged a smile with Devin. "Kids are the same everywhere."

He nodded his agreement, studied her a moment, and turned away to go to Nina.

CHAPTER FIVE

As Benito prepared to leave, Nina spoke to him in Spanish and, at a nod from her grandfather, she came over to Em and hugged her. Then she hugged Devin.

Em couldn't help the tears that stung her eyes. If she had a little girl one day, she'd want her to be just like Nina—smart and loving.

She stood to watch as Benito pulled his truck and trailer out of the driveway. He'd promised to come back early in the following week to catch up to his schedule. Em intended to be there so she could have more time with Nina. In the two days she'd been in Florida, she'd already learned about tropical plants, along with a lot about herself. She knew now that she wasn't willing to give up the idea of becoming a mother, whether she found the right guy for her or not.

Inside the cottage, she grabbed a beer from her side of the refrigerator and wandered out to the porch. She loved sitting there looking out at the moving water, becoming lost in its rhythm, encouraging worries to vanish. After talking to Benito, she understood a little more what work landscaping involved and the time commitment it demanded. Maybe, she thought, she'd take a course or two on design. Though Gran felt she was ready to open a landscape design business right now, Em wanted more knowledge. Her hometown in New York had a shorter growing season than many, and she was intrigued with the idea of winter gardens where people could sit in the sun while the perennials hidden below the surface waited for warmer weather to show themselves.

Em heard a noise behind her and turned to see Devin holding up a can of beer.

"Okay, if I have one of yours?" he asked. "I'll go to the store later and replace it."

"Sure. I've noticed your side of the refrigerator is quite empty. I was going to ask if you wanted to share some food, but my sister made it very clear that you wanted to be left alone."

Devin's eyebrows rose with surprise. "Really? That's what she told me about you."

Em chuckled. "I think we've been 'big-sistered.'"

"What does that mean?"

"It means Elena is looking out for both of us. Not that I need her help. She wants me to find someone, but I have no intention of dating for a long time. I'm apparently not a good judge of character."

"And why is that?" Devin sat down in a chair next to her and popped open the can of beer.

Em couldn't help the flush that flooded her cheeks. "I've been told I need to be more realistic about people and life in general, that I see only the best in other people."

"That's not a bad thing, I would think." Devin shook his head. "We need more people like that."

"I agree, but not when I don't see a person's true nature," said Em. "I've gotten into a couple of messy situations. Once with a married opera singer."

Devin sat back and studied her. "And the latest?"

Em felt her mouth turn downward.

"Ah, I get it. The guy at the wedding. Right?"

Feeling foolish, she nodded.

Devin shook his head. "Somehow, I don't see you with a guy who can't dance. You're the kind of woman who deserves better than that."

"How would you know? You don't even know me."

Devin held up a finger of warning. "I was at the wedding. Remember?" His green eyes crinkled with amusement.

He was, she thought, adorable. Warning signals suddenly erupted throughout her body. She had to be careful.

Fighting the urge to stay, she forced herself to stand. "I think I'll go try a new place for dinner, maybe grab a snack at one of the bars. See you later."

Devin got to his feet. "Mind if I accompany you? As long as we both understand the ground rules, it should be okay. We're not going on a date. Right?"

"Sure." Em flinched at the stab of disappointment that pierced her. "I'm going to change my clothes. I'll meet you out front in fifteen minutes."

"Deal." They went inside, and he wandered into the kitchen, leaving her to admire the view.

When Em emerged from her bedroom, she saw Devin standing by the front door waiting for her. His dark hair was still wet from a shower and hung over his brow, tempting her to take her hand and brush it back. Wearing a golf shirt and slacks, he looked ... well, great.

"Ready?" he asked, studying her with a look of appreciation. "Let's go to The Key Hole down the road. I hear it's supposed to be good. Part of the Salty Key Inn complex."

"Sounds fine to me. I didn't get a chance to go there when I was in the area for Elena's wedding."

Sitting across from Devin at a high-top table, Em was well aware of the looks other women were giving him. He ignored them as he continued to answer her questions about the medical trip he'd recently participated in to help children. When he spoke about his work, his eyes glowed with a satisfaction that caught her interest.

"You love what you do," Em commented.

"It was worth all the effort to get through med school, internship, and residency to be able to do it. My ex-girlfriend wanted me to open an office in an expensive part of her town, but that's not what I wanted. The only way I got my education was through scholarships and other people helping me out. She didn't understand I feel a deep need to pay back for all I've been given."

"Oh, I'm sorry," she said.

He waved his hand in dismissal. "That wasn't the only problem. A colleague asked me to go into practice with him in Miami. I've been working there for a while, but I'm not sure that's what I want. I want to continue my work in other countries." His gaze settled on her. "You say you've had bad luck in the past. I get the whole idea of not wanting to date for a while. I'm there with you. Too many other people are counting on me to help them."

"I was worried about sharing the cottage with you. Now, I'm not," said Em. "You're a nice guy. I'm going to use this time here to work on a business plan so when I get back home, I'll be ready to open a small landscape design business in tandem with working at Gran's flower shop."

"Sounds impressive," said Devin, resting his gaze on her.

"That isn't the only thing I'm going to do. I'm going to figure out how to bring a child into my life on my own. I don't need a man to do that."

He cocked an eyebrow and studied her with a grin. "It's pretty basic science."

She laughed. "I meant that in today's world you can have a donor, do IVF, even adopt in order to have a child."

"True," Devin admitted. His lips curved into a teasing smile. "But you could be missing out on a lot of fun."

"Maybe," she said, "but being here has given me a lot of ideas for future plans. Plans I intend to put to good use."

Devin gave her a little salute. "I say go for it."

They smiled at each other. In that moment, Em realized she'd found a friend.

After sharing a tasty meal of grilled mahi mahi, the best coleslaw she'd ever eaten, and pineapple upside down cake, she patted her stomach, pleasantly full.

As they were about to leave, a couple approached them. "Hey, Devin! Long time no see," teased an attractive redhead.

He laughed, got to his feet, and kissed her cheek. The tall, blond man accompanying her clapped Devin on the back. "Couldn't stay away, huh?"

Grinning, Devin turned to her. "Emerson Jordan, meet two of my best friends, Allie and Doug Masters."

"Ah, you're the housemate at Seashell Cottage," said Doug.

"Yes, just housemates," said Em, wanting to make it clear. It felt good to say it. No expectations from Devin or her.

"Well, I see you've already paid the bill," said Doug, eyeing the leather folder sitting on the table holding the tab. "I suppose we can't ask you to change your minds and stay."

"Thanks, but no," answered Devin looking to Em for confirmation.

She nodded and turned to the couple. "Thanks for the offer. Nice to meet you."

Devin took her arm, and they left the bar.

Back at the cottage, Em made a cup of tea. "I'm going to bundle up and sit on the porch for a while before going to bed. Care to join me?"

Devin shook his head. "Thanks, anyway. I'm going in to my room to watch a basketball game."

Left alone, Em grabbed a blanket and headed outdoors.

A sliver of moon smiled down at her from the dark sky. Surrounded by twinkling stars, the moon seemed a good omen for her future. She liked the idea of being independent, of having plans of her own choosing. The townhouse she'd just bought held a small office she could use for her business. She'd taken an interior design course in college for fun, easy credits. That very course would now be a bonus in developing designs for outdoor gardens. Gran, she knew, would help her with information about plants. Marty Caster, one of Gran's friends, owned a large landscaping business. She intended to talk to him about working together on various projects.

Sitting in the rocking chair, moving back and forth to the sound of the waves hitting the sand and rolling away, she felt a peace settle over her. Like Gran said, it was time for her to grow up and become a woman who knew who she was and where she was going with an open eye to others. Em silently thanked her sister for coming up with the idea of staying at Seashell Cottage.

The next morning, as Em trotted along the sand, she felt a new sense of purpose. The neighborhood's wooden pier, an enticing pathway toward deeper water, lay ahead of her. She jogged to it, walked out to the end, and sat on one of the wooden benches. Three men were fishing, quietly throwing in their lines and reeling them in. It seemed such a peaceful scene. She let out a sigh of pleasure. When her cell phone rang, still smiling, she picked it up. *Gran.*

"How's my sunshine girl?" Gran chirped. "I miss you, but I'm glad you're able to escape the latest snow. We got just enough to be bothersome."

"It's a beautiful morning here. I'm sitting in the sun watching men fish off the local pier. And, Gran, I've come up with plans for the future. Can you give me the cell number for Marty Caster? I want to talk to him about doing some design work for his clients."

"Of course. Hold on. I've got it here in my office. Keep talking while I search for it. What else have you decided?"

"I'm going to set up an office in my townhouse but will continue to work for you as well."

"Wonderful. Your floral designs have been sorely missed, but Marilyn is doing her best to duplicate what you showed her. And Nancy Norris wants you to help her with her garden. You promised you would come up with a design for it. How's the housemate working out?"

"He's fine. We've become friends."

"That's a good sign, Emerson. Sounds like you truly are on an independent path to happiness."

"Thanks," Em said. She wasn't about to tell anyone about her desire to go ahead and have a child on her own. Thinking of children, she asked, "How's Elena?"

"She emailed me a photo. She's glowing like a woman about to have a baby. She and Andrew are so excited about it that it's touching. Oh, a customer is at the door. I'd better go. Talk to you later, sweetheart. Love you."

"Love you too, Gran," she said with feeling. They'd always been close.

Em headed back to the house anxious to enjoy the rest of the day. Last night, she'd looked up information on the Florida Botanical Gardens, and she planned to spend several hours there. Now that she'd decided to continue to work with plants and flowers, she couldn't wait to see and read about as many as she could.

When she jogged back to the cottage, Devin was in the kitchen. Barefoot and wearing only Bermuda shorts, he looked like he'd just gotten up.

"Just made coffee. Help yourself," he said. "What have you got planned for the day?"

"I'm going to visit the Florida Botanical Gardens. You're welcome to come along if you want."

He shook his head. "No, thanks. I'm going to veg out here, catch up on some reading. And then I promised to meet a colleague for dinner. She and I have worked together, and she's now considering coming into the practice in Miami."

"I thought you weren't sure about working there."

"I'm not. But I haven't figured out a solution yet to how I can do both."

"How about working in Costa Rica every fourth week, or five days a month, something like that, and having your new colleague cover for you. Then you'd be doing the work you love and providing service to others in both Miami and Costa Rica. Maybe your friend would be agreeable to something like that, especially if she's new to the practice."

Devin slapped his head. "My God! That's so simple. Why didn't I think of it? It'll relieve my mind if we can figure out a way for me to do both." He grabbed her in an impulsive bear hug and quickly let her go. "Thanks, Em."

Surprised by the hug and her immediate sensual reaction to it, she barely managed to say, "You're welcome." *Wow!*

CHAPTER SIX

Before Em headed to the Botanical Gardens, she placed a call to her real estate agent. "Glad you called," the receptionist said. "Barbara is out of the office for a few days, but she wanted to let her clients at Green Meadows know that final inspections for Building B will be held in two weeks."

"And then I can move in?" Em asked, excitement growing in her.

"It looks that way," came the response. "Barbara said she could be reached in an emergency, but otherwise she's taking a few days off. Family business."

"No problem. I'm delighted. Please be sure to thank her for staying on top of this." Em hung up the phone and raised a fist in the air. "Yes!!" For once in her life, things seemed to be falling into place.

On that optimistic note, she decided to go ahead and call Marty Caster. His AAA Landscape Company was the most prestigious in the area, and she wanted to be able to work with him. When she reached his number, a recorded message told her the landscape company had closed for two weeks for their winter break, but the snow-removal operation could be reached through a different number. She hung up, let out a sigh of disappointment, then told herself it would be better to talk to Marty after she got home. By then she hoped to have a written business plan. For now, she was off to learn more about plants and flowers in Florida and, more importantly, how professional designers at the gardens had put all the pieces together to create a compelling attraction.

###

As she drove to Largo, Em mentally reviewed what she'd read about the gardens. Founded in 1991, the Florida Botanical Gardens emerged from extensive planning with input from citizens, horticulturists, and plant societies. It wasn't until the site was readied that design and construction of the gardens moved forward in 1997. It officially opened to the public in December, 2000, showcasing 10 gardens with 10,000 plants on 182 acres.

She shook her head. This was no small enterprise. She couldn't wait to see it.

Em parked in one of the designated parking lots and headed out. She picked up a map and stared at it, wondering where to begin. She decided to head toward the Butterfly Garden. Butterfly bushes were popular in Ellenton. Maybe she could get some good ideas for designs there.

After viewing the garden and admiring the butterflies that fluttered inside the caged area like pieces of a rainbow tossed in the air, she moved on to the Native Garden. Here, she was enamored by the colors that abounded even though it was winter. Well aware of the limitations of a northern garden, Em took special notice of how greenery with varying shades and textures served as a design of its own and complemented the flowers and other plants.

It was late afternoon by the time Em decided to head home. She'd taken as many photos as her phone would allow without using all her battery power. Inspired by everything she'd seen, she planned to stop by one of the local restaurants for an early dinner. Tonight, she was going to write down her thoughts and glance through the armload of books she'd bought in the gift shop.

###

When Em arrived at the cottage after eating dinner at a nearby seafood restaurant, she was glad to be there. She needed a quiet time to sit and reflect on what she had seen that day.

Devin's BMW was in the driveway. Her lips curved. She was eager to tell him about the gardens. She was still in awe of what she'd seen.

Em carried her books inside and stopped at the sound of voices in the kitchen. Curious, she went to see who was with Devin. She plunked the books down on the kitchen counter and turned as Devin called to her. "Em, come meet Su Lynn Wang. She's the colleague I was talking to you about earlier."

A striking woman with sparkling dark eyes smiled at her and held out her hand. "Hi, I'm pleased to meet you. Devin said you're the one who came up with the plan for him and me to share time. I like it."

Em shook Su Lynn's hand. "Hi, I'm Emerson Jordan. Pleased to meet you."

"You're just visiting here?" Su Lynn asked pleasantly, but there was something in her voice that gave Em the impression Su Lynn was interested in Devin in more than a professional way.

Em quickly reassured her. "Yes ... just a little over a week left before I head north."

Su Lynn's smile lit her beautiful features. She and Devin would make a very handsome couple.

"Have fun! I'm off to do some office work," Em said. "I've got notes to make, and then I'm going to work on my business plan."

"You're in business?" Su Lynn asked with an irritating look of surprise on her face.

"I'm setting up a landscape design business," Em replied, loving the sound of it in her ears. "My grandmother has owned a flower shop for years. I'm taking it up a notch or two by offering design ideas to customers and hopefully working with a landscaper."

"Sounds good," said Devin. "You really are going through with all your new ideas?"

Em gave him a smile. "That's the plan." She lifted the books from the counter. "See you later. Nice to meet you, Su Lynn."

As Em left the kitchen, she heard Su Lynn say to Devin, "You didn't tell me that Em was so pretty."

"Yeah, I guess she is," he answered in a non-committal tone that let Em know he definitely wasn't interested in her.

Em had seen enough business plans at work to know what needed to be done. As she walked the beach, bundled in a jacket and long pants to counter the cool wind off the water on this gray morning, her mind conjured up a mental list of points. Among the first things she needed to do was to prove that the business premise was a valid one capable of profit. That might be a problem.

Ellenton was a small town in upstate New York that wasn't a typical suburb of New York City. Most residents did not commute to the city for work but had been living and working in the area for years. Neighbors knew neighbors, living was relatively simple, and there were no McMansions dotting the area. Sure, there were nice developments, but all were tasteful and not showy. Money was very much present, but understated.

Em sat down on a bench provided by the county next to a public walkway to the beach and lifted her face to the sun, warming her cool cheeks. Her goal would be to convince customers to spend money on upgrading their gardens for their own pleasure. Because winter was definitely a factor of life in Ellenton, spring, summer, and fall were months when residents reveled in being outdoors. That might work in her favor.

Em's mind raced. Maybe Gran's house would be a good place to start. Em could easily imagine changing the look of the backyard from ordinary to stunning by adding a stone wall, a pathway through the wildflowers, and a garden bench beneath the maple tree. Things like a small pond, a gazebo, a waterfall, or other expensive items could be used for those who wanted it. But most of the people she knew would go for something simpler, especially those in the wooded areas near the creek.

She heard the sound of someone approaching and opened her eyes. "What are you doing up so early? I thought you and Su Lynn would stay out late having fun. She seems very nice."

"Yeah, she is," admitted Devin, taking a seat next to her. "She's a very good physician. Last night, we called the head of my office group and talked to him about bringing Su Lynn on board. He was quite receptive to the idea. We're driving over to Miami to meet with him today. Want to ride with me, see the scene there?"

She shook her head. "Thanks, but I'm going to stay here and work. Maybe before I leave, I can find the time to do that, but not now."

He gave her a teasing smile. "No vacation for the new business owner?"

"Something like that," she said. The truth was she was attracted to him and knew she'd fall back into her old habit of projecting a future with him if she didn't stay strong and stick to her plans.

###

That afternoon, left alone at Seashell Cottage, Em felt a stab of loneliness. She lifted the phone and called her sister.

"Hey, there!" said Elena. "How's the weather in Florida? It sounded mighty nice when I checked in with The Weather Channel."

"It's beautiful, but when it's time to leave, I'll be anxious to make my way back home." She told Elena about her business idea.

"Sweet! That sounds perfect for you. You're so creative. And Gran must be relieved to know you'll continue working for her. She's hoping to give you the business one day."

"I'm not sure that's what I want to happen, but it's a very thoughtful idea."

"So, how are you and Devin getting along?" Elena asked.

"Great. As I told Gran, it's nice to be just friends with a guy. That hasn't happened to me in a long time." She chuckled. "Not since grade school, when Chip Robertson and I were best buddies."

Elena laughed. "You once told me you were going to marry him. Too bad Clara Lawry got to him first."

"They're a great couple," said Em. "By the time I reached high school, the last man I wanted to marry was Chip. No sparks at all between us. Clara and I are still friendly. I see her from time to time." Em changed the subject. "How are you feeling?"

"Good. We going to find out the sex of the baby soon. Andrew opted to wait, but I want to know so we can get everything ready for him or her. You know how important that is to me."

"Yes, I do. I'd better go now," Em said, "I hear Andrew calling you."

She clicked off the call and sat a moment. It was wonderful that everyone was pleased she'd help Gran with the flower shop, but owning the shop was a 24/7 deal with no or few vacations. Em wasn't sure that's what she wanted. Having freedom in Florida had helped her develop plans for the future, plans that might not give her the time she'd need to both help Gran and own her own business. Though she hated to disappoint them, she might have to talk to her family about it. First, she needed to make her business a reality.

CHAPTER SEVEN

Hoping for additions to the collection of ideas she was gathering, Em decided to visit several resorts in the area to study their landscaping. When she asked Devin if he wanted to join her, he jumped at the chance. After he and Su Lynn had visited Miami to meet with his group of doctors, he was due to go back to work two days early and wanted simply to hang out.

She put the top down in her VW convertible and slid behind the wheel. “Can you get in all right?”

Devin chuckled as he folded his legs into the passenger seat. “Feeling a little like a sardine, but it’s fine, believe me. I just want to relax and go along for the ride.”

She made a game of driving up to a hotel entrance and deciding whether they should get out of the car. Landscaping along the beach was pretty consistent with a variety of palms, bougainvillea, hibiscus, jasmine, oleander, and other well-known plants in the area. But Em was after how each hotel strived to make the arrangements unique.

They decided to have lunch at the Sandpearl Resort. Sitting beachside at the Tate Island Grill, Em drew in a breath of the salty air and let it out again in a sigh. She loved being able to eat outside in February.

“How about a Mojito?” Devin said as a waitress approached. “My treat.”

Em hesitated. She never drank during the day.

“They’re very light and refreshing,” said Devin. “But if you’d rather order something else, that’s fine.”

Realizing her time in Florida was drawing to a close, Em said, "A Mojito sounds festive." She glanced at the menu she'd been given. "I'll have the Strawberry Basil Mojito."

Devin grinned. He looked up at the waitress. "My guest will have the Strawberry Basil Mojito, and I'll have the Traditional."

The waitress beamed at him. "Yes, sir. I'll bring those right out to you." Her gaze lingered on him before she walked away with a sashay to her step.

Em couldn't help laughing.

Devin caught her eye and shook his head. "It isn't funny."

"I'm sorry, but she was so obvious." Sitting across from him now, Em wondered how she could have failed to pay attention to him at Elena's wedding.

They sat in comfortable silence watching the people on the beach. Em liked that about him.

After they'd finished their drinks, Devin said, "What are you having for lunch?"

As the waitress approached, Em perused the menu, delighting in the choices. "I think I'll go for the shrimp salad." Served with baby greens, plantains, mandarin oranges, and a number of other things, it sounded delicious.

The waitress took Em's order and turned to Devin. "And what can I do for you?" she asked, batting her eyelashes at him.

"I'll have the Jerk Chicken Sandwich," he said without taking his eye off the menu.

"And water, please," added Em to the waitress, noticing she'd failed to bring any to the table.

After the waitress left, Devin glanced at Em. "That girl is probably half my age."

"How old are you?" asked Em.

"Thirty-six. Way too old to tangle with a teenybopper."

Em laughed. "Teenybopper or not, she'd like nothing more." She grew serious. "You've never married?"

"I came close to it once, but some people have a misconception about doctors and their incomes. With all the required malpractice insurances and government intervention in the last couple of decades, it's a hard life without all the financial benefits once expected. With the kind of work I do, I make a good living, but I'm not rich. Especially with my debt load."

"The women you dated wanted more, huh?"

Looking miserable, he nodded. "That's what happened to me over a year ago. Between the time away and the lack of prospects for a prosperous lifestyle, I was not what she wanted. Or so it turned out when I found her in bed with my neighbor."

"That hurts," said Em softly. "I'm sorry."

He shrugged. "Sometimes it takes something like that to make you rethink what you're doing and where you're going."

"True," she said, understanding that is what had happened to her.

She asked him about his work in Costa Rica and listened as he came alive discussing the need for medical attention there and elsewhere. "I've become close to a few of my patients. Especially one mother and her daughter. I'm not sure how it will end because when I treated her child, I learned her mother is dying from cancer."

Em suspected that was one of the reasons Devin's eyes turned sad when he talked about his work. By the time the meal was over, she considered him one of the most decent and caring men she'd ever met.

They left the hotel and continued to weave in and out of other properties on their way back to Seashell Cottage.

The sun was lowering in the sky as she parked her car in

the driveway. Em got out and stretched. "I'm going for a walk on the beach."

"Enjoy it," Devin said agreeably. "I'm going to meet my friends at the Salty Key Inn for an early dinner. They leave tomorrow morning." He paused. "Thanks for today. I enjoyed your company."

"My pleasure," she responded, wondering what it would be like if things were different between them. But then, friendship was nice too. Her future depended on her gaining her footing and doing things for herself.

Some days later, as Em was sipping coffee on the porch, she heard the roar of a truck entering the driveway and eagerly rose to her feet. It sounded as if Benito had arrived. She hoped he'd brought Nina. She'd formed a bond with this little girl and learned a valuable lesson. She didn't have to share genes to grow attached.

She hurried out to the driveway and waved at Benito as he got out of the truck. "Did you bring Nina?"

"*Si*. She wanted to see you again." He went around the truck and opened the back door. "Nina, someone wants to see you."

"Em?" Nina said clearly.

A flush of tenderness flooded Em. As soon as the child ran toward her, Em picked her up and swung her around. "Hi, Nina! *¡Buenos dias!*"

The girl smiled shyly at her. "Good morning."

Surprised, she turned to Benito. "She's learning to be more comfortable with English."

He gave her a look of pride. "Yes, my daughter is working with her."

Em set Nina down on the ground. "There. Let's go inside. I

have a treat for you and, if you like, we can do some art projects together."

Benito explained that to Nina in Spanish and the little girl clapped her hands with excitement.

"I went to the Florida Botanical Gardens. Have you been?"

Benito shook his head.

"It's a wonderful place to visit. I hope you get to see it someday. I learned so much."

"Good. I have a gift for you." Benito reached into his truck and brought out a beautiful white orchid plant. "From my daughter and me for taking an interest in Nina."

Tears stung Em's eyes. "Thank you," she said, accepting the plant he handed her. "It's so thoughtful, and believe me, the pleasure is mine. Nina is a darling child."

Benito beamed with pride. "We think so too."

While Nina scampered around them, Benito and Em walked around the house checking the plants, talking about what needed pruning and what could wait.

"I will be working with such different plants up north, but it's so helpful to hear how you handle landscaping here," she said to Benito.

"Yes, I understand. Now I must do what I've talked about."

"And I'll watch Nina," said Em. She turned to the little girl. "Want to come inside?

Nina looked at her grandfather and then said to Em. "Yes, inside."

In the kitchen, Em laid out the coloring book and crayons she'd found in one of the cupboards. She fixed some lemonade and put a couple of cookies on a plate and set them on the table.

Nina's eyes lit at the sight of them. "*¡Por favor!*"

Em held the plate while Nina looked over the cookies and daintily lifted one off the plate. "*¡Gracias!*"

"*De nada,*" said Em, wishing she remembered more Spanish from her college classes.

Em worked beside Nina coloring a page of the Cinderella activity book.

"See how blue and yellow make green?" Em asked.

Nina blended the colors of the crayons Em handed her. "Pretty!"

Though they didn't speak much, there was a sense of warm camaraderie between them.

When Nina indicated she had to go to the bathroom, Em said, "I'll help you." She made sure Nina had what she needed, and afterwards, helped her wash her hands.

"Okay, now let's watch a movie. Which one do you want to see?"

Nina looked through the pile of old movies and picked Cinderella.

Later, when Benito came in to check on them, Nina and Em were watching the movie on the television screen. Benito gave Em a satisfied salute and returned outdoors.

As she sat facing the television, Em looked down at Nina's hand in hers, and her heart filled with contentment. She knew having a child was something she really wanted. It felt right.

When it was time for Benito and Nina to leave, Em gave each of them a hug. "I won't see you again, but thank you, Benito, for allowing me to spend time with Nina. She's a special little girl. And thank you for talking to me about plants and landscaping. I hope to put it to good use soon."

He bobbed his head. "You are a very nice lady. Someday you will be a very good mother."

"I hope so," said Em, blinking rapidly, touched by his words and the way Nina had wrapped her arms around her legs for a hug.

After they'd driven off, she walked down to the beach,

hoping to put her restless mind at ease. She had a lot to think about—a move to the condo, setting up her office, forming a business, and creating a full life for herself.

First things first, she reminded herself, and with a last look at the seagulls circling in the sky above her, she turned and went into the cottage to begin.

She'd just finished a list of items to buy for her condo when Devin arrived. Still in his gym clothes, he said, "How about lunch? If you share what you have in the refrigerator, I'll take you out to dinner tonight. It's my last night here."

"Okay, that's a deal," she answered, dismayed by the fact that he was leaving. She'd be alone for another couple of nights.

Em made sliced chicken and ginger relish sandwiches, set out potato chips and bottles of bubbly water, and went to get Devin.

He emerged from his bedroom in shorts and pulling a golf shirt over his taut abs. At the response to his sexiness, Em held her breath and let it out slowly, telling herself it might be a bit naughty to think of a friend like this.

"Thanks. I'm starving," said Devin, moving past, unaware of his impact.

Em followed him into the kitchen, relieved he'd be leaving soon. Seeing him like this had her thinking it might be difficult to keep him in the friend zone.

But as they sat at the kitchen table eating, their relationship settled into their old routine. And when Devin announced he was doing errands that afternoon, Em forced herself to stop weaving fantasies about them being together and went back to forming her plans for the future.

CHAPTER EIGHT

Em stood in front of the mirror assessing herself. Devin had told her to dress up because he'd decided to take her to Gavin's at the Salty Key Inn for dinner.

The black, sleeveless sheath fit her body well, her skin had tanned nicely with just a scattering of freckles across her nose, and her blond hair pulled away from her face was firmly tied at the back of her head. Altogether, not a bad look for her.

"Well, Em, as Gran would say, it's as good as it gets," she said, turning away from her image.

She stepped out of her bedroom and walked into the living room.

Devin's eyes widened when he saw her. "Wow! You clean up nice!" he teased.

She laughed, though her cheeks had gone from warm to hot.

"Ready? Let's go! I made a reservation for seven-thirty, but the restaurant will be crowded. We might have to wait for a while."

"I've heard Gavin's is one of the best restaurants along the coast."

Devin nodded. "Yeah, it's earned four stars from more than one food critic."

"I can't wait to see it! Thanks for taking me."

"It's the least I can do for having such a good housemate during this stay. I needed this break, and you've made it easy for me."

He held out his elbow, and she took it.

After Devin helped her into his car, he went around and climbed into the driver's seat. Though the Salty Key Inn wasn't very far, Em was glad he hadn't mentioned walking there. Her high-heeled sandals were cute but no good for walking any distance.

When they pulled through the entrance to the hotel, Em glanced around eagerly. The story of the three sisters who owned it was well known in the area. She'd read an article about them in a magazine left at Seashell Cottage.

Devin pulled up to the valet area and braked the car. A young man hurried to open the door for her. She stepped out onto the pavement and inhaled the delicious aromas coming from the restaurant. Butter, garlic, and other odors combined in a mixture of anticipation.

Inside the restaurant, wood-paneled walls were highlighted by crystal sconces that provided a soft glow around the perimeter of the room. Overhead, crystal chandeliers complemented the side lighting, washing the room in gentle light.

They followed a hostess to a table set in a tiny alcove that overlooked an outdoor garden. Fascinated by the way the design of the small garden made it a feature of the alcove, she took the seat offered to her and gazed out the window.

"Pretty, huh?" said Devin, taking his seat opposite hers.

"Yes, very elegant. I like it."

"I'm glad you agreed to go out with me tonight." He smiled at her. "I've made final arrangements with my colleagues, and I'm going to be very busy for the next few months traveling back and forth to Costa Rica. It was your simple suggestion that made this possible."

"I'm glad I could help," she said, pleased to see a happy glow on Devin's handsome face.

He grew serious. "I've been told I was selfish for trying to work something like this out. And others have ridiculed my lack of business sense for wanting to do humanitarian work. In a way, I understand. I have debts I need to pay back. I'm not going to be a wealthy man."

She reached out and patted his hand. "But you will be in every other way."

"I like you, Emerson Jordan," he said, giving her fingers a squeeze before pulling his hand away.

"Thanks. I like you too," she responded.

The wine steward arrived at their table. While Devin and he discussed wines, Em studied the twinkling lights woven among the greenery outside the window. In leafing through the books she'd bought, she'd seen enough pictures of gardens at night to realize that lighting might be another way to dress up what would otherwise be a simple garden.

"Hope you don't mind, but I've ordered champagne," said Devin. "I wanted this to be a special night to thank you for your encouragement."

"It sounds lovely." She'd tasted champagne occasionally at the weddings of some of her college friends, but hadn't had much.

The wine steward returned with an ice bucket on a stand containing a dark-green bottle and two flute glasses. He placed the glasses on the table and lifted the bottle out of the ice to show Devin. At a nod of approval from Devin, he opened the bottle, offered the cork to Devin, and poured a small amount of wine into Devin's glass to taste.

"Very nice," said Devin, nodding and smiling his approval.

The steward poured some champagne into Em's glass and refilled Devin's.

"Enjoy," said the steward, quietly leaving the table.

Devin lifted his glass to her. "Here's to success. Yours and mine."

"Yes," said Em, clicking her glass against his before taking a sip. The bubbly wine tickled her nose. A giggle escaped her before she allowed the rest to slide down her throat.

"That good, huh?" teased Devin, his eyes sparkling.

"It's delicious. Just took me by surprise." Her next sip was smaller.

"Let's order a nice appetizer to go with this. Anything but the caviar. I don't want you to end up washing dishes to pay for the meal."

She laughed, liking the fact that there wasn't any pretense about him. Jared had tended to be a little flashy.

They ordered shrimp puffs—lemony shrimp in a buttery, crisp wrapping of puff pastry.

Relaxed, Em began talking about the idea of adopting a child. "I have to look into the laws and regulations in New York, and I'm not ready to move forward until I have my business secured."

"I'm familiar with several adoptive families. For the most part, it turns out to be a wonderful solution. There are instances when families are unaware of medical histories and have to adapt. But kids everywhere can be a challenge." He studied her. "Are you up to it?"

"A few months ago, I would've told you no, but I truly do think I am. Enough to move forward with it when the time comes."

"Fair enough. Sounds like you've thought it out. What about a non-white child? How would you feel about that?"

"I've never considered it would be a problem. And now, after bonding with Nina, I feel stronger than ever that wouldn't stop me from adoption."

"I'm glad to hear it. I hate to see kids without a good home. It happens here in this country more often than one would think."

"Yes, and I'm sure you've seen a lot of it in your travels," commiserated Em.

A sadness filled his eyes. "Oh, yes. I guess being an only child, raised by a hardworking, single mother who struggled to find a safe place for us to live has made me more aware than others, but it exists everywhere and at any age."

"Where's your mother now?" Em asked.

"She died when I was eighteen. Cancer. Another reason to go into medicine."

The waiter came to their table to get their order, and the talk between them moved to a happier subject. Em ordered a pompano dish, and Devin ordered roast pork with an apple and walnut stuffing.

After the waiter had taken their orders, conversation turned to Em's family and more specifically the fact that Elena and Andrew were expecting their first child.

"Andrew has already asked me to be the baby's godfather," Devin said proudly, and for the first time, Em could sense a deep loneliness about him.

"I'd better be the baby's godmother," said Em in a teasing way. "I can't wait to see him or her. That baby is going to be spoiled for sure."

Devin laughed. "Nothing wrong with that if it's done right."

As they ate their meal, they talked about everything and nothing, each savoring the food. Em's baked fish with a citrus sauce was delicious.

Too full for dessert, she suggested going back to the cottage for a cup of coffee or tea.

Devin readily agreed.

After he settled the bill, they left the restaurant.

On the way to Seashell Cottage, Em gazed out at the water and observed the gold-tipped waves reflecting light from the moon and realized she'd truly miss Florida with its beaches, palm trees, and bright-colored flowers. But Ellenton was where her family was and where she needed to be. With Elena in Philadelphia, her parents and grandmother depended on her to help out. She'd do the best she could while working to set up her own business.

Devin parked the car in the driveway and helped Em out of the car. "Shall we sit on the porch for a while? I can bring a blanket out to you."

"Sounds good. And then I'll make coffee, if you want."

"Great."

Em lowered herself into a rocking chair and waited for Devin to bring her a blanket. The air at night in February was cool.

"Here you go," said Devin, coming from behind her and handing her the blanket.

She wrapped it around herself and smiled up at him. "Thanks. It's so lovely out, I want to enjoy the moonlight on the water. It still seems magical to me that I'm so close to the beach and palm trees are swaying nearby."

"I love the semi-tropical atmosphere too," said Devin. "I don't plan ever to live up north. I figure I can always visit if I want to see snow."

She laughed. "I don't like snow. It would be different if I skied."

After several minutes of silence, Devin got to his feet. "I'm going to leave early tomorrow morning. I have a meeting in Miami first thing. So, if you don't mind, I'm going inside."

"How about the coffee I mentioned earlier?" she said, unraveling the blanket from her shoulders and rising.

"I think I'm going to skip it."

"Okay. Well, I guess I'd better say goodbye," said Em, wondering if she should shake his hand.

Devin studied her, and gently pulled her into his arms. "I'll see you sometime, I'm sure. Probably at the baby's baptism."

She looked up at him. "Yes."

The world around them disappeared as they stared at one another.

Devin's lips came down on hers, sending waves of sensation through her. She closed her eyes and let herself fall into the moment.

"Ah," Devin said softly. He pulled away and stared at her wide-eyed.

"Wow!" Em gazed into his eyes and saw the surprise she felt. Aware she was headed for trouble, she quickly stepped away from him.

Devin cleared his throat. "Guess I'd better go. You've got work to do, and so do I."

"Yes, good idea," she lied, wishing he would stay.

He went inside, leaving Em feeling so alone she wanted to cry.

CHAPTER NINE

The next morning Em lay in bed, awakened by the sound of Devin's car pulling out of the driveway. Thinking of the kiss they'd shared, she felt as if her emotions were on a roller coaster. The magic of their kiss was inspiring to say the least, but they'd both willingly stepped away from it, each intent on pursuing their own path.

Still in her nightshirt, she got up and padded into the kitchen in bare feet and stood a moment. It was quiet. Too quiet. She noticed a note on the kitchen table and lifted it up. "Goodbye, Emerson Jordan. Good luck with all your plans! Devin."

She stared at the scrawl on the paper and sighed. Time to pull up her big-girl panties and get organized for the future she'd carefully planned.

After making coffee, she poured herself a cup and headed into the bedroom to work on her computer. She had a head start on her business plan, but no name for it. "Landscape Design by Emerson Jordan" was pretty boring. She tried a number of names and finally settled on "Living Designs". She liked the idea she could change the words around and do some cute advertising with it.

With that big decision made, she changed into her clothes and headed out to the beach, thinking inspiration for other aspects of the plan could be found there. Walking along the water's edge, hearing the cries of the birds, inhaling the smell of the water, her mind opened up to possibilities.

As she splashed her toes into the foamy edges of the water,

Devin's face came into her mind. He'd looked shocked by their kiss, but then his eyes had become shuttered. She understood his need to protect himself. She'd felt the same way.

After strolling along the sand, Em filled with fresh energy and hurried back to the cottage. Today, she was going to drive to Sarasota to visit the Marie Selby Botanical Gardens, well known for their orchids among other tropical treasures. It would be her last excursion in Florida because tomorrow she'd have to begin organizing for her return. She was hoping to make some stops along the way heading north.

Later, standing in the Conservatory at the Marie Selby Botanical Gardens, she was emotionally overwhelmed. The beauty of the orchids surrounding her was breathtaking, the flowers so perfect that tears stung her eyes. It might seem foolish to others, but by visiting botanical gardens in the last couple of days, she felt a renewed sense of creativity. She'd always been artistic, able to see colors in a different way from some people, and had always admired the textures and colors of living plants and flowers. But now she was better able to visualize what she could do for clients. First, she'd have to convince them she could do it.

By late afternoon, she was once again sated by all she'd seen. She loved all the gardens but, for her, the air plants in the Epiphyte Garden and the shapes and textures in the Bromeliad Garden were the most intriguing.

She headed back to Seashell Cottage exhausted but inspired. She'd grabbed a quick bite at the café but was looking forward to a simple supper at the cottage, maybe an omelet. And once more, she wanted to sit on the porch to unwind.

Back at the house, Em unloaded the books she'd bought,

poured herself a glass of wine, and walked out to the porch. The clear skies and bright sun had warmed the day. Taking off her shoes and wiggling her toes, she reminded herself to enjoy the moment. Snow and ice awaited her at home.

Sitting alone on the porch, it seemed empty without Devin's presence. She wondered what he was doing and how his next trip to Costa Rica would turn out for the dying mother and her child. Jared would make fun of Devin for being such a bleeding heart, but Em admired Devin for all he was doing.

Her cell phone rang. *Elena*. Smiling in anticipation, Em clicked on the call.

"Hey, mama sis. How's it going?" Em asked.

Elena laughed. "The mama part is doing well; the sis part is wondering how you are. Tomorrow is your last day at the beach, right?"

"Yes. I'll be heading up north early the following day. I must admit I'm going to miss being here. I've gone to two botanical gardens close by and am definitely opening my own landscape design consulting business. As soon as I get home, I'm going to talk to Marty Caster about working with him."

"That's so exciting! You've wanted to do something like this for a while now. Good for you." Elena hesitated and then said, "So, how did you and Devin get along?"

"Great. He's a nice guy. We've become good friends ..."

"Yes, I've gathered that. He told Andrew that you made it very clear that you were not interested in anything more right now."

"I've got plans for the future, plans that don't depend on any man to make them happen. We talked about it, and Devin made it clear he, too, was not about to get involved. He took off this morning before I even got up."

"I see," said Elena, sounding disappointed. "You're both so devoted to your professions and don't want to get tangled up in a relationship that it's probably a good thing Devin feels the same way you do."

A sharp pang of disappointment hurt Em. Part of her wished things could be different, but wishing didn't change reality. She'd learned that lesson the hard way.

"No news on the baby's sex?" she asked, changing the subject.

"Not yet," Elena said. "The big day is this week. I'm thinking it's a girl. I hope so anyway."

"Done any decorating yet?" Em asked. As Elena had admitted earlier, she was and always would be a planner.

"Well, I've been thinking of doing a color scheme of pale gray accented with either blue or pink colors, depending on whether the baby is Desi or Lucy."

"What? You're kidding, aren't you?"

Elena laughed. "Don't worry, that's not going to be the baby's real name. It's just how Andrew and I have been teasing our families."

"They're actually cute names," said Em.

"I know, but we're going to use family names when the time comes. First grandchild and all." Elena lowered her voice. "Did you hear that Gran had a date the other day?"

"Nooo, I didn't know that," said Em. "Guess I'd better get home and find out all about it. She's always been so independent."

"Anyone can have a change of heart, Em," said Elena, sounding more like a big sister.

"I know," Em replied. "I'll get the scoop when I get home and fill you in."

"Thanks. I'm feeling a little left out."

They talked about the weather and what Em might expect to find on the drive home and then said goodbye.

Putting the phone aside, she stared out at the water and the darkening sky. She'd yet to see the "green flash" everyone talked about, but knew the atmosphere had to be just right when the sun's orb lowered behind the horizon. Tonight, it was too cloudy for her even to try to see it.

Feeling a sudden chill, she went inside to fix dinner. Tonight, she'd watch a movie on television and then slide into bed, trying not to think of a certain doctor who wanted nothing to do with her.

The next morning when Em awoke, she decided to enjoy the day as much as possible. The idea of leaving filled her with sadness. Though she might never return to Seashell Cottage, it would remain a very special place to her—one of healing, new ideas, and of a rare friendship. Devin was a good man, steadfast in his beliefs.

She got out of bed, wrapped herself in the terry robe the cottage provided, and made her way into the kitchen to make coffee. The memory of having coffee each morning on the porch would, she hoped, warm her on winter days up north.

Outside, she lowered herself into a rocking chair and watched the early morning crowd seeking seashells. Bent over, they resembled long-legged crabs scouring the sand for treasures. During her stay at the cottage, she'd found a couple of shells to take home. But when walking the beach, she tended to look up into the sky to watch the birds above her and allow the sun to warm her face.

When she went inside, she rummaged in the refrigerator for the fixings for breakfast. The food she'd bought when she'd first arrived was almost gone. She'd leave what she could for the next person or the cleaning crew.

She was finishing her scrambled eggs when her cell phone rang. *Mom.*

"Hi, Mom! What's up?" Em asked cheerfully.

"It's Gran. She's fallen on ice and broken her left ankle. When we talked last, you mentioned you might stop at the Lewis Ginter Botanical Garden in Virginia on your way home. I hope, instead, you'll come home as soon as you can. Gran would never ask you to handle the flower shop and to forego any other plans, but I am. You know how she is about having that shop open six days a week. She's fussing about it already."

"Oh no! Is she badly hurt? Was it just her ankle?"

"Her knees are bruised and sore from where she landed, and her hands have scrapes. They kept her in the hospital because of a bump on her head."

Em heard the worry in her mother's voice and swallowed hard. She hated the idea of Gran being in pain and unable to keep busy in her shop. "I'm on my way."

"Oh, hon, I'm sorry. I know this is your last day, and you probably had plans."

"It's okay, Mom. I want to be there for Gran. I'll pack up and call you tonight when I check into a hotel."

"You're a darling daughter and a wonderful granddaughter," said her mother with feeling. "Thank you!"

Em clicked off the call, poured herself another cup of coffee, and set to work packing up. She checked weather reports along the route and breathed a sigh of relief. It looked like winter storms along the coast were heading out to sea.

Until she had to lug them all to her car, she hadn't realized how many books she'd purchased. But they would serve her well in her new business and would look good in her office.

Once she packed up, she checked the house for anything that might have been left behind, opening drawers in her room and surveying the closet one more time. She hesitated and then went to the bedroom Devin had used.

As she stepped over the threshold, she inhaled the spicy

citrus aroma of his aftershave lotion. She closed her eyes and imagined him standing there, waiting for her to say hello. A voice in her head whispered, “Foolish girl,” and she snapped back to reality.

After checking for anything left behind and finding nothing, she left the room, carefully picked up the orchid plant from Benito and his daughter, and hurried to her car. She had to get home to Gran.

Worry pushed Em northward, keeping her on the highways longer than she liked. And then, lying in bed in a motel, all she could see in her mind were cars flying by her or cars in front of her traveling much too slowly.

Two days later, exhausted, she pulled into her parents’ driveway.

As soon as she climbed out of the car, she saw her mother walking gingerly toward her.

“You’re here!” her mother exclaimed. “Be careful! It’s still icy. We’ve put down sand and salt, but it’s still slippery in spots.”

At the memory of her toes wiggling in sand just days ago, Em sighed, and she moved toward her mother. “I came as fast as I could. How’s Gran?”

Her mother shook her head. “She’s furious I called you, but secretly she’s glad.”

“Well, then, I’m happy I’m here. Don’t worry, Mom. I’ll make sure things are right at the flower shop.”

“Unfortunately, because of her injuries, she’s become frustrated over the effort it takes to do some of the simplest of tasks. As she gets used to the cast, she’ll adjust better. Can I help you with your luggage?”

“Sure,” Em said. “I didn’t have a chance to tell you that I’ll be settling on the townhouse condo by the end of the week and moving in as soon as possible."

"Your father and I will miss you, but it's only right for you to have your own space. Thank goodness, selling your share of the apartment in the city to a friend gave you enough funds to buy the condo here."

"I know," Em agreed, happy now that she was out of the rat race of life in the city and able to do things here. Relaxing in Florida had confirmed a slower pace produced more creativity in her.

Em suddenly stopped. "Oh my God! I forgot to ask. What is Elena having? A boy or a girl?"

Her mother grinned. "It's a girl. I'm thrilled."

Em hugged her mother and twirled her around. "A girl? That's great!! As soon as I get my things inside, I'm calling Elena."

Her mother grabbed the smaller suitcase and a canvas bag loaded with shoes. Em took hold of the larger suitcase and decided to leave the books where they were. They'd need to be carried into her townhouse in a matter of days. She could hardly wait.

As soon as her things were settled inside, Em called her sister.

"A girl?" Em said, holding in a scream of joy.

Elena laughed. "I guess Mom told you. I didn't want to distract you on the drive home. Everyone is so happy you came right home. Thank you, Em."

"You're welcome. Talk to you later. Congratulations to both you and Andrew. I'm thrilled for you."

Em hung up wondering what their little girl would look like. The image of Nina came to her. She felt a pang of longing and quickly pushed it away as she punched in the number for her grandmother.

"Hi, Gran, I'm home! I'm so sorry about your fall and I'm here to help. I'll meet you at the flower shop as soon as I can."

"Oh, dear child, that would be wonderful! I'll feel so much better knowing you're here to help me. Marilyn does her best, but she isn't you!"

Em was both pleased and worried by Gran's words. She wanted to be there for her grandmother. She had a bit of time to get things settled before the first signs of spring would appear, but she also had her own tasks to do before then. If necessary, she'd talk to her mother about the difficulty of doing both.

CHAPTER TEN

When Em stepped into Rainbow's End and saw her grandmother sitting behind the counter, her vision blurred. Now 76, Gran had always been full of energy, flitting from one end of the shop to another, but today she looked tired and ... old. Gran struggled to her feet and stood as Em rushed to her and gave her a hug, careful of her body.

"I'm so sorry about your fall, Gran." Her mother hadn't mentioned to Em her grandmother's cheek was bruised.

"It was black ice on the sidewalk. I never had a chance," Gran said. "But I'll heal fast now that you're here. I've been so worried about the store. With all the competition I face, even one day closed can make a difference."

"We'll have to make sure we have a backup for when we can't be here. Marilyn didn't want to do it?"

Gran shook her head. "She's a dear person but not great about handling a lot of details. She does the best she can with flower arranging, though. I have to give her credit for that."

"Well, okay. Do you need me to go over the books for you? Is that it?"

"Yes. I made sure deposits were made, but we need to check inventory and place orders, if need be." Gran's eyes watered. "Guess this old lady needs all the help she can get."

Em gave her a stern look. "No more talk about your being an old lady. You were doing just fine before I left, and you'll be back to your old self soon.

Gran sighed. "You're right. I guess I'm just feeling sorry for myself."

"Mom told me a fall like yours can take a toll on anyone. Let's chalk it up to that. By the way, I hear you went on a date. Was it with Michael Leaman by chance?"

Gran's cheeks turned a pretty pink. "Yes, we went out for dinner. I thought I'd enjoy getting out with him, but I'm too old to change my ways."

"You could have a change of heart," teased Em.

Gran laughed and waved her hand in dismissal. "I doubt it, but you're just the tonic I need. C'mon, let me show you the gifts you and I ordered for spring. They came in yesterday."

Em grinned. "It always feels like Christmas when we get a new order. And, Gran, I want to add a whole bunch of lawn ornaments that can be used in my business."

"Right," Gran said. "You can set up an account through Rainbow's End. I've earned quite a good discount with some of the companies I've worked with for years."

Em grinned. Gran was sounding more like herself.

Gran sat while Em opened several boxes, carefully unwrapping ceramic rabbits, tin wall baskets for flowers, special containers for flower bulbs, and an assortment of items to be placed around the shop, transforming the feel of it from winter to spring.

Em grinned as she looked down at the gifts lying at her feet. "The shop is going to be so pretty. I love when we can change the décor."

"Yes. I wouldn't trust anyone else to do that. I adore your mother and your sister, but they don't have the artistic talent you do."

"I used to get teased at school because I wasn't as smart as my big sister."

Gran shook a finger at her. "You can't always measure

talent like yours in a mathematics class. You're each gifted in your own way."

Em gave her grandmother an impulsive hug. "You always make me feel so good."

Gran hugged her back. "There's every reason to feel good about yourself. Now, we need to get these things shelved and the boxes put away."

"That's the editorial 'we,' right?" teased Em.

Gran laughed. "You've got that right."

Later, sitting at the dining room table at her mother's house, Em's head began to bob with fatigue. "If you don't mind, I'm going up to bed," she said, struggling to her feet. "I'm exhausted from the trip."

"Of course, dear," her mother said. "We appreciate your being home. It means so much to all of us."

"Especially Gran," her father said. "You're her favorite. No doubt about it."

"Wait until Elena's baby comes along. I'll be bumped out of that spot," said Em smiling.

"It's going to be fun getting ready for this baby. I just wish Elena and Andrew didn't live so far away," said her mother.

Em gave her parents a little wave. "I'm off to bed."

It felt good to be home where she was loved and treated well. Her thoughts turned to Devin. He was alone in the world and had probably never known this kind of life. She thought of how many children grew up without the basic things of a roof over their heads, food in their bellies, the opportunity to learn. She promised herself that she wouldn't give up on the idea of adoption.

###

The next morning, Em tiptoed across the cold tile in the bathroom. She longingly recalled how warm Florida had seemed to her and wrapped her robe tighter around herself. She'd have to get used to the cold all over again. Floridians sometimes complained about the humid heat of summer, but right now it sounded pretty wonderful.

Downstairs in the kitchen, she poured herself a cup of hot coffee and wrapped her hands around the ceramic mug. The heat in the house, she knew, would be turned up shortly, but now the space contained a chill enhanced by a cold wind outside that rattled the windows. February usually produced a winter storm. It appeared one was on its way.

She was sitting at the kitchen table when her mother walked into the room. "The weatherman says it's going to be a nasty day tomorrow. I'm glad you made it home before bad weather struck."

"Me too," said Em. "It's a good day to do some work at the shop, and I intend to drive over to the condos. Even though the official inspection is later this week, I want to get a good look at my place."

"Want company?" her mother asked. "I'm very curious to see how it turned out."

"Sure. You can help me add to a list I started of all the things I'll need. I've got some stuff from the old apartment, but I know I'll have to buy furniture. I have enough in my budget for the major pieces, but will probably have to wait for the rest."

"The town's rummage sale takes place in April. That might be a good way to pick up some things."

"Right. Craig's List will be good source for me too."

"It's amazing how the internet has taken over so many aspects of our lives," her mother said, shaking her head.

"You sound like an old lady," Em teased.

Her mother straightened with indignation and then laughed along with her.

The thought of having her own place was enticing. Her parents were generous and tried to make everything easy for her, but Em longed for the privacy she'd been lacking. And she was long past the time to be treated like a kid.

Driving into the Green Meadows condominium complex, Em felt a great sense of pride. She'd been very careful about saving her money while working in the city. And then, because she'd bought into an apartment with Kat and two other women in a neighborhood with increasing property values, she'd made money when she sold her share of it to a friend—enough to put a down payment on the condo.

Though construction was still going on and would for a while, she could easily envision how the area would look when spring came, and plants surrounded the buildings, and the trees that had been planted earlier leafed out. Butted up next to a wooded area near the river in town, the complex was designed to fit in with nature with clapboard and stone exteriors in neutral colors.

Em parked in front of her building. With four units in each of eight three-story buildings, she was pleased to have been able to secure an end unit with extra yard space along the side of it, a space she intended to use for a private garden.

"The complex is looking very nice even with snow on the ground," said her mother, smiling her approval.

"Wait until you see the inside. It looked great when I last saw it. I can't wait to see the finished product." Em got out of her car and hurried to the lockbox attached to the handle of the front door. She punched in the code to unlock it, lifted the key out, and held it up for her mother to see.

As the key slid into the lock and turned with a smooth twist, Em felt as if this was the beginning of more than a new life; it was the beginning of the new person she hoped to be.

She ushered her mother inside and stood a moment, studying the area in front of her. The entry hall bypassed a half bath and a small nook and led into an open space that contained a large family room with a fireplace on the outside wall. White book shelves lined the walls on either side of the fireplace. Beyond that space, one could clearly see the modern kitchen that Em knew held ample storage, a pantry, and a large eating area next to a bowed window that would one day look out onto the side garden. Between the living area and the kitchen, a sliding-glass door led to the outside where a small concrete pad had been poured. Behind the kitchen was a combined laundry and mud room that led to the two-car garage.

"They've done a wonderful job with the finishing touches. The wooden trim, painted white, looks fabulous with the pale gray walls," her mother exclaimed. "Let's see the upstairs."

The second story contained the master suite, and two smaller bedrooms separated by a Jack-and-Jill bathroom.

The third floor was more like an attic with sloping ceilings, lots of storage along the inner walls, and a small, open room off to the side that Em intended to use for her office. The wide window in that area would, she thought, allow her good light for sketching and studying color schemes for her work. Best of all, the built-in window seat was a good place to perch and think.

Em twirled in front of her mother. "Here's the future office of Living Designs, my new company."

Her mother clapped her hands. "How exciting! Love the name!"

"I've checked online for the name, and it's clear. Before I

came home, I filed with the state to form the company. I should be able to be in business soon."

Her mother lowered herself onto the window seat and patted the space next to her. "We haven't had a chance to talk. The other day, Dad and I were speaking about maybe having you buy out Gran's flower shop. How would you feel about it? Gran knows nothing about this and would be furious at us for thinking she can't handle it, but the truth is, she's approaching the time when it's going to be way too much work for her."

Em sank onto the seat beside her mother and stared out the window, giving her time to settle her racing thoughts. Finally, she turned to her mother. "I can't make any such commitment right now. I need to get my business up and running, and then maybe I'll be able to take a different view of it. Besides, after being at Seashell Cottage, I learned how much I like a warmer climate."

Her mother gasped and placed a hand on her chest. "What? You'd move to Florida?"

"I didn't say that, but it's something I've been thinking about lately. That, or having time to travel there in the winter months."

"Is it Devin? Is that why you're talking like this? I thought you said you were only friends."

Em patted her mother's arm. "We are only friends. That's all."

Her mother's sigh whispered in the air. "Elena was hoping you and Devin would connect, and Devin would move to New York. I guess she's as much of a dreamer as you." Her mother's smile was loving. "Devin is a fine young man. I liked him immediately when I met him. He's so kind, so thoughtful. Do you remember how sweet he was when he asked me to dance at the wedding?"

Em shook her head, feeling like a fool all over again for

focusing her attention on Jared when Devin was around. She thought back to Devin's remark about not being able to see her with a guy who couldn't dance.

"Was he a good dancer?" Em asked her mother.

"Very good. Why?"

She shrugged. "I don't know. He said I deserved to be with a good dancer, not someone like Jared." A chuckle bubbled out of her. "Jared was an awful dancer."

"Jared was wrong for you for so many reasons, but you wouldn't see it."

"I know. I've learned a lot about myself just being away for a while." She faced her mother. "How did you know Dad was the one for you? The kind of man who would always be there for you?"

"First of all, we were friends, then lovers. That gave us enough time to really know one another. Today, so many young people skip that first part that they end up being hurt. Lust can happen right away, but love takes time, and good, lasting love even longer."

Em thoughtfully nodded. "Okay, I get it. Maybe while I'm here, I'll start dating again."

She knew her mother's look of relief had a lot more to do with the idea of Em sticking around than having her start dating again.

As they were heading down the stairs, Barbara Arnold, the real estate agent in charge of the complex, called up to them. "Emerson? I need to talk to you."

"Hi, Barbara!" Em said, and introduced her to her mother. "I'm so excited about closing and moving in."

"Yes, that's what I wanted to talk to you about. For a few days, you'll be the only person living here at the complex. The construction team will be here during the day, and the real estate company is hiring nightly security, but I wanted to warn you in case you'd be afraid to stay here by yourself."

Em's mother frowned. "Oh, hon! I don't think it's a good idea ..."

"I'll be fine," said Em, giving in to her desire to be more independent, even as she fought a sense of unease.

"Okay, I'm technically off until Friday when we sign the papers," said Barbara, "but I saw your car and wanted to check on you. You have a beautiful new home. It's become one of the favorites with the colors you've chosen, along with the extras you've added."

"Thanks." Em walked Barbara to the door. "We'll leave now too. I'll see you on Friday." She handed Barbara the key. "Thanks for your help."

As Em and her mother walked to her car, she could sense her mother's concern, hear the clucking of her tongue in her mind. Em was worried too about being here alone even if it was temporary, but she couldn't start off her so-called new life of independence unable to move into her new home because of fear. Besides, her unit and all the others were wired for security. That would protect her.

CHAPTER ELEVEN

Gran was already behind the counter when Em arrived at Rainbow's End.

"Hi, Em! Just in time. We're about to start on the weekly business orders. The country club is holding a mid-winter dance, and in addition to the bouquet for the center hall, they want us to do arrangements for the ballroom. And then we have one anniversary bouquet and one birthday garden arrangement."

"Good news," said Em, loving the idea that her grandmother had built up such loyal clientele over the years. But then, Rainbow's End provided outstanding arrangements—classic to unique.

As Em hugged her grandmother, Marilyn Fields emerged from the back room. "Hi, Em! Am I glad you're back! I need your expertise for our new orders."

"Glad to help," Em said cheerfully. She liked having a lot to do, and after seeing the flowers in Florida, she was inspired to try some new things. When she went to hang up her coat in the office, she saw a lot of paperwork on the desk and realized Gran had left a lot of office work for her too. She told herself to take a deep breath and not worry about it. As Em tried to explain to Marilyn about the use of small, green plants and succulents for the garden baskets, it became clear to her that Marilyn was good at following directions but lacked enough creativity to come up with her own designs. Em sighed inwardly. They'd have to hire additional help as Em's business took off—something Gran was always reluctant to do.

Em quickly drew a design for the anniversary bouquet and left Marilyn to work on it while she checked paperwork in the office. As Gran had told her, the deposits had been made. But invoices needed to be paid and all information put into the online bookkeeping system.

First, she had to check the order book and determine what flowers they might need. Several years ago, Gran had arranged for a fellow florist to make the trip into New York City to the flower market in Chelsea to buy flowers for her. When she lived in the city, Em had worked in tandem with him, discovering the wonderland provided by flowers from all over the world. Of all the family members, she was and had been the most involved with the flower shop, working there after school and on weekends in high school, taking design, art, and horticulture courses in college, and helping Gran now.

Em quickly made a list of flowers to use for the upcoming week and then, with Florida in mind, added a few new greens for experimentation.

"What do you think, sweetheart?" Gran said, holding up the anniversary bouquet Marilyn had made.

"Nice. I want to add a touch or two, though. I'll ask Marilyn to help me."

"Good. I thought you'd say that." Gran hesitated. "I think we should put an ad in the paper announcing spring and your return to the shop."

"Let's hold off for a while. I need to see how everything is going to work out on the move to the condo and setting up my new business."

Gran gave her an apologetic look. "Oh, right, of course. I keep forgetting that. I'll leave you to your work."

Worry filled Em as she watched Gran leave the office. The fall had taken a lot more out of her than Em had thought.

She'd always thought of her grandmother as strong and eager for any challenge. Now, she seemed almost broken.

Rather than go home for dinner, Em went down the street to the Ellenton Diner, grabbed a hamburger, and brought it back to the office. Once she got started making the financial entries, she didn't want to stop. They were on target. That was the good news. The bad news was that Gran's usual tidiness was missing. She'd had to search for receipts and other papers to do the input.

After closing up and locking the office, Em made her way to her car. The storm that had threatened earlier was already beginning to let loose. Wet snow driven by the wind struck her cheeks with cold. She wrapped her arms around herself and found her way to her vehicle. The car seemed to curl with the cold as the wind shook it, making it seem as if the little convertible was shivering.

She hurried to it and climbed inside, anxious to get home.

The next morning Em sat in the kitchen, sipping coffee and gazing out at the white blanket of snow covering the ground and laying atop tree branches like icing. An early morning snow was the one time she loved it. Soon, though, the inconvenience of waiting for snow plows, the muddying of the roadways, and the marring of the snow's whiteness would erase the magic of it. Today, she thought, she'd take advantage of the quiet time to do some online shopping for the condo.

Her mother hurried into the kitchen in a pink, fluffy robe. "You're up so early!"

"I couldn't sleep," Em admitted. "Those numbers of Gran's shop kept circling in my mind."

Her mother stopped and frowned. "Everything's all right, isn't it?"

"Oh, yes," Em said. "But it's going to be a challenge to keep the numbers up if Gran can't stay at the job. She's the reason business is so good. Her customers love her, and so do the suppliers."

"And they love the work you do, Emerson," said her mother sternly.

'I know, but I think we're going to need to hire a professional floral designer. I can't do everything myself and run another business too. And, Mom, I want the chance to see what I can do on my own."

Her mother sat down at the kitchen table and squeezed her hand. "You deserve that. Give Gran enough time to understand that she might need to have professional help brought in so you can have more flexibility. She'll fight the idea at first, but I know she wants you to be happy."

"And you and Dad will wait to see how I do before you mention the offer for me to buy her out?"

"Yes," her mother said sheepishly. "Your father and I were so excited about having you come home that we jumped too quickly to try to make things right for both you and Gran. That's something you two will have to work out on your own."

Feeling better, Em took another sip of hot coffee.

Later, Em sat in front of her computer studying furniture from various companies, listing her choices and their costs. She knew she couldn't buy everything she wanted, but it gave her a better idea of what she liked and what would fit nicely in her condo. Later, she'd visit the nearest furniture stores and see what she could find.

On a whim, she put an ad in the local newspaper looking for a floral designer. She knew it was chancy to go ahead without Gran's approval, but she wanted to see just how far afield she'd have to go to find someone willing to work in Ellenton.

She reviewed her business plan and called Marty Caster. His voicemail announced he was back in town but busy with snow plowing and to please leave a message.

Em hung up, deciding to bide her time. She wanted to face him in person and give him a professional presentation of what she had in mind.

On Friday, Em drove to the realtor's office to sign final documents for the purchase of her condo. Barbara met her with a cheery hello and introduced her to the lawyer handling the sale for the development company.

An hour later, after all details were taken care of, Em was handed the keys to the condo.

"Congratulations," Barbara said, giving her a hug. "You have a beautiful new home."

The lawyer representing the development company came over to her. "Congratulations. You bought into the project at a good time. Prices for the condos are already up ten thousand dollars."

"I like to hear that," Em said. "You're settling on the three other condos in my building soon?"

"Yes, within two weeks," the lawyer said. He studied her. "'Sure you don't want to wait a week or so before moving in?"

"I'm sure. I'm having some of my furniture delivered tomorrow, and the cable guy is scheduled to come this afternoon."

"Okay, then. As mentioned earlier, the developers have hired a night guard who will keep an eye out for you and your unit, along with the rest of the property."

"Thanks," Em said, anxious to leave for her new home.

She'd been excited to purchase a car, but this was ten times bigger.

As promised, her mother met her at the condo.

Carrying a beautiful bouquet of flowers in a square vase, her mother smiled at her. "Gran had me pick these up for you as a housewarming gift."

"How nice." Lilies, freesia, and pink roses were a favorite combination of hers. "Let's set it down and get to work."

Together, they unboxed things she'd brought from the city. And then Em attacked the boxes recently shipped from online sources. Her excitement grew with each new item purchased for the condo unwrapped. And when the cable guy showed up to make sure her television and internet access were set up, she was thrilled. Now, the condo was home.

"Are you sure you don't want to sleep at the house?" her mother asked. "Your bed won't be here until tomorrow."

"I want to sleep in my own home for my first night here."

"How about dinner?" her mother asked, smiling.

"I'm ordering JC's Pizza," Em said. "It's the best."

Her mother chuckled. "Okay, then, I'm off to meet your father." She kissed Em and hugged her, then with a wave she was gone, leaving Em to rejoice in her surroundings.

She walked up to the second floor to check on the air mattress she'd placed there. Taking a blanket from the linen closet she lay it on top, then grabbed the pillow she'd brought from home. Satisfied she'd be comfy and cozy, she went back to the kitchen to open the half-bottle of champagne the realtor had left in the refrigerator for her. Time to celebrate.

She poured the wine into one of the new glasses she'd ordered. In the past she would've refused to celebrate alone, but now, with her plans for the future intact, she thought it fitting.

In the living room, she turned on the gas fireplace and sat

on the soft carpeting in front of it. Enjoying the warmth of the fire, studying the almost empty bookshelves, she could hardly wait to fill them with more books and small art objects.

She realized she was hungrier than she'd thought and lifted her cell to call in her pizza order when it rang in her hands. *Kat*. Thinking it might be something about a future wedding with Jared she didn't answer. Then her phone pinged, indicating a message. *"Em, I need to talk to you. Kat."*

When the second call from Kat came through, Em reluctantly answered it. *Best to get it over and move on,* she thought*, but I refuse to be in the wedding*.

"Hello, Kat," Em said calmly, though she still was hurt by Kat's betrayal. They used to share a fun friendship.

"First of all," said Kat, "I want to apologize to you again for hurting you. I never meant to do that. I guess I was so caught up in my relationship with Jared that I let that take over everything."

"I get it, Kat. So, when is the wedding? That's what you're calling me about, isn't it?"

Kat's snort told a different story. "I've broken up with Jared. It turns out it was only talk. Like you, I've discovered he's the type of guy who won't or can't make a commitment."

"What? After all you told me? No way."

Kat's sobs stopped conversation.

Shock kept Em quiet, and then she said, "When did this happen?"

"While you were in Florida. I wanted to call you earlier, but I thought you probably hated me, and I needed time to get up my nerve to call you." Kat's voice shook with emotion. "Em? Do you think we could ever be friends again?"

Em hesitated. "I don't know."

"It's important to me," said Kat. "We were friends once. Please, could we start over?"

"We can try," Em said honestly. "But it comes with a promise not to hurt one another."

"Yes, oh, yes. I promise," said Kat.

"You really hurt me."

"I know. It's something that keeps bothering me. When are you coming to the city? Can I meet you somewhere?"

"No, not for a while," Em said. "I'm sitting in my new home having some bubbly champagne to celebrate."

"New home? Wonderful? Is it the condo you were thinking of buying?"

"Yes. It's my first night here."

"I want to hear all about your plans, see your new home, everything."

"After I get settled," Em said, "I'll call sometime."

"Thank you, Em. So glad we can be friends again."

"Mmm," Em said, clicking off the call before she changed her mind. Her thoughts spinning, she leaned back and stretched out on the carpet. Jared could be very charming. She understood how Kat could have fallen for him, but she also knew she'd be careful if the time came for either one of them to be in her future.

She realized it was getting late and called in her order for pizza. Tomorrow would be an early day. Her furniture was scheduled to arrive first thing in the morning.

As she waited for delivery of her veggie pizza, one of her favorites, she gazed out the front window. The complex was going to be lovely when it was completed.

At the knock on her door, Em jumped and went to answer it. Keeping the safety chain on, she peered out to see a young man wearing the familiar baseball hat with JC's Pizza's logo on it.

She opened the door, gave him a tip, and accepted the box he handed her.

"Wasn't sure I had the right address," the young man admitted. "Looks like yours is the only unit occupied."

"Yes, I know. We're looking forward to getting new neighbors soon," she said, hoping to give him the impression that she was living with someone.

"Good thing," he said, glancing around.

As he trotted to his car, Em quickly locked the door.

CHAPTER TWELVE

When Em's alarm sounded, she jolted out of sleep. She'd had a rough night of awaking to every strange sound in her condo. It was close to morning, she knew, when she must have fallen asleep.

Later, as the first piece of furniture was unloaded off the truck, Em's parents arrived.

"Thought you could use a little extra help getting the furniture placed," said her father, giving her a hug.

"Thanks," she said, happily accepting his embrace. David Jordan was a college professor of history who was blissfully unaware that most of his female students fell a little in love with him. He and her mother were a devoted couple who kept their marriage alive by sharing many similar interests in travel, the arts, and tennis. On the tennis courts, they were not quite as devoted, trying to outdo one another with tricky shots. Raised by Gran alone, her father was molded to be polite, kind, and attentive to the female sex.

After the delivery truck roared away, a couch, an easy chair, and coffee table were placed in the living room, along with an end table, a table lamp and a standing lamp. A new television sat inside a box ready for hookup. Upstairs, her father was assembling the bed Em had ordered. One of the end tables meant for the living room was going to be used as a night stand until she could find a bargain to replace it. On the third floor, a new desk, chair, and chair mat sat in the office Em planned. An overstuffed chair in a funky print and a book case were on backorder.

"It's a good beginning," said her mother standing in the living room. "You've done a great job of picking out items."

"I'm going to fill in with little things from different places when they go on sale," she said. Already she could envision how she wanted things to be.

The doorbell rang. She hurried to answer it.

"Happy new house!" cried her sister. "I couldn't miss out!"

Em pulled Elena into her arms and hugged her hard. "I'm so glad you're here. Come in."

"How'd you get here?" cried Em's mother, rushing over to them.

"Andrew drove. He and Devin are looking for a better place to park. Construction trucks are all around."

Devin? Em felt her knees weaken and grabbed hold of her sister's arm. "What are they doing here?"

"They have a conference to go to in the city tomorrow. So, I decided to come along." She turned. "Here they are now."

Elena's husband, Andrew, was a well-built man with brown hair, hazel eyes, and an open face that easily broadcast humor along with a sense of decency. His patients adored him. Em glanced at him then turned her gaze to Devin.

He grinned. "Hi! I didn't expect to see you again so soon, but Andrew and Elena insisted I come for a visit and then ride up with them to the conference."

Em fought for nonchalance. "It's good to see you again. Come in, all of you. I can offer you coffee, tea, water, and left-over pizza."

Elena laughed. "Thought so. That's why I made the guys stop at the supermarket before coming here."

"Yeah, we were told not to bring the bags of groceries in until Elena was ready," Andrew said.

"And she threatened us if we ate anything before then," said Devin, giving Elena a playful wink.

Elena laughed. "We all better go down to where Andrew parked the car and grab a bag or two."

"What a sweet idea, darling," Em's mother said to her.

Em followed the others to Andrew's Lexus and stopped in surprise. The whole back end of the SUV was filled with grocery bags.

"Enough to feed an army," Em's mother said.

Elena turned to Em. "I know how good it feels to have a kitchen well-stocked. This should be a good beginning."

"Thanks," said Em, giving her sister a quick hug. "Mom said the same thing. A good beginning. I think so too."

Devin caught her eye and nodded.

Still lost in his gaze, her heart felt ready to burst. Her life seemed very good right now.

While Andrew and Devin set to work on getting the television hooked up, Em, Elena, and their mother put the groceries away.

"Let's make sandwiches for the men," Em suggested. "Dad must be hungry, and I bet we could entice Andrew and Devin to join him and the rest of us with a good lunch."

"Perfect," said Elena. "I don't know why it is, but I feel hungry all the time."

"I can't wait to see that baby," said Em. "I'm going to be the best aunt ever!"

"And a good mother too," said Devin walking into the room and giving her a smile.

The looks of surprise on Elena's and her mother's faces sent heat to Em's cheeks. "Devin and I met a little girl in Florida, the granddaughter of the gardener, and I became very attached to her."

"I see," said her mother, looking from Devin to her

thoughtfully. "You've always wanted a big family."

"Before I do anything else, I'm going to get my business up and running," she said quickly, hoping to break the speculation that hovered in the room like a puffy cloud full of rain about to spill all her secrets, drop by drop.

Later, as they sat eating ham and cheese sandwiches at her new dining table or standing at the bar in the kitchen like Devin and Andrew, Gran entered the room, moving a little awkwardly with the walking boot on her left foot. Fortunately, her break wasn't as bad as it could've been, so she'd avoided needing crutches, which could have been a real problem.

Her father rose from his seat. "Hi, Mom. Come sit down. I'm almost done."

"Thanks, son," Gran said, smiling at him as she slowly made her way to the table. "I had to come see Em's new place."

"How about lunch?" Em said, jumping to her feet to give her grandmother a hug.

"Thanks. It has to be a quick one. I don't like to leave Marilyn alone in the shop for too long." Gran's gaze turned to Devin. "Ah, how are you, sweet boy? Ready for another dance with me?"

Devin laughed. "Any time, Gran, though. I see you're not quite ready to do that."

"Not yet." Still chuckling, Gran hugged Andrew and made her way to Elena. "And how's the mother-to-be?"

Elena grinned and hugged her. "Still trying to come up with a name for the baby."

"I've always thought Julia was a nice name," Gran said, bring laughter to the group.

As Gran sat down, she squeezed Em's mother's hand affectionately and turned to Em. "I've got a surprise coming to you. It should be delivered this afternoon."

"Oh? You know I love your kind of surprises."

Gran's face lit with pleasure. "When Elena and I talked earlier this week, she mentioned she might make a visit. So, this should help."

"If it's what we talked about, it's perfect," said Elena.

"Are you going to go ahead and tell me, or do I have to wait until later?" Em said, placing her hands on her hips.

"Later," Elena said. "Definitely later." She turned to Gran. "It's nice that you can drive. I'm glad to see you doing so well. I know how frustrated you'd be otherwise. How's business since it happened?"

"It's a slow time of year, but with Em here to make sure we get the store all decorated for spring, things will pick up, I expect." She patted Em on the shoulder. "I hope you'll be able to handle the shop on Monday. Your mother insists on accompanying me to my doctor's appointment."

"Okay. I've set up an appointment with Marty later in the week regarding my business. And I've placed an ad for a flower designer to help us at the shop."

Gran's eyes widened, but she said, "I suppose it's time to do that."

After Gran and her parents left, Em stayed at the kitchen table talking to Elena.

Andrew turned to Devin. "C'mon. I'll show you the town."

"Sounds good." Devin turned to her. "Thanks for lunch."

Em laughed. "Don't thank me. Thank Elena and Andrew. It was all their stuff."

"Okay then," Devin said with a little bow, "I thank all of you for a great lunch."

Alone with Elena, Em struggled to hide her emotions. Her sister wasn't anyone she could fool. Sure enough, when Em faced her, Elena's smile was smug.

"So, the two of you are just friends. Is that it?"

"Yes. We're both busy professionals."

"Really? Is that what you tell one another?" Elena shook her head. "Amazing."

"I don't want to go back to my old self, dreaming up possibilities that aren't there. Besides, nothing could come of it. I'm setting up my own business here. It's important. I need to know I can make a go of it, or I'll always wonder if I wasn't good enough."

"Ouch! I've obviously touched a nerve," said Elena. "I'm sorry. I really am. Let's talk about the floral designer you want to hire. Any ideas where you'll find someone like that?"

"I'm hoping to get someone nearby. Ellenton is a nice town. Maybe someone would even move here. By the way, Kat called me yesterday."

Elena's eyes gleamed. "That was nervy of her. Tell me all about it. What did she want?"

By the time Em had filled in her sister with the details, they were both shaking their heads.

"You were so smitten with Jared that you wouldn't listen to any of us. I guess he affected Kat the same way," said Elena.

A knock on the door brought both of them to her feet.

"I bet it's the delivery," Elena said smiling.

When Em opened the door, she saw a delivery truck with the name of a company she loved. She turned to Elena. "Oh, my word! What has Gran done?"

"You'll see. You're the one who told me about it," said Elena, refusing to say more.

The minute Em saw the headboard come off the truck she clapped her hands. "Now I can sleep someone in my guest room. Wonderful!"

Elena grinned "And now I'm able to comfortably spend the night. Gran knew I'd want to, and she also knew she'd feel better if you had someone with you."

"She's the best," Em said, directing the delivery man inside the condo.

Later, after the bed had been put together, Em and Elena made up the bed with the clean sheets, blanket, and quilt that had been purchased with the bed. Standing back looking at it, Em's heart filled with love. Her family was the best.

The sound of feet on the stairs caught her attention. She turned to see Andrew and Devin.

"Come see what Gran gave Em for a housewarming gift," Elena said. "I'm going to spend the night here so Em isn't all alone in the complex."

Devin frowned. "What do you mean, all alone?"

"The other condos are being sold, but no one has scheduled to move into the complex for another five days or so," Em explained.

Devin continued to frown but didn't say anything.

The rest of the afternoon was spent with the four of them lounging in the living room watching an action movie the guys loved. Em fixed microwave popcorn, and with the four of them sitting together on the couch, she thought it was the perfect way to celebrate her new home.

After they'd ordered and eaten a Chinese dinner, Em sat in the kitchen with Elena, Andrew, and Devin chatting about the forthcoming baby and how it could change anyone's life.

Em hesitated and then blurted, "I'm thinking of adopting a child or maybe even becoming a foster parent."

"Whaaat?" said Elena. "What about having children of your own?"

"I want that too, but I may never meet the right person—someone who's willing to live in Ellenton. In the meantime, I'm building a life and a business here. In addition, I don't want to disappoint Gran. She's worked hard to make her flower shop a success. And now Mom and Dad want me to buy her out."

Elena shook her head. "Em, I think they believe they're helping you, but they're not if it means you don't feel free to do your own thing."

"Yeah," said Andrew. "You can work with plants and flowers anywhere, if that's what you really want."

"But my family is here," she said, wondering why she was defending herself when, in reality, she sometimes felt frustrated by the obligations that had been placed upon her.

"Oh, my God! I'm going to be sick! It must have been something I ate," said Elena, rising and gripping the edge of the table. Her face turned white. She ran out of the room toward the half bath near the entrance.

Em started to go after her but stopped when Andrew hurried to catch up to her.

She turned to Devin. "Is she going to be all right?"

He gave her a reassuring smile. "I'm sure she'll be fine."

A few minutes later, Elena and Andrew returned to the living room.

"I'm sorry, Em, but I think I'd better stay at Mom and Dad's house tonight. Andrew thinks it's a good idea," said Elena. She looked awful.

"Why don't I stay here with Em? I don't like the idea of how alone she is here." Devin turned to her. "Is it okay if I stay?"

"Thanks. I'd feel better if someone were here," she admitted, "but I don't want to put you in an uncomfortable position. I slept here alone last night."

Elena gave her a knowing look. "And how comfortable was that?"

When she hesitated to answer, Elena said. "I thought so. Devin, it would be wonderful if you took my place tonight and stayed here."

"Consider it done," Devin said, giving Elena a nod of assurance before turning to Em with a grin that made her wonder if this situation might be more dangerous than being left alone.

CHAPTER THIRTEEN

After Elena and Andrew left, Em tried to think of how to fill the awkward moment. Devin saved her by saying, "Why don't we take a walk? I think it's important for you to know your surroundings. Then you might not be so concerned about staying alone." He studied her. "You don't want to stay with your parents a few extra days?"

She shook her head. "I know it may sound silly, but I want this to be the start of something new for me—my own house and my own new business."

"I get it," he said. "Let's take a look around."

Em grabbed her jacket, and they walked out the door.

Hers was the second building in the complex. The others formed a circle around a courtyard that held the clubhouse, which was in the midst of construction, and a swimming pool. Lights shone from the outside walls of the clubhouse and from the street lights that had been installed on the property. But in the dark, there were a lot of spaces that clung to shadows.

"This is going to be very nice when it's completed," Devin remarked, indicating the clubhouse and the rest of the property. "I'm happy for you."

"Thanks. Did Andrew show you the rest of the town?" she asked.

"Yes. It, too, is very nice. I understand why you don't want to leave here." He shook his head. "I couldn't wait to leave my hometown."

She stiffened as a tall, heavy-set male figure walked toward them.

Though Devin lifted a hand in a wave, he drew closer to Em.

"Hey, there!" said the man. "What are you doing here? This property is private." He studied them carefully as he stopped about ten feet from them.

Em let out the breath she hadn't realized she'd been holding. "I live here."

"Ah, are you the woman in B #101?"

"Yes, Emerson Jordan," she replied. "And this is my friend, Devin Gerard."

The men shook hands. "I'm Nick Munro, the night guard."

"Are you here every night?" Devin asked.

Nick shook his head. "Five nights a week. I'm off Sunday and Monday nights. Then I'm not sure who's on. It changes from time to time."

"I'm glad to meet you," Em said.

"You have only a week or so, and then there's going to be a lot more activity. I'm told that your building is sold out and the next one too. Be careful walking around, though. We wouldn't want anyone to get hurt in the construction area and, as always, be careful with strangers."

He went on his way.

Devin turned to her. "Feel better? He looks like he could take down anyone."

"Looks like a former football player to me. And, yes, I do feel more secure knowing he's around."

"Good," said Devin, taking her hand. "Better not trip. Now let's look around."

As they walked around the complex, they talked easily with one another about their plans, the latest weather report, and recent news on television. Em enjoyed the fact that Devin responded to her remarks without judgment. With some of the other men she'd dated, Jared, in particular, she'd been forced to measure her words carefully.

When they got back to the condo, Devin's suitcase was sitting by the front door with a note from Andrew saying that he'd pick him up at six-thirty the next morning.

"Guess we'd better get you to bed," said Em, blushing when she realized how that might sound. "I mean you've got to get up early, and it's late."

His eyes twinkled with humor. "I know what you meant."

Later, standing in the living room and staring at the couch, she said, "Are you sure you want to sleep on the couch? The guest bed is made up with fresh bedding. It might be more comfortable for you there."

"I think it's better if I stay down here. I'll be fine. And this way I won't disturb you in the morning; I'll just quietly slip out of the house. But I would like to use the guest room bathroom to take a shower now, if you don't mind."

"Not at all. Let me make sure you'll have everything you need. I'm pretty sure we put fresh towels in there, but I'll check."

Em hurried up the stairs to the guest room. The thought of Devin naked in her condo sent her imagination into overdrive.

When she was certain he'd have everything he needed, she left the bathroom and went downstairs to the kitchen to fix herself a cup of hot tea.

Later, when Devin appeared in the living room carrying his Dopp kit with his personal gear and wearing only a pair of jeans, she knew she was in trouble.

"Guess, I'd better say goodnight and goodbye," she said, standing. "I'm sure I'll see you again. At the baby's christening, if not before."

Devin set down his belongings on the couch and walked

over to her. "It's been great seeing you." His gaze lingered on her, sending her nerves on high alert.

He held out his arms, and without hesitation, she stepped forward into his embrace.

When his lips met hers, she closed her eyes as desire rolled through her in sensual waves. In all her years of dating, she'd never been kissed like this, and it felt so ... so delicious.

After a few moments, Devin lifted his head, stepped back, and drew a shaky breath. His green eyes darkened with concern. "I'm sorry. I shouldn't have done that. It only complicates matters, and I'd never want to hurt you."

"Oh, but ..." Her voice trailed off. He was right. He had his important work to do in Florida and Costa Rica, and she had obligations in Ellenton. She fought her disappointment and smiled at him. "I'd still like to be friends. I'm able to talk to you freely about things, and I know when the time comes for me to build a family, I'll need your advice."

"Consider it done. You have my phone number." He reached out and stroked her cheek. "Text me anytime."

Tears stung Em's eyes. She quickly blinked them away. "Thanks. Help yourself to anything you need in the morning. And safe trip, Devin." She gave a little wave to him and hurried up the stairs, wondering why the timing of things never seemed to work for her.

The next morning, Em heard the sound of the front door closing, rolled over, and stared out the bedroom window, listlessly observing morning light slipping through the cracks in the blinds. She pushed aside her disappointment and thought of the time ahead. Today, if she was lucky, she'd be able to talk to Marty Caster about a partnership of sorts, allowing her to do consulting with some of his clients. With renewed energy, she bounded out of bed.

She was in the kitchen eating breakfast when Elena called. "Hi! I'm so sorry about last night. How did it go with Devin?" Her voice lowered. "Anything you want to tell me? It was the perfect time for you two to be able to figure things out."

"Elena, it's not that way between us," she said as forcefully as she could, though she was beginning to think Elena was right all along. Devin was perfect for her in many ways. "Are you feeling better?"

"Yes. Now it's just the usual ickiness that comes and goes with pregnancy. Mom made me her special tea, and I felt a lot better. Guess once you're a mother, always a mother."

A pang of envy pinched Em's insides, but she brushed it away. In good time, her day would come.

"Want to meet for lunch?"

"Lunch sounds great," said Elena. "Nothing fancy. How about the Lettuce Leaf?"

"Great. They have delicious soups and salads. I'll pick you up at noon unless I have to do something for Gran. If so, I'll call you."

Sitting inside the Lettuce Leaf restaurant, Em was amused by the number of people who came over to their table to congratulate Elena on having a baby and to say hello to her.

"So nice to see the Jordan girls together," warbled a friend of Gran's. "Emerson, Julia is so glad you're home and able to help with the flower shop. It means so much to her."

"Yes, I know," Em said politely. "I'm happy to help her and will also be starting my own business."

After Gran's friend left the table, Elena gave her a soulful look. "I understand now why it would never work between you and Devin. Like you said, you each have big commitments."

They finished their Caesar salads in silence.

"How about dessert?" Em asked, giving Elena a sly look. "Want to split their famous Butter Cake?"

Elena grinned. "Only if you don't mention it to anyone else. I was complaining about how hard it is to grow from my usual size to something that is beginning to look like I swallowed a melon."

"It's a deal," said Em. "I haven't had one of these deserts in a long time, but I know it'll be worth it."

"Oh, yes," said Elena.

After they ordered it, they continued talking as they waited for its arrival.

"Mom has already spoken to me about christening the baby here in Ellenton at our church. We thought maybe 4th of July weekend. How would you feel about that?"

"It sounds nice. Much nicer than the last one. I can't believe how foolish I was," lamented Em.

"I've already asked Devin to save that weekend. Will it be awkward to see him again?"

Em frowned and shook her head. "No, of course not. In fact, it might be very good. He may help me with a couple of ideas I have."

Elena arched her eyebrows but said nothing as their waitress approached.

"Enjoy," said the waitress, smiling, setting down the cake on the table, and handing each of them a dessert spoon. "It's my favorite of all."

Em and Elena looked at the huge bowl in front of them and laughed.

With a knife, Elena drew a line down the middle of the cake topped with a mound of vanilla ice cream drizzled with caramel sauce.

Em chuckled at the careful way Elena had divided it. She

and her sister had shared a lot of things through the years.

By the time they were ready to leave, Em's belly was comfortably full.

Elena patted her round stomach. "I'll have to walk a few extra blocks to burn off the calories, but I'd do it again. That was delicious."

Em drove Elena to their mother's house, ran inside to say hello, and then drove to her condo to do a little more unpacking.

The next morning, Em hurried to Rainbow's End. She had an hour to start decorating the store before she was to meet Marty at AAA Landscapes.

Gran and Marilyn continued work in the back room as Em took apart the Valentine display in one of the front windows and began transforming it into a spring scene complete with pussy willows, tulips, daffodils, and hyacinths. Sprinkled throughout, ceramic bunny rabbits paused, plants filled flowery pots, and small gifts added fun and texture.

A woman outside the store stopped and waved at her before entering. "I love the new display. Can I buy a few pieces from there?" the customer asked.

"No, but we have duplicates."

Gran entered the store. "I heard the bell." Seeing the customer, Gran said, "Well, hello, Margery. Good to see you!" They hugged and then Gran said, "What can we do for you?"

Em went back to work, putting a finishing touch to the display.

"Can I help?" Marilyn asked, standing by.

"Yes, all these things from the Valentine window display need to be tagged for sale and put in our sale corner," Em answered. "I have to leave for a meeting, but I'll be back before we close." Excited and not a little nervous, Em grabbed her coat and her small briefcase and headed out, hoping for a good meeting. It would be the beginning of what she hoped would be a successful venture.

CHAPTER FOURTEEN

Marty Caster was a trim, white-haired man whose tan, leathery skin showed the signs of working in the sun for most of his life. But the light-brown eyes that studied her were full of life, belying his age.

"So, little lady, you're opening your own business?" he said, giving her a smile from where he sat behind his desk in the cluttered office.

Seated in front of him, Em bristled and then reminded herself that in every business there were others ready to belittle you if you let them. She pulled out a copy of her business plan and handed it over to him.

"I think you'll find all the information you need here, but let me break it down for you. What I'm asking for is the ability to market my business through you. In return, you would have the opportunity to provide plantings and maintenance to those properties I work on through deals made with the owners. Though I would also be advertising on my own and through Rainbow's End, it seems natural for us to work together. Our two businesses complement one another. It would, I believe, be of financial benefit to both of us to team up."

Marty sat back in his chair, looked up at the ceiling, and chuckled.

Offended, Em tensed and waited for him to speak.

"My God! You're Julia Jordan's granddaughter all right. That's the kind of talk that got her business up and running. And now that I know you're just like her, I would be inclined to say yes, but you're going to have to convince me that I should even consider it."

He gazed at her intently. "Why should I take the risk of introducing you to my clients, when your business is untested, unproven? It could be disastrous for me and my business."

Em felt her mouth grow dry. Her mind went blank.

"There are other landscape designers I've sometimes used in the past, and I'm happy with those relationships."

"But ..." she began, her mind whirling.

"What do you bring to the table that they don't have?"

Em felt her cheeks grow hot and forced herself to straighten in her chair. "I appreciate your need to ask those questions. I'll try to answer them one by one. This is a small town in which many people know me from my work with flowers and plants at Rainbow's End. It's true I haven't set up my business before now, but it's not true I don't have any experience with landscape design. I studied it in college. Several people are aware of that and have asked me to come and look at their gardens for ways in which they can be improved."

"Really? Interesting," said Marty. "Go ahead."

At his encouragement, some of Em's confidence returned. "I'm not pretending, as others might, that I have all the answers. The reason I'm coming to you is to take advantage of your knowledge of this particular growing area and use it along with my creativity to design and implement a plan that will satisfy our joint customers."

Marty's eyebrows shot up. "So, we would, in essence, be partners?"

"Only on certain projects," Em said, hoping that wouldn't ruin the deal, but she wanted to run her own business.

"What I bring to the table is a lifetime love of flowers and plants, along with an ability to see how they can be integrated into pleasing, easy-to-care-for designs."

Em sat back in her chair and kept a steady gaze on Marty's face though she felt sweat break across her brow. "I believe my business and yours can work well together and I intend to prove it to you."

"Okay," Marty said, holding up the business plan she'd given him. "Give me time to look this over before making any final decision. If necessary, and I think it might work, we can tweak it. Sound like a plan?"

Em smiled happily. "Yessir, it does."

"Good." He rose. "You're a smart woman, Emerson. I hope we can work together."

After they shook hands, she walked to the front door of the large greenhouse feeling as if she could fly.

She drove to the flower shop in excitement. Even if she had to make a few concessions to her plan to work with AAA Landscaping, she knew it was a big win.

That night, Em dragged herself into her apartment tired to the bone. She'd worked frantically to complete the transformation of Rainbow's End from a Valentine theme to one of spring and setting up a display of new gift collections for sale. The end result was worth every ache in her body.

Too tired to think of fixing dinner, Em pulled out a can of bubbly, flavored water from the refrigerator. After she sat a while, she'd make herself a sandwich and go to bed.

She wandered into the living room and clicked on the television. The news was depressing. She was about to get up and go back to the kitchen when she heard the sound of her doorbell.

She hurried to answer it, hoping Elena and Andrew had decided to stay another night.

She peeked through the peephole in the door and stared at a man wearing the baseball cap with the name of her favorite pizza place on it. *Had Elena surprised her*?

Keeping the chain on, she opened the door a crack.

"Sorry, I didn't order any pizza."

"Not to worry. A friend ordered it for you."

Smiling at the kindness of her sister, Em opened the door wider to accept the pizza.

The delivery man handed her the box, then pushed her inside and followed.

"Wait! You're not the delivery boy!" Em said, getting a closer look at the man's face, his glassy eyes. She dropped the box of pizza onto the entry tile. "Get out! Get out right now!"

He laughed, slammed the door shut behind him, and locked it. "I'm not going anywhere until you pay me. Besides, I think you and I ought to have some fun. How about it, sweetheart? You look like you could stand a little excitement."

Em glanced at her cell phone lying on the table next to the couch, and wondered if she'd have time to make a dash for it and call 911.

The man noticed where she was looking and lurched toward the phone to grab it.

With his attention on the phone, she ran to the door. She screamed when he grabbed an arm. With the other, she managed to flick the front porch lights on and off a few times before he dragged her back into the hallway.

"Okay, I've got you. Let's start with the money and then we'll move on to the entertainment," the man said, chuckling in a menacing way.

Gagging at the thought of him touching her, she indicated the kitchen with a nod of her head. "My purse is in there." *Maybe*, she thought, *I can grab a knife.*

Holding onto her arms painfully, pinning them behind her

back, he dragged her over to the television.

"What are you doing?" she asked, trying to hold in her panic even as adrenaline pumped through her.

"I don't want nobody to hear you scream," he said, turning the volume on the television way up.

Em's breath left her in a gasp of terror as he forced her to walk toward the kitchen. Afraid of what might happen there, she fought him with everything she had. She soon discovered she was no match for his size, his strength. In the struggle, he released one arm and slapped her across the face so hard she saw stars. She clasped a hand to her cheek and barely managed to stand on her feet.

A loud bang shattered the air, and her front door flew open.

Nick Munro charged toward them.

The man behind her was as shocked as she, released her arm, and staggered back. "What the fuck?"

Em was pushed aside as Nick quickly wrapped large, muscular arms around the man's body and pinned his arms before he kicked his legs out from under him, threw him face down and then sat on him, pinning him to the floor.

The man struggled to resist, but he was no match for Nick.

Stunned, struggling to stay on her feet, Em watched Nick quickly bind the man's hands behind his back with a large zip-tie he'd pulled from his jacket pocket.

Breathing heavily, Nick stood up and straightened. "I saw the flickering lights and came running. I've called the cops. They should be here shortly"

Confused, she said, "But it's Monday. You're day off."

"Your boyfriend paid me extra to stay on until he was sure you were safe."

Em began to cry deep, wracking sobs of relief, her body so weak she barely made it to the couch before sinking onto it. The horror of what had almost happened to her made her feel faint. She lowered her head between her knees and fought for air to fill her lungs. How, she wondered, could she ever thank Devin? He had, in his own way, saved her life.

Two policemen came running in, said hi to Nick, and then lifted the man to his feet, handcuffed him, and took him into custody. One of them took the man away, and the other walked over to the couch and sat down beside her.

"Are you okay, Ma'am?"

She nodded and whispered, "I think so."

"Okay, I need some answers."

Nick stayed right at her side as she told the policeman as much as she could.

"Do you have family to call?" Nick asked her gently when the questioning ended and the policemen left.

"Yes. My father," she said numbly. She knew how upset her parents would be, but she'd already decided she needed to spend the night here, or she'd never be able to be alone in her condo again.

"I'll get some of the carpenters here to fix the lock on your front door. When I kicked the door in, part of the door jamb shattered, but it can be fixed easily."

Later, sitting in the living room with her parents, Em fought the urge to curl up in her mother's lap as her father paced the room.

"No way you're going to be alone here at night until you're completely ready. We'll sleep here tonight until I can be sure you'll be safe. You don't mind, do you, Donna?"

"Of course not, dear," her mother said. "Emerson's safety is the most important thing." She gave Em another hug. "I wish you hadn't decided to move in right away."

Tears filled her eyes. "I know, but I can't go back to living at your house. It's important for me to be here."

Her father came to her and held her in his arms. "Your

mother and I are here for you, Em."

She knew then she'd made the right choice to stay in Ellenton.

The next day, Elena called her first thing. "I heard all about the intruder and the close call you had. I'm shaking just talking about it. Mom also told me about the thoughtful thing Devin did in hiring the guard to protect you. If that isn't the sweetest gesture, I don't know what is."

"I will always be grateful to him for that. Last night's episode was the worst thing I've ever been through. I thought he was going to rob and rape me before killing me." Em's voice wobbled with emotion. "I was so scared."

"Mom said you fought the guy."

"Yeah, but I couldn't stop him. That's the most frightening thing of all."

"Is there anything I can do for you? I feel so helpless."

"Just be well and happy. The thought of being an aunt is a pleasant one, giving me strength to get through this."

"Okay," said Elena. "Call me anytime you need someone to talk to. Promise?"

"I promise," she said. As she clicked off the call, she checked to make sure the chain was locked in place on the door, the deadbolt lock secured, and all the windows on the ground floor safely locked.

That afternoon when Em arrived home from the flower shop, her father was waiting for her at the front door. He held a small bag in his hand. "Here. Your mother and I bought these things for you."

After going inside, she opened the bag. "What's inside?"

Her father winked at her. "Your mother did a little research online. These are the five things you should carry with you to get you out of an uncomfortable situation."

She lifted out a can of pepper spray, a small personal alarm, a whistle, a small flashlight and a hollow piece of plastic labeled a Kubotan. "Wow! These are great!"

"Yes," her father agreed. "And your mother and I would like to pay for a self-defense course if you're interested."

Smiling, Em nodded. "Thanks, I'll look into it."

Her mother arrived carrying a casserole. "I thought you could use a nice, hot meal." She smiled at Em. "It's your favorite lemon chicken casserole."

"Thanks, Mom," she said. She loved their concern but didn't want to give up the idea of being independent.

With dinner over, her mother gone home, and her father resting on the couch in front of the television, Em went up to her office to work on logo ideas for her business. She loved the name Living Designs but wanted to add a tagline for it. After noodling around on the computer, seeking other names for businesses like hers, she came up with" Living Designs – Fresh Ideas, Beautiful Results.

Pleased, she started working on designs for the name.

She was trying to decide between a green background or a brighter color when her cell rang. Seeing Devin's name, she grabbed up the phone.

"Hi, Devin! Bless you! You saved my life!" she gushed. "I have to tell you what happened to me."

"Elena just called me. Are you all right now? And are you going to be okay staying at your condo?"

"Yes, thanks to you. Hiring the special security guard for me is the sweetest thing anyone has ever done for me. How can I thank you? Nothing I say can express my gratitude."

"I'm just glad you're fine. I didn't like the idea of you there alone and wanted to be sure you'd be safe. What's the development company doing to make it safer for you and everyone else?"

"I got a call from them today. They're going to make it a gated community, and they've hired more guards. One of my closest neighbors is moving in tomorrow and three others this weekend."

"Sounds good," said Devin. He hesitated. "I've thought a lot about you and what you want to do with your life. I may need your help with something. I'll be in touch."

"Oh, yes," she said. "I'm happy to hear from you. Call me anytime."

"Thanks. I'll do that," he said.

Em could hear the smile in his voice and knew him well enough to understand how pleased he was. Listening to him, realizing how much he cared, she felt safer already.

As the days passed, she continued to feel stronger, even as she became more aware of her surroundings as she'd been warned. Talking to Devin on a regular basis helped too. They talked about everything. In one conversation, he quizzed her on her desire to adopt, and when she assured him that she wanted to do that in the future, he said, "I have something in mind." That was a piece of information she kept to herself. Though the idea of a possible adoption was thrilling, she didn't want to do anything to take away from Elena's excitement about her baby.

When Kat called to invite her to lunch in the city, Em hesitated a moment and then accepted. She hadn't been in New York City for some time, and she was in need of a change. She'd been feeling housebound with bad weather and working at the flower shop.

Traveling on the train into the city, she recalled how excited she'd been with her first job while temporarily living at home. Meeting Kat and her other roommates at the advertising agency where they all worked was a tremendous help. Not only did they work together, they played together. Two of them had married and moved on, but Kat and another friend still stayed at work and in the apartment that Em once owned with them.

As agreed, Em was to meet Kat at Rennie's, a small, neighborhood bar they both loved not far from Kat's workplace in midtown. Rennie's was known for its excellent bar food—anything from oysters on the half-shell, to fresh, crisp salads, thick deli-style sandwiches, big burgers, and beyond. Em wasn't sure how they did it, but she'd never had a bad meal there. And for her, the servings were large enough to provide leftovers to take home for another meal.

At one o'clock the place was jammed. Em looked around and saw Kat sitting at a small high-top table in a corner. Em elbowed her way through the crowd to get to her.

Kat jumped off her chair to hug her. "It's so good to see you! I feel as if it's been years, not months."

Em smiled. "I know. So much has happened in those months. It feels good to be back, but I'll be happy to get home too. I'd forgotten how crowded, how impersonal the city can be. So much activity, so much noise."

"Wow! You sound like a country girl. You're really happy in Ellenton?"

"Yes," said Em, realizing how deeply she felt. "It's home. Tell me all about you. Anything new on the dating scene? What's happening at work. The boss still the same?"

Kat laughed. "Boss man will never change. Nothing too great on the dating scene. I still see Dave from time to time. How about you?"

"I've met a special guy. We're not dating, but he's a wonderful man. He's a doctor who lives in Miami and does volunteer work in Costa Rica."

"A doctor, huh?' said Kat, wiggling her eyebrows. "A nice, rich catch. If you're just friends, maybe you can introduce me to him, huh?"

Em looked at her with surprise. "First of all, being a doctor doesn't necessarily mean you're rich. Besides, he devotes time and money to children in Costa Rica. In fact, he knows I'm looking to adopt a child and may be able to help me."

"Whaaat?" Kat shrieked. "You adopt a child? What for? You're not even married?"

Em held up her hand to stop her. "Hold on! Hear me out! After Jared dumped me, I realized that what I've wanted all along was a big family. And then I understood I don't need to be married to do that. There are thousands of children everywhere who need a good home. Not only here in this country but in places like Central America and Africa. Why not adopt? And if I find a suitable guy along the way, fine. But that isn't my main goal now."

Kat frowned. "But a lot of these kids are from different ethnic backgrounds or don't have much intelligence, that kind of thing. Why would you saddle yourself with someone like that? You'd be stuck with them for the rest of your life."

Listening to her, Em suddenly realized she didn't like Kat very much. First, there was the betrayal issue with Jared and now, this. Thinking back through the years, there were many other incidents that should have caused alarm. In the past, she'd kept quiet to maintain peace between them. Now, she couldn't. Not after seeing Kat for who she really was—greedy, unkind, and selfish.

"You know, Kat, I think I'd better go. I made a mistake agreeing to meet you here, and it's best if I leave now."

Kat scowled at her. "What are you talking about? Are you still pissed about me and Jared?"

"No," Em said calmly. "I've just learned to see things more clearly. Thanks for asking me to lunch, but like I said, it's time for me to go."

As she walked back to Grand Central Station, Em thought about the changes she was making in her life. She'd always been too quick to see any situation, any person in the best light, even when common sense warned her against it. She realized it was better to see people as they really were, even if it sometimes hurt.

CHAPTER FIFTEEN

When Em arrived back at the flower shop, a message was attached to her desk phone. "Please call Allison Belle about the job you advertised." The number listed was a local one.

Excited about the prospect of finally finding someone to help, Em sat right down and punched in the number. Since her fall, Gran hadn't felt able to come into the store every day, and Em was tired of spending most of her time in the store either alone or with Marilyn. As it got closer to summer wedding time, Marilyn would expand her hours. And unless Gran came back to work, they might even have to add another employee.

A lilting voice answered, "Hi. This is Tinker."

"I'm calling Allison Belle. This is Emerson Jordan from Rainbow's End."

A soft giggle floated in Em's ear. "Oh, yes. That's me, Allison Belle, but everyone calls me Tinker. I'm interested in the floral arranger job you advertised."

"Good," said Em. "The flower shop is in Ellenton. Do you live close by?"

"Next town over, in Hornwell," she said. "I love flowers and love to arrange them. It's something I've always done. In high school I worked at the Town Florist after school and on weekends."

"Where are you working now?" Em asked.

"That's just it. I quit college, or I should say the college quit me. My scholarship money ran out. It's a long story."

"Email me your resumé, and then I'll call you for an appointment."

"I'll send the resume right now, and I can come this afternoon if you would like," Tinker said with hope in her voice.

"All right. We'll see how well you fit the job." She gave Tinker the directions to the store and her email address. "Call if you're not going to make it."

"Oh, I'll make it all right. I need the job," said Tinker. "See you soon."

Em clicked off the call with a smile. There was something so ethereal about the voice she'd heard that she actually thought of Peter Pan's Tinkerbell.

That afternoon, she looked up from behind the counter to see a small, young woman enter the shop on light, dancer's feet. She knew immediately it was Tinker. With her short, curly, auburn hair and bright green eyes, she looked every bit a creature of fantasy.

"Hi, you must be Tinker," she said rising and holding out her hand. "I'm Emerson Jordan, Em, the store manager for my grandmother."

"Hello, Em," said Tinker shaking her hand. She twirled around, gazing at her surroundings with curved lips. "This store is wonderful! It seems almost as if I'm in a magical garden."

Pleased, Em said, "I like to think of it that way myself. I received your resume and am ready to talk."

"Great." Tinker pulled a small notebook and a pen out of the large purse she carried.

"Why don't you look around the shop while I take care of one more thing," Em suggested, already knowing she was going to hire her unless something unexpected stopped her. She knew from the skinny pants and stylish sweater Tinker wore and the artful way she'd tied a floral scarf around her neck how naturally creative she was.

In reviewing Tinker's resumé earlier, Em discovered that the young woman had always worked through high school and the almost two years of college. That meant a lot to her, as did the letters of reference from both previous employers and two of her teachers.

"Okay," said Em, laying down the paperwork she'd been filling out, "let's talk. First of all, is there anything you'd change in the store? Placement of items, perhaps? A different take on the arrangements in the refrigerator?"

Tinker studied her. "Is this a test?"

"Of sorts," Em replied. She had to hire someone she could trust to be honest with her, someone who could handle and improve on what was being done while she was busy building her own business.

Tinker drew a deep breath and then said, "Okay, if that's what you want, I'd rearrange things in the sale corner of the gift area so it's easier to see each one, maybe arrange them in groups. Where you have the Easter display, I'd offer an arrangement of silk flowers, maybe a spring wreath." She gave Em a worried look.

"Go on," Em said. "What about the live floral arrangements in the refrigerated case? Any in there that could use a little different touch?"

Tinker sucked on her lip. "That one, the one with the lilies needs more texture, either with greenery or something like baby's breath or lily grass."

"I agree," said Em. Marilyn had done that arrangement on her own. She was a sweet lady but she wasn't a floral designer, more like a very good helper. "Let's go into my office and talk some more."

Tinker followed Em into her office and took a seat in the

chair offered to her. Em sat behind her desk and studied the young woman.

"Tell me about yourself. You were studying at the community college so you could get a degree in art."

"Yes, I wanted to get both a business degree and as many art courses as I could take. But I goofed up, got involved with the wrong group, and when my grades fell, my scholarship went away." Tinker's cheeks flushed a pretty pink. "It was stupid, but here I am."

"You gave your address as being in Hornwell. How long have you lived there?"

"For almost a year. I live with my boyfriend. My mom is single, and I don't want to live with her in New Jersey."

"So, you don't expect to move away?" Em asked.

Tinker shook her head. "No. Rob and I are planning on getting married next December. He's already bought the house we're living in."

Satisfied, Em nodded. "Okay, let's go over hours, salary, and benefits, and if you're satisfied, you can begin tomorrow."

A half-hour later, Em studied the smile on Tinker's face and matched it. She stood. "Let me show you around the store, and tomorrow I'll introduce you to my grandmother, who owns the business. She's cutting down her hours while she recuperates from a fall, but she tries to get in as often as she can. Marilyn Fields is our part-time employee, but is someone who needs direction, if you know what I mean."

"She did the lily arrangement?"

"Yes, but we'll be careful how we manage her."

"Not a problem," said Tinker.

"Ah, no wonder you had such glowing letters of recommendation," Em said, liking Tinker more and more.

###

As soon as Tinker left the store, Em called Gran. "I've found someone who's going to be a great designer for us. She's starting tomorrow."

"Oh, my! The woman must be good if you hired her on the spot. You checked her background and all?"

"She came with several recommendations." She filled Gran in with all the details. "I'll talk to some of the people but I think she's for real. She even made some suggestions for the store."

"She's not going to be one of these people who wants to change everything, is she?" asked Gran with a note of worry in her voice. "I've done very well for myself over the years."

"No, Gran, no. I think you're going to be very pleased with her. I told her I'd introduce her to you tomorrow."

"Okay. I'll be there. I'm sure the cold I've been fighting will be better tomorrow."

"Me, too, Gran. Wait and see. Tinker is like a breath of spring air."

"That sounds good. Can't wait to get through the final days of March and into April."

"Me, too. Talk to you later." After hanging up, she realized it had been over a month since her visit to Seashell Cottage. She decided to call Devin. They'd talked a few days ago, but she loved her conversations with him and sharing news of her days. She described Tinker to him. "I swear if she had worn booties and carried a bag of magical dust, I would believe it was actually the Tinkerbell in the storybook."

"Sounds as if she's a real talent if she's able to give you suggestions comfortably. Good for you. I know how bound to the shop you've felt. Now you'll have a chance to devote time to your business plan."

"Yes. It's going to be a big help. How about you? When are you taking off for Costa Rica?"

"Su Lynn and I are going together. We leave tomorrow. I

want to introduce her to the staff and volunteers."

Em hesitated and then said, "Well, have a successful trip." Inside, she wondered just how close he was to Su Lynn.

Devin cleared his throat. "I believe I've found a little girl you'd be interested in adopting, but there are a ton of details to be worked out."

"Really? Someone there? Someone like Nina? How wonderful! I know adoption is never an easy thing to arrange, but I think about it frequently."

Devin's voice softened. "Has anyone ever told you what a nice person you are?"

Warmth traveled through her at the sound of appreciation in his voice. She forced her imagination to remain grounded, though, for a moment, she imagined how it would feel if he were looking into her eyes soulfully while telling her this. How he'd tell her how much she meant to him before sweeping her up in his arms.

"Well, I've gotta go. Talk to you later, Em," he said, breaking into her thoughts, jarring her back to reality.

"Safe travels," Em said, clicking off the call and sighing. Too bad fate had planned nothing more than friendship between them. But as she saw it, they each had their own responsibilities. Besides, she was about to get her first big job, and she couldn't allow herself to get distracted by thinking about him. Not when the idea of being able to support a child might become a real possibility.

The next morning, Em headed to Rainbow's End filled with excitement. She'd scheduled the time to meet Tinker at the flower shop an hour before the store opened to show her how the cash register operated and what usual morning routines were involved in opening.

When she arrived, at the storefront, she was surprised to see the lights on, the sidewalk sign out, and a buzz of activity inside. She parked her car, put her car keys in her purse, and drew out the self-protection devices her parents had given her.

As she approached the door, she let out a chuckle. Gran was sitting behind the counter watching Tinker vacuum.

Em opened the door and walked inside. "I see you've met Tinker, Gran."

Tinker turned off the vacuum. "I came early. Mrs. Jordan showed me around."

"I've told Tinker about the importance of keeping the shop clean. She's got what it takes. Everything is sparkling."

"Yeah, well I've worked for a cleaning company and know how to take care of things."

Em grinned. "You're going to be a terrific addition. Are you ready to learn about the cash register with me?"

"Yes. Just let me put this away, and I'll be right with you." As she left, Tinker lugged the vacuum cleaner behind her.

Gran watched her go and then turned to Em with a smile. "Emerson Jordan, I think you've found a treasure. Tinker's such a sweet young thing and so very eager to do a good job. It eases my mind to know she'll be here to help you."

"Thanks. Let's hope Marilyn feels the same way. She doesn't like it much if I adjust any arrangement she's done, and Tinker already wants to change one of them."

Gran nodded sympathetically. "I know Marilyn hasn't been the best at the job, but she needed something to do while dealing with the grief over her sister's death."

"Let's see how it goes," Em said, looking up when Tinker returned to the room at the same time Marilyn entered the store.

Em introduced Marilyn to Tinker. They smiled at each

politely, but when Em explained that Tinker's job was to design and oversee floral bouquets, Marilyn's smile wavered.

"I've learned so much from you, Em, I don't believe I'll need much guidance."

"Why don't we give Tinker a fair chance at the job and take it from there," Em said brightly. "Though Tinker is young, she has a lot of experience."

Marilyn studied Tinker. "Okay, I'll give it a try. But both you and Julia need to know I'm thinking of moving to Phoenix. My sister's family wants me there."

"How nice for you, Marilyn, but I would hate to see you go," said Gran.

"I haven't decided yet," Marilyn said. "The only reason I'd stay is because of this job. I love it."

"And we love having you here," said Gran, giving Marilyn a hug.

"Well, I've got to go. I'm meeting with Mrs. Jansen on Maple Avenue to do a consulting job for Living Designs," Em said proudly. "Wish me luck."

Em got into her car, drove the few minutes to Maple Avenue, and stopped in front of an old Victorian house. Well-maintained, the house stood proudly on a sizeable lawn beside one of the oldest, widest streets in town. She drew a deep breath. *I can do this!*

She gathered her materials and left the car determined to make this work. Cynthia Jansen was a middle-aged woman who'd been an active member of the Ellenton Garden Club for as long as Em could remember. If Em pleased her, her business would take off nicely.

She rang the doorbell and waited impatiently for an answer.

The door opened. "There you are!" said Cynthia, smiling. "Come on in! I'm eager to see what designs you've come up with for my garden. I told Charlie I want something new and different."

"I think you'll like some of the ideas I have," said Em with more confidence than she felt. Some people wouldn't be as excited about change, and Em had taken Cynthia's request to heart.

Cynthia led her to the dining room off the hallway. "I thought you could spread your material out here on this long table. By the look of things, you've got a lot to show me."

"This will be fine." She may have overdone it for this first consultation but she wanted to draw up as many options as possible.

"From my kitchen window, I saw you marking off distances, and I'm very curious," said Cynthia, eagerly taking a seat next to Em.

Em turned to her. "You have plenty of yard space, which is a big plus. I think we should stick to the Victorian theme of the house but play it up a bit. You have room for a gazebo for one thing."

"Oh, I love that idea!" gushed Cynthia.

Em smiled at her enthusiasm. "Instead of having the gazebo nestled to the ground, I'm suggesting you might want a semi-formal garden with brick or stone walkways with steps leading up to it. We'd make use of the small incline and set it on top of the higher elevation so those inside could look out. As for the rest of the yard, I think keeping it simple with a border of your choosing would dress it up a bit. There are many choices of plants and flowers to use for adding depth and color to the scene—roses, hollyhocks, hydrangeas and a list of other things we can discuss."

"It all sounds wonderful!" Cynthia said, beaming at her.

"Well, we don't want to make it difficult to keep up. I understand you use AAA Landscape on a weekly basis to maintain your yard, but we want to keep the cost of upkeep in mind."

Cynthia sat back and studied her. "My word! When your grandmother told me about your services, I had no idea what a treasure you are. Let me show your ideas to Charlie and I'll get back to you."

"By all means, take your time. Part of my fee is to oversee the actual implementation of my design. I want both of you to be happy with it and me, because I hope to do a lot of work in the area."

"Oh, I believe you will," said Cynthia. "I love the way you've drawn the designs in color so we get a good idea of how things might look."

They discussed various flowers and plants, and then Em rose. "I believe I've given you enough to think about. My card with all my information is attached to the packet. Call me as questions come up. At the moment, I have you scheduled for a follow-up appointment next week. I'll call you to reconfirm." She knew the importance of giving a client time to think about things, but the need also to nail down a time to set things in motion.

Cynthia was still bubbling with excitement as she led Em to the front door. She waited until she got outside before enjoying a mental dance down the sidewalk to her car. *I really can do this!*

Life became even busier as Em spent time with the Jansens coordinating changes with AAA Landscaping. At one point, Marty called her into his office.

Wondering if she'd allowed her clients to make too many changes from their original choices, she entered his office warily.

"Sit down, we need to talk," Marty said crisply from behind his desk as he hung up the phone.

Concerned by his tone of voice, Em took a seat in a chair opposite him ready to fight.

He studied her a moment and then said, "You and I discussed financial arrangements for your participation in having us do work for your clients. We agreed on twenty percent of any work you brought to me. I realize now that it's wrong."

"But ..." Em began to protest. Through the Jansens' work, she was providing him with the opportunity not only to replant the yard but to continue maintenance at a higher rate.

He held up a hand to stop her. "I'm talking about making it twenty-five percent."

"Oh," she said blinking with surprise. "Good, because I have another contract that I think you're going to like."

Marty grinned. "You've got a great sense of design and color. When specific plant or flower choices need tweaking, that's something we can easily talk about. The soil here can be tricky. Lots of clay. That can affect the growth and long-term success of whatever is planted."

Happiness rolled through her in a wave. "It would be wonderful to have you help me with plant choices. Thank you."

"I like you. You're not only creative, you're a hard worker and smart as a whip. Like your grandmother."

She felt a smile spread across her face. Gran would be so pleased by his words.

"Okay, now let's talk about the Jansen project. There's one change I'd like to see," said Marty.

By the time she left his office an hour later, her head was spinning with new ideas. Marty Caster knew plants and this area. Not only could he give her suggestions, he also gave her the reasons for choosing any plant he talked about. She felt as if she'd just attended a college class.

Em became even busier, but as she told Devin during one of their nightly calls, it was a dream come true to be able to have her own business. "The only problem is that Tinker and Marilyn aren't getting along. I'm waiting for Marilyn to become discouraged and leave on her own. In reality, I need her to step up or give me the opportunity to hire someone else."

Devin chuckled. "I love seeing this change in you, Em. You sound like a boss. Are you happy with your life now?"

"I love being here in Ellenton with my own business, but I haven't given up on the idea of adoption. I've always wanted to be a mother. I had more baby dolls than anyone I know. In fact, I've saved a couple for a little girl of my own."

"You sound like a real mom. It suits you."

"I don't mean to sound pushy, but do you have any news on the child we discussed? I know, I know. I need to be patient."

Devin chuckled. I'm working on it. There are details to sort through. The moment I have news, I'll let you know. Okay?"

"Yes. That's all I can ask of you."

They talked about his work and then ended the call. But long afterward, Em thought of their conversation. She hoped the day would come when she had the chance to set her idea of adoption into motion.

CHAPTER SIXTEEN

As her business grew at a steady rate, Em found herself pulled back time and again to Rainbow's End. While she chafed at the responsibility, she knew she had no choice but to spend more time there until things settled down. Gran would hate for Em to notice, but she was getting forgetful. One night, she left the store to go home with the lights on and the front door unlocked. Thankfully, Em had decided to drop by a while later and found it that way. Gran had become angry when she'd mentioned it. Em understood she was embarrassed and decided to say nothing to her family about it. Even so, she was determined to talk to both Tinker and Marilyn to make sure they were aware of the situation.

And, while covering for Tinker, when Em discovered Marilyn had made a huge mistake in reconciling the money taken in that day, mistakenly crediting an account rather than charging it, her worries increased. She decided to talk to Tinker about becoming manager of the store.

After store hours, Em and Tinker walked to Jake's, a small bar off Main Street that had a great choice of wines and tasty appetizers.

Seated at a small table in the corner, Em and Tinker quickly ordered. The place was filling. They talked about the new spring design Tinker had drawn up for one of the businesses for whom they did regular jobs. "I love the work you're doing, Tinker, with both the business end and the floral designs."

Tinker's face brightened. "I'm pleased you're happy. It means a lot."

Em took a sip of her red wine, mentally crossed her fingers, and said, "I'd like to offer you the position of store manager. I think you're ready for it, and so am I."

Tinker's face fell. "I'm sorry, but I have to say no. I've recently received new scholarship money, and I just signed up for some college courses. I can't let anything stand in my way of earning a degree. I promised both my parents and Rob. But I'm very happy to continue working for you on a part-time basis."

The air in Em's lungs escaped in a puff of disappointment. "My own business is growing so fast, I need to have someone reliable to take over for me. Marilyn will admit to anyone that she's not very good with numbers, and her work with flowers is just okay."

Tinker studied Em, her blue eyes troubled. "Ordinarily I wouldn't say anything, but Marilyn is definitely thinking of leaving. She told me she's planning on telling your grandmother soon."

Em felt the blood leave her face and return in a flush of dismay. She'd just taken on two new clients with the promise of getting the work done quickly. Filling in for Marilyn in the store and adding flower design to her schedule would impact her available time. She couldn't mess up her new business. Her reputation would be ruined if she couldn't keep her word about getting the jobs done on a timely basis. Leaning forward, she heard her note of desperation as she asked, "Do you know anyone who could help me?"

Tinker's brow furrowed and then smoothed as her lips curved. "Bart Lovell was a wonderful mentor to me before he sold his share of Town Florists."

"He's retired, isn't he?"

"Yes, but I think he realizes he made a big mistake leaving the business. He can be a bit of a perfectionist, but he's smart, and his designs are cool. I learned a great deal from him."

"Hmmm, I wonder how he and Gran would get along?"

Tinker chuckled. "It could be very interesting. They're a lot alike."

"Do you think he'd be amenable to working for two women?" Gran had hired a man to work for her early on and, when it didn't work out, she'd vowed to hire only women.

"I think he's bored enough to give it a try," said Tinker. "Though it took time to get used to his manner, I like him a lot."

"Okay, give me his information, and I'll give him a call. I need someone right away."

The waitress brought over the pear and blue cheese flatbreads they'd ordered.

"Let's relax and enjoy this time together," said Em. She liked Tinker and was eager to know more about her. She'd just taken a bit of her appetizer when a young man approached the table.

"There you are, Tinker. I tried calling you, but no answer. I left a message telling you I'd be late getting home."

Tinker grinned. "So, will I. Rob, I'd like you to meet my boss, Emerson Jordan. Em, this is my fiancé, Rob Gardener." She chuckled. "And, yes, the name is perfect for me."

Em laughed with her, liking the way Tinker and Rob were gazing at each other as if they were not only lovers but best of friends, as well.

"Please join us, if you can."

"For one minute," he said. "I'm meeting a client interested in purchasing a building for a new business." He smiled at Em. "Tinker likes working at Rainbow's End. I've seen some of the work she's done, and I think it's great."

"She's very talented," Em agreed. "I wish I could get her to be my manager, but she says she has to work on getting her college degree."

Rob turned to Tinker.

"I was offered the job, but turned it down," Tinker explained. "If I don't get my degree now, it'll never happen."

"It's your choice, but I agree." He checked the door as a middle-aged man entered. "Gotta go. Wish me luck." He gave Tinker a quick kiss on the lips and left the table.

"Rob's trying to make it big in the commercial real estate business," Tinker said. "He's off to a good start."

"He's very friendly and pleasant. I'm sure he'll do very well."

"I'm hoping to get my degree in Interior Design so I can help him with projects in the future," Tinker explained. "We hope to have our own business buying properties and rehabbing them."

Em hid her surprise. Tinker's appearance seemed playful, but she was a serious person.

Conversation turned back to Rainbow's End, and after a while, Em left to go to the flower shop to call Bart Lovell. Even if he might be a little difficult to get along with, she had every intention of hiring him. The true test would be if Gran liked him.

Before Em placed a call to Bart Lovell, she googled his name and came up with major details about his life. She liked the idea that he'd lived in Hornwell for most of his life and was active not only with Town Florists but with a number of charity organizations. To look at his craggy, handsome features and stern expression on his promo file, one would not expect him to be a softie dealing with flowers.

She punched in the number with high hopes. If, as Tinker had said, he was bored without his business, she might be in luck.

The voice that answered was low and crisp. “Hello.”

“Mr. Lovell, this is Emerson Jordan calling for Rainbow’s End. Tinker Belle suggested I call you. I’m wondering if we might set up an appointment to discuss having you manage the flower shop.”

“Tinker suggested it, did she?” Bart said.

“Yes, sir,” Em said. “I understand you’ve retired from Town Florists and might be willing to help us out.”

“Does Julia Jordan know you’re calling me?” he asked.

Surprised, Em floundered. “Uh, not really, but I’m managing the shop for my grandmother, and after setting up my own design business, I find I need someone to take over a lot of the duties of running Rainbow’s End.”

“Well, if Julia agrees to my discussing it with you, call me back. She and I have known each other for a long time.”

“I see. Let me talk to her, and I’ll get back in touch with you either way.”

He chuckled. “Got a bit of spunk in you, like her. Okay. Let me know.” He clicked off the call before Em could say goodbye.

As she did many nights, Gran walked into the store as Em was going over the daily figures. “What’s new, sweetie? How’d we do today?”

“Not bad for a Wednesday. I think the new ad campaign featuring ways to make your room ‘more alive’ is working with both plants and flowers. How are you feeling?”

“Very good. Better than I have in a long time since the fall.”

“Great, because I have something that I wish to discuss with you. I’ll finish up here, then I’ll lock up, and we can move into the back office.”

"Okay. How about a cup of tea?" Her grandmother winked at her. "Or some of my sherry."

Em laughed. "Do people even drink sherry anymore? Let's open the bottle of wine the Winston Hotel sent you. This has been quite a day, and we need to talk about a lot of things."

"Sounds serious. Okay, wine it is."

After Em finished going through the tally for the day, she shut off the lights and went into the back office.

Gran was sitting there with two glasses of white wine and a plateful of cheesy crackers from the gourmet shop a few doors down. "Ready whenever you are."

Em sank down into a chair with a sigh. She lifted her glass of wine and clicked it against her grandmother's. "Here's to Rainbow's End. May it continue to thrive."

"I'll toast that," said Gran. "It's taken me years of hard work to get to this point, but we're holding on against the fact that every grocery store around now sells plants and flowers."

"Our commercial accounts make the difference. Businesses of every kind love the service and the products we give them. Among other things, I'm thinking of hiring someone on a more permanent basis for our flower delivery service."

"Oh, but Jeffrey has done that for me for years," protested Gran.

"I know. And now his grandson, Sonny, wants the job. He's working his way through college. After seeing what Tinker has gone through to find the finances to go to school, I want to give Sonny the chance for a regular income."

"I see," said Gran. "I suppose Jeff will continue to be as involved as he can be. He has aged, poor soul."

Em hid the smile that was tempted to cross her face. She wondered what Gran would say if she knew people talked about her that way. "I understand Marilyn is going to be leaving us."

"Oh? She's made up her mind?"

"Apparently, she spoke to Tinker about telling you sometime soon. Tinker told me after she turned down the offer to manage the store for us."

"She turned it down? But why? And when did you offer her that?"

"Earlier this evening, she and I talked. She's found scholarships for her college courses and has signed up for them. She'll continue to work for us on a part-time basis but can't take on the job of being manager. However, she did recommend someone to me."

"Oh?"

"Tinker worked under Bart Lovell at Town Florists. She speaks very highly of him. He's sold his share of that business but might be persuaded to work for us because he's bored."

Gran set down her wine glass on the desk, her eyes ablaze. "That pirate!"

"Whoa! What's that all about? He told me he wouldn't consider the job unless you approved. What's up with that?"

"It's a long story," said Gran, looking away from her.

"I've got time to listen," Em said gently.

Gran turned to her. "This will call for another glass of wine."

Em gave her grandmother a puzzled look. Gran never had more than one glass of wine. She poured her a little more of the chardonnay and sat back to listen.

"Bart and I became friends back when your father was young. I was fairly new in town, left alone to raise my son." Her memory formed a smile. "He was a handsome man, someone all the single women in town much admired. But after we dated, he told me I was the only one for him. Me, with a child? Of course, I didn't believe him. Turned him down cold. I'd been deeply disappointed by one man, why would I want to marry another?"

Em studied her grandmother. She was still a beautiful woman, but now, a woman she didn't really know. "Then what happened?"

"Shortly after that, I convinced one of the local banks to lend me money to open the flower shop. The only reason they gave me the money was because they'd heard the rumor that I was about to marry Bart. I, of course, didn't let them know I'd turned him down. If they'd known that, they would never have given me the funds." She shook her head. "Back then, sexism existed to a much greater degree. Single women had a tough time of getting loans, even if they owned a home."

"So, you got the loan and opened the flower shop. What then?" prompted Em.

Gran straightened in her chair and pounded the desk with her dainty fist. "Bart found a partner and decided to open Town Florist to compete with me. That's what!"

"He did that just to spite you?" Em couldn't hide her surprise. The background information on him indicated a very charitable man.

"Well," Gran replied. "He said he was doing it to help out a friend, but I knew it was to get back at me. He had other businesses in the area. I was certain that he didn't actually need a flower shop."

"Maybe he likes working with plants and flowers," Em suggested. "Tinker said she learned a lot from him."

"Humph," muttered Gran.

"Would you have a problem working with him?" Em asked. "Surely, there's no reason to hold a grudge this long, and, just think, he'd be working for you. Nice way to end the situation, I'd say."

Gran's brow knit with worry, then she grinned. "We could try it. In a way, it would be sweet revenge."

"But, Gran, if we hired him, we'd all have to get along. It doesn't sound as if you want to have him here. Not really."

"We're a much bigger, more successful operation than his. Maybe that would be a good way to end this quiet battle between us, my being his boss."

Em looked at the gleam in her grandmother's eye and laughed. "Bart Lovell is a well-respected man, a generous person noted for all his charity work. Surely, he can't be that bad."

"He isn't bad at all," Gran said. "It's just that we never got to work out our differences. He was married within a year after my turning him down."

"Well, then, let's see if he's willing to come on board. It might be a good way for both of you to forgive and forget."

Gran studied her. "You know, you've grown up a lot since you've been back in town. If Bart is willing to work here, I say go for it. But if any of that old-fashioned attitude of thinking he can tell me what to do comes back, he's gone. Understand?"

"Yes," Em said quickly and firmly. She was dying to see how this unknown bit of drama would play out. "I'll call him first thing in the morning and let you know. Would you like to be there when I phone him?"

"Absolutely not," said Gran so stiffly that Em knew how much she cared.

CHAPTER SEVENTEEN

The next morning when Em called the number Bart had given her, he answered on the second ring. Amused, she said, "Good morning, Bart! How are you?"

"Just fine. I suppose you're calling to tell me Julia has no interest in my helping her at Rainbow's End."

"Actually, I'm not. She's happy to have you join our staff. In fact, I was wondering if you could come over to the store this afternoon for some training. I'm busy with my personal clients this morning but could meet with you around two."

"That would be acceptable," he said with enough crustiness that she wondered if they'd made a mistake to think of hiring him. He didn't sound like someone eager to take orders from her or anyone else.

She hung up the phone and called her mother. After the usual pleasantries were exchanged, Em said, "Did you know Gran and Bart Lovell were once serious about each other a long time ago?"

Her mother chuckled. "I've heard stories about it from your grandmother, but I have a feeling that her version is only one side of things. Why?"

"Last night, Gran and I decided to go ahead and hire him on a trial basis to manage the flower shop. Tinker turned down the offer but suggested we hire him. He's sold his share of Town Florists and is looking for something to fill his time."

"Oh, my! Julia was okay with this?"

"Gran was okay with being his boss. Tinker says he was great to work for and taught her a lot. I don't have the time to train someone who is not capable nor a good business person. I'm too busy with Living Designs."

"Well, if you need me to referee them, let me know, and I'll be there unless I'm at Elena's for the birth of the baby. Just a few more weeks to go."

"I hope it's a May Day baby," she said. "I've always thought that was such a romantic day."

"You've always loved the little baskets of flowers the shop makes," said her mother. "I'm off to a tennis game, but keep me informed."

"And you keep me informed if any of your tennis friends want to spruce up their gardens or even their yards."

"Will do. Love you," her mother said, hanging up.

Em checked the clock. Time to go to her next appointment. It was a small job, but Em didn't care. Her business was growing.

Driving through the family-friendly neighborhood, Em studied the bicycles, carriages, and toys strewn in front yards. She knew in today's world her drive to have a child might seem strange to the mothers she'd overheard complaining about their roles or the kids who were nothing but a trial. But no matter what they might say, it didn't lessen her wish for a big family.

The Thompsons lived in a large, one-story, contemporary house with wood siding. She parked in front of it and took a second look at it. She'd already come up with a few good ideas but needed this opportunity to see if there was anything she'd missed. As she remembered, the curb appeal was very limited because the mess by the entrance quickly drew one's attention.

She made her way up the stone-block pathway to the front door, bypassing the bicycles and outdoor toys thrown on the ground beside the small entry porch.

A mother of four boys, Sarah Thompson was a tiny woman with brown hair cut in a pixie style and gray eyes that missed nothing. Her two older boys towered over her, and even the baby of the family, a toddler around three, looked like he would rapidly approach her size. Em knew the family from newspaper articles on local sports teams that always seemed to feature one of the boys.

At the moment, Sarah looked a little flustered as she waved Em into the house. "Sorry, it's been a crazy morning. The baby has a cold."

She led Em into the cluttered kitchen, moved aside a bowl of half-eaten cereal, picked up a couple of juice glasses and set them on the counter, swept up crumbs into her hand, and quickly wiped down the table all within a matter of what seemed like seconds.

"Have a seat. We can talk here. How about a cup of coffee?" Sarah asked.

"That sounds nice. I take mine black."

"I can't wait to see the plans," Sarah said, flitting around the kitchen, grabbing a coffee mug, and filling it.

She handed the mug to Em and fixed one for herself before sitting down next to Em at the long, pine table.

"Whatcha got?" she said, giving Em a curious look.

"You complained that the house and yard always looked a mess and that one of the neighbors across the street spoke to you about it. I have an idea that will help both of you."

Em pulled out the sketches she'd made, showing a simply constructed wooden fence that was essentially vertical pieces of wood encased at the top and bottom by plain wooden rails. A gate opened to the walkway. The contemporary design of the fence matched the style of the house. More importantly, she'd sketched in plantings on both sides of the fence to provide an attractive border to the front of the property for neighbors, blocking the view inside the yard.

"I love it!" Sarah said, clapping her hands. "It will give me the chance to have some flowers where the boys aren't likely to trample them."

"Yes, they'll still have the space for the basketball court to the side, and I think I've figured out a way to keep bikes and toys away from the front entrance. The gate to the walkway will help, but we'll construct large flower boxes on each side of the front door entry, protecting it and preventing kids from throwing their bikes down alongside it."

Sarah clasped one of Em's hands. "It all seems so simple, but I would never have thought of it." She shook her head. "Sometimes I wonder how I can ever survive my boys. I love them to death, but I can't help wondering what it would be like to raise girls." She held up her hand. "But this is it. Four kids are enough."

"I've always thought it would be fun to have a large family," Em commented.

"Oh, it is," said Sarah. "I wouldn't have it any other way."

They shared a smile.

"As soon as you officially approve the design, I will get in touch with the fence provider and talk to AAA Landscaping about the both the flower boxes and the plantings. We'll give you an estimate for planting them or, if you wish, you and your husband can do your own planting. I would suggest, however, that it be professionally done. It can be completed in a day or two."

"Okay, let me check with my husband, and I'll get right back to you. I'm thrilled, positively thrilled with what you've suggested." She grinned. "My birthday is coming up, and Tom never knows what to give me. This will save him a lot of time and trouble."

Em laughed. "Sounds like a plan. You've got my business

card. Give me a call as soon as possible. My schedule is filling up quickly. By combining the fee for the plan with the work of AAA Landscaping you save a lot of money. It's an agreement I have with them that I pass onto you. And remember, I'll be here to oversee the work."

Sarah gave Em a quick hug. "Thank you so much. I can't wait to begin."

Em left the Thompson house feeling good about her work. Her design seemed simple, but it was well thought out. And when the actual work began, she'd be right there to see that everything turned out right.

Em waited with Gran in the back office for Bart's arrival, as anxious as she. Luckily, Tinker was working that afternoon and would, Em hoped, provide a nice buffer for their first meeting with him.

When she heard the doorbell chime announcing a customer, Em glanced at Gran and got to her feet. "Here goes. For better or worse."

The two women walked into the front room to see Tinker all but dancing in front of Bart. "I'm so glad you're here," said Tinker. The sound of her voice trilled in the air joyfully. "I told Em how much I learned from you."

"You were a good student." The smile left Bart's face as he studied Julia. "Good afternoon, Julia. I assume this is Emerson, your granddaughter."

"Oh, yes," said Em, hurrying forward to shake his hand. "I'm pleased to meet you."

Bart's hand was warm. She looked into his eyes and saw kindness there and relaxed. "Come into the back office. We can discuss the situation there. Would you like coffee or tea?"

"A glass of water sounds nice," he commented.

"I'll get it, Gran," Em said, eager to give her grandmother and Bart a few moments alone. They'd pretty much ignored one another.

As she was carrying the glass of water to the office, Tinker called out to her. "Em, I need to know how you want me to handle this order. It was just called in long-distance."

"Hold on, I'll be right there." Em hurried into the office, set the glass of water down on the desk in front of Bart, and said, "I've got to talk to Tinker, and then I'll be back." As she left the room, she heard Bart say, "You're looking well, Julia."

Em couldn't hear what Gran replied, but her tone was a bit chilly. *Interesting. Gran was nervous.*

After Em went over the proper procedure for the out-of-state order, she left Tinker to another customer and returned to the office.

"Ah, here she is," said Gran, obvious relief in her voice.

Em took a seat behind the desk and decided to hold nothing back. "You sold your share of Town Florists; why would you consider working here?"

Bart's eyebrows lifted in surprise. "A straight shooter, huh? Well, I'll go ahead and answer that. Town Florists was only a part of my life. I have several other business interests. Years ago, I opened the store on a dare, and while I continued working there from time to time, my partner and I began to have conflicting views of how things should be done. I didn't need the job, and he desperately wanted to take over so his son could run it as his own."

Em frowned. "But you don't really need this job either, do you?"

Bart shook his head. "No. Not in the way you think. I live alone now. My wife has been deceased for several years. With the florist shop sold, I realized I missed getting out and meeting people on a daily basis. I've always loved that aspect of the business, and I do like working with flowers, designing attractive arrangements. Being creative is good for anyone's soul."

"I agree," said Gran, nodding at Bart. "It's been a part of what's kept me healthy and happy through the years. Being alone without contact with others is the road to unhappiness."

While they studied each other, Em wondered how to break the stiffness between them and blurted, "It will be wonderful to have your talents here at Rainbow's End, which has continued to do very well, mostly because of Gran's influence. Our customers love her."

"Yes, I know," said Bart. "I've kept an eye on the store for a number of years." He turned to Gran. "I remember how determined you were to succeed on your own."

"I'd learned not to trust anyone to take care of things for me," Gran said. "And I had David to raise." Her voice faltered. "I couldn't fail him."

"And, indeed, you didn't. He's a fine man." He glanced at Em and back to Gran. "You've done a wonderful job with him and his family."

Em was surprised by the watery shine in Gran's eyes as she said. "Thank you, Bart. That means a lot to me."

Silence followed.

"How do you feel about working for us? We've got a smooth operation here, but one of our helpers is leaving, and I'm becoming busier and busier with my own business. You know Tinker and how dependable and creative she is, and, of course, Gran will be here."

"I think it's going to be very pleasant," said Bart, glancing at Gran. "I assume you still have your buyer and delivery people in place?"

Gran straightened in her chair, alert. "Yes. I'm envisioning your doing the creative work and attending to some of the business requirements. Em is taking over the business, but the simpler aspects of running the store, we can give to you. I'll continue to do the PR work with my clients, along with Em. As you will discover, our commercial contracts are important to us."

Amused, Em watched conflicting emotions cross Bart's face, but in the end, he smiled and nodded. "I'd be happy to do so."

"Why don't you spend some time with Tinker? She can show you how to run the cash register and give you a tour of the property," said Em. "Gran and I will discuss hours and pay and then, if you're still interested, we can settle those issues."

Bart stood, and Gran and Em joined him.

Em led Bart out to the front and gave instructions to Tinker to show him around and how to use the cash register.

When she returned to the office, Gran was staring out the window to the little garden they'd planted in back of the store.

Em came up beside her. "Wow, Gran! I had no idea Bart was so handsome or that he still had feelings for you."

Gran turned to her with a puzzled look. "Why would you say that? We're just old friends." A pink blush crept up her cheeks making her look like the attractive young woman she'd always been.

As Em told Devin that night, "I think the next few months are going to be very interesting."

He chuckled. "Indeed."

Something about his response made Em pause to wonder why he'd sounded so mysterious.

Over the next couple of weeks, Em left the training of Bart to Gran and Tinker. She was now the proud overseer of four different projects. As she watched AAA Landscaping workers dig and plant as she directed, she thought how lucky she was to be in charge of her life, meeting the challenges of her new business, and loving every minute of it. When she'd drawn up her business plan in Florida, she'd been very uncertain about her future, her own abilities.

She was watching the last of the flowers being planted at the Thompson's house when she received the phone call she'd been waiting for.

"The baby's here and she's beautiful," said Andrew. His voice broke. "And Elena is a super mom already."

"Oh, Andrew! I'm so glad. Everything went well? How big is the baby? How tall? Tell me everything." Tears of joy formed in her eyes. "She's our May Day baby!"

"She's seven pounds, two ounces and nineteen-and-one-half inches long. I think she's going to look like a Jordan," Andrew answered with noticeable pride. "We're calling her Lillibet. I'm going to text pictures of her to everyone after I call my parents."

"Oh, how sweet! Can I talk to Elena?"

"She said she'll call you later after things have calmed down. Just wanted you to know."

"Congratulations, dad! I'm so happy for you!" Em's voice wobbled as fresh tears filled her eyes. "Tell Elena I love her, and I already love the baby."

"Will do," said Andrew. He clicked off the call.

Em wiped her eyes, drew in a deep breath, and slowly let it out to meet the air. Filled with the happy news of her niece's birth, Em swore the spring morning was even brighter.

When she got back to Rainbow's End, she put together an arrangement of silk flowers in a tiny, white-wicker May basket. It would be the first of many for the baby.

###

Though she stayed in Ellenton to allow time for both her mother and Gran to travel to Philadelphia to be with Elena and the baby, Em talked with her sister daily, viewed pictures her sister sent, and watched videos of Elena and the baby. She loved hearing about the progress of the little girl she couldn't wait to meet in person.

Em opened the store every day before going off to take care of her own business projects. At night, she checked in with Bart to discuss the day's activities. Working with Bart at Rainbow's End, she learned he was not the stiff, crusty man he'd first presented to her. His laughter, when it could be drawn out of him, was deep and rich. Tinker, especially, had a way of putting him at ease. And watching how he was with Gran, Em saw a tenderness in him that was touching. Unfortunately, Gran mostly ignored his advances for a deeper relationship, becoming flustered in his presence.

One morning, Bart brought in hot coffee to Em in her office. "Thought you could use this. It's been a hectic week."

Pleased, Em accepted it and waved Bart to a seat in one of the two chairs facing her desk.

"How's it going, Bart? I hope you like it here. You're doing a great job, and I really need you."

He smiled. "I like keeping busy. I'm amazed at the way Julia built her business into such a steady operation. She's very clever."

"Yes, she is," Em replied proudly.

Bart stared out the window and then faced Em. "I'm hoping to be able to convince Julia to come to my house for dinner. I'm a great cook, and I've missed cooking for someone. We used to be good friends, way back when."

"So, I've heard," said Em, amused by the earnest expression on Bart's handsome face.

"Ahhh, so you may have heard we even talked marriage. At

least I did." He sighed. "I couldn't convince her she wouldn't have to give up her independence. But now, I hope she'll have a change of heart, and we can have the relationship we might have had all along."

"I see," said Em, leaning back in her chair and studying him. "I'm not promising to champion your cause, but I can tell you that her favorite meal is roast chicken with all the accompaniments. She isn't much of a cook herself, but she loves a tasty meal."

"Thanks," said Bart rising. "You're the gem your grandmother thinks you are. I'll give it a try."

Gran arrived at the store, looking fresh and happy. Em had been too busy to notice before, but Gran had had her hair cut and styled and wore a new pair of pants that fit her figure nicely.

Em gave her grandmother a kiss and waved goodbye to Bart. "I'm off, but I'll check in with the two of you tonight. Hope it's a good day."

At the last minute, she turned at the doorway and looked behind her. Gran and Bart were smiling at one another.

"Hmmm," thought Em, grinning herself.

CHAPTER EIGHTEEN

May sped by quickly, pushing its way into June with unexpected energy. With the rush of spring planting over, Em began working on larger, more time-consuming projects for customers. She loved seeing the faces of her clients light up with surprise and pleasure when she placed her drawings of suggestions in front of them.

As she told Devin one night, "Even though I'm drawing ideas on paper, it feels as if I'm standing in the garden as I envision it."

"Part of your creativity," he commented. "I like that you can picture things like that. I'm more of a science guy myself."

"By the way, how's that little girl you kept talking about, the one whose mother died? You haven't mentioned her in a while."

"I think we've found the perfect situation for her," he replied. "It's been difficult. She's well aware that her mother has died, and needs to know that she won't be alone, that other people will love and take care of her. Before she died, her mother and I talked alone and then the three of us discussed the circumstance together. Cancer is a relentless disease, but at least we had the time to discuss this child's future."

She heard voices in the background and then Devin said, "Sorry. I've gotta go. Good to hear from you."

Em hung up the phone, grateful she and Devin could talk about anything. In the last few months he'd become the best friend she'd ever had.

The days trotted ahead with no relief in sight. June was full of long, hard days for her. The idea that she would see Devin soon kept her spirits up when she dragged herself home sweaty and dirty from working with the crew of AAA Landscaping. She'd hoped to have her own patio rebuilt by the time July first rolled around, but it hadn't happened yet, and with her days so busy, she realized it probably wouldn't.

The flower shop kept pace with Em's busy schedule. Though she still kept tabs on what was happening there, she quickly learned how much of a help Bart had become. She observed Gran and Bart together with amusement as he took on a greater role. They bickered like an old married couple.

"Guess Bart is doing a good job," Em said, one evening. "I haven't heard you complain about him in a while, and you don't call him a pirate anymore."

"No. Actually he's quite the gentleman. He even invited me to dinner one night."

"And?"

"And he's a good cook."

"I see," said Em, knowing for a fact that Gran had now gone to dinner at his house at least three times, usually on a Saturday night after the store closed.

July arrived with a visit from Elena and the baby, a few days ahead of the baby's christening and the Fourth of July celebration.

Em drove to her parent's house filled with excitement to see Lillibet. She pulled into her parents' driveway, looked up, and saw Elena waving to her from the front door. Em climbed out of the car and hurried toward her.

As Elena moved toward her holding her baby, Em's gaze

rested on Lillibet. Tears filled Em's eyes. Even from a short distance, she thought Elena's daughter was the most beautiful baby she'd ever seen. At eight weeks, the sweet little girl had round, pink cheeks, dark-blue eyes, and light-brown hair.

Em carefully lifted the infant in her arms and nuzzled her cheeks. The smell of baby—lotion, milk, and sweetness filled her nostrils. "You darling, darling girl," she murmured. If she was not mistaken, Lillibet was smiling at her—a secret little smile between the two of them.

"She's beautiful, huh?" Elena said, gingerly stroking the baby's cheek with a finger.

"Oh, yes. She truly is. I'm so happy I finally get to see her in person. It was hard to wait to actually hold her, but I couldn't leave the businesses. I hope you understand."

"Of course, I do," said Elena. "It's a very good thing we could Facetime though, because you're the one person I wanted to share her with." She took the baby from Em as Lillibet started to fuss. "It's time for her to nurse."

Em smiled at her sister. "I'm so happy we'll have a couple of days together before Andrew and Devin arrive for the christening."

"Me, too. I've already planned to take you to the Lettuce Leaf. I've been dreaming about their Butter Cake dessert."

Em laughed. "Tomorrow, we'll have Mom and Gran babysit while we indulge in it."

Elena patted her stomach. "I have to be careful, but somehow I think I might deserve a treat. Or so I tell myself ..."

Em threw her arm around Elena's shoulder. "I'm telling you too. You've done a wonderful job. Mom was so impressed by the way you've easily handled the baby from the beginning. She said you have a natural instinct."

"So will you when the time comes," said Elena. "Now, sit with me while I nurse Lillibet. I want to hear all about the business. It sounds as if things are going well."

"Very well. Much better than I ever dreamed."

They went inside their mother's house and into the guest room where Elena was situated. Em had offered to have her sister stay with her, but their mother had put her foot down and insisted the baby should sleep at the grandparents' home, declaring it a grandmother's privilege.

Seeing all the baby gear Elena had brought with her, Em realized that preparing for a baby might not be as simple as she'd thought.

Em lowered herself onto the bed while Elena sat in the rocking chair with the baby. She filled Elena in on the business. "Sometimes I don't know how I can get everything done—overseeing the store and handling my business. I think because I don't charge outrageous fees, people are willing to take a chance on hiring me. And then, when we get started, they want more and more direction from me. That's the exciting part. The hard part is finding the time to do everything."

"I thought Tinker and Bart were doing a good job with Rainbow's End," said Elena.

"They are. But I still have to take care of the business end—keeping the books, handling the purchasing of gifts, and overseeing inventory. Bart is a help, and Gran's doing some of that, but sometimes I need to double-check their work. Not that I'm letting them know. I'm also working on marketing for the store, but hope to have Tinker take a greater role in that."

"I've forgotten how much work goes into operating that little shop. It's deceptive because it's always seemed so easy with Gran running it," said Elena.

"She's the magic behind the business because her big customers love her and trust her. Now that she's aging and stepping away, I'm finding a lot of the details need to be worked on. I'm trying to weave my design business into Rainbow's End, but it's been a helluva of a few months trying to get a handle on it."

Elena lifted the baby to her shoulder to burp her and gave Em a look of admiration. "I know teachers made it tough for you following me in school, but, Em, you're way smarter than I am. I could never do what you're doing by yourself."

A warm feeling flowed through Em. She'd always been made to believe by some that she'd never measure up to Elena with her perfect grades.

Elena rocked back and forth, patting the baby's back rhythmically until Lillibet went to sleep. "What's happening with you and Devin? I know you've been doing a lot of texting and talking back and forth."

Em couldn't help the smile she felt crossing her face. "He's become such a good friend. We can talk about most anything. It's really nice."

Elena sighed. "It sounds as if you're totally perfect for one another."

"We know how much we like each other, but what's the point of taking our relationship to the next level if Devin is living in Florida? Besides, he told me he's bringing someone special here this weekend. He wants me to meet her." She glanced at Elena. "Do you know who she is?" The thought of Devin bringing another woman to the celebration sent acid to Em's stomach.

"No." Elena's eyebrows knotted. "Come to think of it, he's been very secretive lately."

"He told me I was his best friend and he needed my input on something very special." Em tried to hide her feelings, but the idea that Devin might want her opinion on a new girlfriend made her feel queasy.

Elena gave her a sympathetic look. "I'm glad you're friends.

He's one in a million. A great guy devoted to helping others."

"I've never had that kind of friendship with a man before. I'd miss it, if it ended." Em swallowed hard at the thought.

Their mother came into the room and hurried over to Elena. Smiling down at the baby, and rubbing her hands together in anticipation, she said, "How's Lillibet doing?"

Elena chuckled and handed the baby to her. "She's through nursing and is starting to wake up."

"I'll change her and then spend some time with her so you two can talk."

Em and Elena looked at one another and grinned. Their mother was all about being a grandmother. It was sweet to see her so excited about this little one.

That evening, Em was posting daily sales in the back room at the flower shop and going through bills when she came upon an envelope from the local hospital. Wondering if Gran had agreed to donate something, she opened it and stared with dismay at the words on the page. It was a notice indicating a biopsy of her left breast was inconclusive, and it was recommended that another test be done again as soon as possible. Em hadn't even known Gran had had the procedure. Her stomach churned. The thought of anything bad happening to Gran was devastating. She'd been too busy with her own business to keep an eye on her.

She heard a tapping on the front door. She went to see who it was and stopped in surprise. Devin was staring through the glass into the store and waving to her.

Seeing him, happiness shot through her, making her body come alive. Grinning, she hurried to open the door. "Hi!" She stepped back to allow him inside. "I didn't think you were going to be here for another day or so. Come on in."

As she began to lead him inside, he caught her arm and turned her around to face him. Smiling and gazing into her eyes, he pulled her closer. “I had to see you alone, had to know if I was right about you, about us, all along.”

Before she could ask what he meant, Devin lowered his lips to hers, warm and sure. The sensations she remembered from their other kisses exploded inside of her. She lifted her arms around his neck as he drew her even closer against him, near enough for her to know he was aroused.

His lips settled on hers again. Heart pounding, she allowed herself to be carried away by the sensual feelings that pulsed through her and settled in her core with a sense of urgency. She wanted him, pure and simple. And by the way he was holding her, kissing her, stroking her, he wanted her too.

When they finally pulled apart, Devin grinned at her. “No question about it. I was not only right about you, I was right about what I have in mind for us.”

“What are you talking about?” she asked, her mind racing with ideas of her own.

“I’ve got a lot to tell you. Right now, come with me.” He walked her over to the chair behind the counter.

She settled on the seat as he indicated and watched in surprise as he knelt in front of her. He lifted a black velvet box out of his pants pocket, took hold of her hand, and gazed at her. She drew in a breath and let it out. It was a moment she’d been waiting for all her life.

A tender smile softened his features as he began to speak. “I love you Emerson Jordan, more than anything on this earth. I want you to be my wife and the mother of all the children I hope to have with you. I’ve never felt the way about anyone the way I feel about you. You’re my best friend, the one I can count on to be honest, the nicest woman I know, someone who already makes me very happy. And I know you're going to be a great mother someday. Will you marry me?"

His green eyes glistened as he opened the velvet box to show her a large, square diamond surrounded by many smaller ones set in platinum.

Em clasped her hands together and sighed. She felt as if she were taking part in one of the fantasies she used to create about the perfect man she would marry one dy. Now, her wish had come true. He was everything she'd ever wanted in a husband.

"Well?" Devin asked.

"Yes, oh yes! I will marry you, Devin Gerard!" she cried joyfully. What was it her mother had said? *Lust can happen right away, but love takes time, and good, lasting love even longer*. Their talks over the last months had formed a friendship that was true. And the attraction? It had been there all along. They had all the ingredients for a strong, lasting marriage—chemistry, communication and caring.

Devin's hand shook as he slid the ring onto her finger. He looked up at her, his eyes welling. "Emerson Jordan Gerard. I like the sound of that name."

"Me, too," said Em.

She laughed when Devin rose, swept her up in his arms, and twirled her around as he hugged her to his broad chest.

Tears of joy gathered in her eyes.

He stopped and gazed at her. "I love you, Em. I love you so much."

She smiled at him even as tears rolled down her face.

"Is that thought so horrible," he whispered, thumbing the tears away.

She chuckled. "You know I don't feel that way, but after all the mistakes I've made, it's a little scary, because I love you too. So very much."

"Nothing to be afraid of," Devin said, hugging her tight.

Em leaned against him, thinking she was the luckiest woman in the world.

Devin drew away. "You'd better sit down. I've got an important question for you. Something you need to think about seriously."

She did as he asked, but noted the look of worry that crossed his face and wondered why he was suddenly acting nervous.

From his back pocket he pulled out a photograph and handed it to her. "This is Ava Torres. She's six years old."

Em's fingers shook as she took the photo from him. She studied the picture of the little girl, noting her dainty, pretty features, her uncertain smile. Ava reminded her of Nina, and her heart opened with tenderness.

"Is this the someone important you said you were bringing to the christening celebration?" Em asked softly.

His eyes bright, Devin nodded. "Yes. She's the girl whose mother recently died from cancer. When Ava's mother knew her days were numbered, she asked me if I would find a good home for her. I've mentioned both Ava and her mother to you. This was about two months ago... about the time I was asking you if you thought it was dangerous for me to get too close to my clients. Remember what you said?"

Em smiled. She'd told him that sometimes people needed closeness and help from others, and those that could give it should.

"I told Ava's mother about you and showed her one of the pictures you sent me. She was very pleased. She said she can tell by your eyes what a wonderful woman you are. I took her words to heart and began talking to some officials in Costa Rica about adopting Ava. We had to pull a lot of strings to make it happen, but she's officially mine. Now, I need to know how you'd feel about having this little girl in your life."

Em's heart beat so fast she thought she might faint. "Are you asking me to be her mother?"

His eyes grew suspiciously moist. "We both are."

She reached up and cupped his face in her hands. "I would be honored to be her mother."

Devin grinned and hugged her close. "I thought so."

"Where is she now?"

"With your sister. I can't wait for you to meet her. I'd like to pick her up and take her to your condo so the three of us can have some privacy. There's a lot we need to talk about."

Em clasped her hands together. "Oh, Devin. This is such a wonderful day!"

"The best." He gave her a lingering kiss and then left to pick up Ava.

Nerves quivering, Em waited inside her condo for Devin and Ava to arrive, feeling as if she was about to take the biggest, most important test of her life. Standing by the front door, she realized how empty the condo felt now that she knew it might soon be shared with the little girl she hoped would grow to love her and the man she already loved like no other. Thinking of how that poor child must feel about losing her mother and coming to America, Em's heart once more opened to her.

And then Devin and Ava were there.

Mouth dry, Em stepped out into the warm air to welcome them, her gaze glued to Ava's figure walking beside Devin. She looked so tiny, so vulnerable. Somber eyes from a warm brown face studied her uncertainly.

Impulsively, Em knelt on the ground and held out her arms. "Hi, Ava. I'm Em."

The little girl stopped walking and stared at her.

"I'm glad you're here," continued Em. "I know we're going to be special friends."

"That's Em, the woman your mother and I told you about," prompted Devin. "You'll love her, just like I do. Go ahead and say hello."

Ava started forward slowly, then suddenly began running.

Em hugged Ava to her, rocking her in her arms as they both quietly wept, their tears blending.

Still sniffling, Em talked quietly to Ava about how sorry she was that her mother had died and promised Ava she'd always be safe with her.

Ava stood and patted Em's cheek, still damp from tears. "*Mami.*"

Em couldn't stem the flood of new tears that trailed down her cheeks. She rose and lifted Ava into her arms, hugging her close, savoring the press of that little body against hers, overcome with maternal feelings.

"Well, that certainly went well," said Devin, his words cloaked with emotion. "I guess talking about you ahead of time with her mother helped Ava to understand the new situation. She's taken to you right away."

Em nodded, touched by the feelings Devin couldn't hide.

He cleared his throat, "C'mon, ladies, let's go inside. We've got a lot to talk about."

After she showed Ava and Devin around the condo, Em settled Ava in the kitchen with paper and some of the colored pencils she used in her business.

"How about a snack?" Em asked Devin. "We're due at Mom and Dad's for dinner, but I can offer the two of you something light to eat."

"Sounds good," said Devin.

She put together a tray of cheese, crackers, grapes, and nuts.

"This ought to hold us over," Devin said, offering the tray to Ava.

Ava very carefully picked up one of each offering.

"She's still not used to having a lot of food," Devin explained. "That's one reason she's so tiny."

Em nodded her understanding. "She's beautiful. I've learned some Spanish, but I guess I should learn more."

"*Si.* And she needs to learn perfect English. That's important. She's quite fluent already. A tutor has been working with her."

After Ava was content in the kitchen, Devin took Em's hand. "Come with me."

He led her to the couch in the living room, sat, and patted the area beside him. "Let's talk here."

Em settled on the couch wondering what was next. There was so much to get settled. Her mind was spinning with ideas of how best to handle the addition of a child to her household. She knew life wouldn't always be easy, but together, she and Devin could handle anything, even helping a six-year-old orphan girl become a permanent part of their lives.

"What are you doing?" came a little voice.

Em turned to see Ava staring at them. "Come here," she said. "We're making a family, and you're part of it too."

"That's my love," Devin said, beaming at her and hugging Ava, forming a circle of love.

After Ava went back to her coloring, Em sat in a daze beside Devin on the couch in the living room. He caressed her face in his hands and smiled at her, sending waves of happiness through her.

"I think I've loved you from the first day I saw you at Seashell Cottage. It scared me to death how much I wanted you, but I knew how you'd been hurt, and I didn't want to do anything that might send you running."

She sighed and returned his smile. "I love you, too, Devin. I fell for you when you told me I deserved a guy who could dance. Then, when you hired the security guard to protect me, I knew you were someone who cared. And you've always understood my desire for a family. Devin, you're so very special."

He cocked an eyebrow at her playfully. "I guess you really didn't remember me from your sister's wedding. We did dance once, you know."

She felt heat rise to her cheeks. She'd been such a fool then. He was the kind of man she wanted now, needed now. But she knew life wasn't that simple. She had commitments, and so did he.

"What are we going to do about us? There's so much to resolve. I can't just leave my businesses and move to Florida." The thought of disappointing her family was painful.

The grin that spread across his face lit his eyes. "How would you feel about my practicing medicine with Dr. Stone in town? He's ready to slow down and is looking for a partner. He and I have already had several conversations about my joining his practice and continuing to work with the underprivileged. He's agreed to my terms. I told him I'd give him a final answer soon."

"You'd move here? You'd do that for me?" Em's breathing hitched and her vision blurred. "You really do love me. I mean, I know you do, but this … this proves it."

His smile became teasingly sly. "I have much better ways to prove it."

She laughed. "Oh, Devin. It was such a lucky day for me when I met you at the Seashell Cottage."

CHAPTER NINETEEN

The minute Em walked into her parents' house, Elena rushed over to her. "Let me see! Let me see!"

Em held out her left hand and stared at the sparkling stone, still having trouble believing all the changes that had taken place in her life.

"It's beautiful!" Elena cried. "I knew the two of you were perfect together." She hugged Em and turned to Devin. "I'm happy to have you for my brother-in-law. You've been such a good friend."

Laughing, Em and Elena embraced.

Em took hold of Ava's hand and squeezed it. "You've met my family?"

Ava bobbed her head. "*Gran familia*. Big family."

"Just the beginning," Em said, thrilled with thoughts of all that was to come. "Let's say hi to your grandmother."

"*Abuela*. Grandmother," said Ava.

Em laughed when she realized Ava was teaching her Spanish. "Right. *Abuela*. Grandmother."

Ava nodded proudly and moved toward Em's mother, who was giving her an encouraging smile.

"Mom's going crazy thinking of two granddaughters, not just one," said Elena, beaming at her. "I'm so happy for you, Em. I really am."

"Me, too. It still feels like one of my fantasies. We have a lot of details to work out, but Devin and I are excited about taking this next step."

"When's the wedding?" asked Elena.

"I'm not sure. We haven't discussed the date, but I'm hoping for a Valentine's Day wedding," Em said, unable to hold back the smile she felt stretching across her face.

Elena laughed. "Perfect. What you've always wanted."

"What has she always wanted? Me?" said Devin joining them.

"A Valentine's Day wedding," Elena answered, chuckling.

Devin turned to her. "Is that right?"

She nodded. "But now, I don't care as long as it's you and me."

Devin gave her a squeeze. "After we put Ava down for the night, we have a lot to talk about. Now let's go see what our girl is up to. Looks like she has your father wrapped around her dainty little finger."

Em laughed. "Looks like it." Ava was sitting in her grandfather's lap, playing a clapping game with him.

After a family barbeque in her parents' backyard, Em sat with her sister and mother in chairs outside gazing up at the stars beginning to appear in the growing dark. Ava sat on her grandmother's lap, trying not to fall asleep. Gran sat next to them, still holding onto Ava's hand.

It surprised Em that Ava had so quickly taken to her and her family, but then her family had always been a welcoming one, and Em suspected Ava was starved for affection. Shy at first, Ava seemed to realize how genuinely happy they were to include her. Em was smart enough to know this initial phase might not last, that there would be tears and struggles ahead as Ava made the transition, but for the moment, it all felt right.

"I can't tell you how happy I am that Devin is moving his practice here," said Gran. "I couldn't ask for better news." She winked at Em. "You'll be able to continue at the shop."

"Now if we could just get Andrew to come here," Em's mother said.

Elena shook her head. "We're not that far away, Mom. And I've already promised you I'll bring Lillibet here as often as I can. Besides, you can come for a visit anytime you want."

"You're right, dear. I'm going to be busy, visiting one grandchild and having Ava here for me to spoil." She frowned. "What are you going to do about your condo, Em? Is it big enough for your new family?"

Your family. Em fingered her engagement ring, needing the touch of it to make it seem real. "I don't know. We haven't even talked about it yet. We have so many things to decide."

"First things first." Gran hesitated and then said, "How can you and Devin live together as a family with Ava in this small town without getting married?"

"All in good time, Gran. I'm sure she and Devin will work things out in a satisfactory way," said Elena kindly. "Besides, Valentine's Day isn't that far off."

"I just want you to be happy." Em's mother fingered Ava's dark curls as she lay sleeping against her.

"I can't believe this has happened. It's all so wonderful," gushed Em.

Devin approached. "I think it's time to take our girl home. If we're lucky, we can quietly transfer her to my car and into your condo."

As Em said her goodbyes to her family, she gave Gran an extra tight hug and whispered, "You and I need to talk about a certain test you had."

Gran's eyes widened. She spoke quietly, "It's all going to be fine. Don't you say a word to anyone else. This is a time of celebration for the family."

"We'll talk later," Em said, unwilling to let it go. Even though she was forming her own family, she would never abuse the special love she and Gran had always shared.

At the condo, Em and Devin got Ava comfortably settled in one of the guest rooms and went downstairs.

Devin patted the space on the couch next to him and grinned at her. "Alone at last."

Em nestled against him. "I feel like I'm in a dream. So much has happened in the last few hours."

"Some of the best moments of my life," Devin said. "I'm so happy you've agreed to be mine. Mine and Ava's. After discussing adoption with you for so long, I thought it might not be a problem for you to take on both of us, but it was something I needed to ask you in person. When her mother asked me to adopt her, I wasn't sure I was ready to take on a child. Not without you. I needed to be certain in my own mind about our relationship. And then I know how strongly you feel about the commitment to your work and to your family."

"When did you become certain about us?" Em asked.

"When you mentioned you were thinking about getting a puppy."

Em sat up. "Whaaat? A puppy is a far cry from a husband and daughter."

Devin chuckled. "I know. This is far better, yes?"

"Yes," Em said, hugging him. "So much better."

"Seriously, I've always known you'd make a good mother, but as our relationship grew through our conversations, I realized how deep my feelings for you went. And then I couldn't bear to think of my life without you in it."

Em sighed with pleasure. She felt the same way about him.

She sat up and faced him. "When are you moving to Ellenton? Where do you want to live? With me? When do you want to get married?"

Devin chuckled. "I'll be moving to Ellenton September 1st so I can get Ava enrolled in school. That will give me time to work out an agreement with the others in my practice in Miami. Right now, I'm on a leave of absence."

"Do they understand you might not be coming back?"

"Yes," said Devin. "Su Lynn knows I'm in love with you and that I want to make our relationship work."

Em's eyes welled. Devin made her so happy, secure in his love for her. She'd never been as sure of anything before.

"Hey, what's this?" Devin stroked her cheek and gazed down at her with such tenderness a tear slipped from her eye and trailed down her face.

"I'm just so happy," Em said, laughing when he shook his head and muttered, "I guess it's all good."

He tugged her to him. "Let's talk later. I've waited too long to hold you in my arms." He stretched out on the couch and drew her down next to him.

She loved the way her body melded into his. And later, when they began to move together, she loved it even more.

Em awoke, startled by an unfamiliar sound. When she realized it was Ava crying, she got out of bed and tiptoed through the dark into Ava's room.

Seeing her, Ava sat up in bed and held out her arms. "*¿Mami?* Is it you?"

"It's Em. You're all right. I'm here."

"I want my *Mami*," Ava cried.

Em sat on the edge of the bed and hugged the little girl to her. "Shhh. I know, darling. She's not able to be here, but you're safe with us." Em rubbed her back in comforting strokes. "We love you, Ava, and are so happy you'll live with us."

Ava nestled against Em's breast and gazed up at her sleepily. "Em?"

"Yes ... it's me."

Ava emitted a long, trembling sigh. "Em," she said, and closed her eyes.

Em continued to cuddle Ava, loving the way the little girl felt in her arms. She vowed to try her best to be a good mother to her.

Carefully, so as not to disturb her, she slid Ava under the covers and stared down at the little girl who would soon be hers. She felt a hand on her shoulder and turned to Devin.

"She okay now?" he whispered.

"I think so," Em replied.

"I love you. Now, come back to bed. I miss you."

She smiled in the dark, knowing she'd never tire of hearing those words from him.

In the morning, Em awoke to find Ava standing beside the bed. "Good morning, Ava," Em said cheerfully, wondering if she would remember crying in the night.

"I'm hungry," said Ava.

Em grinned, pleased that things seemed to be okay. "Give me a minute and I'll get up and give you breakfast."

Devin stirred beside her. "Did I hear the word 'breakfast'?"

Em poked him. "Yes. What do you want?"

"At the moment, I'll have to settle on food. But tonight? A different story," he said, giving a playful tug to her hair.

Ava studied them solemnly. "*Papi* and *Mami*."

Em glanced at Devin and turned to Ava. "Yes." She got out of bed, slipped on a light robe, and took hold of Ava's hand. "Let's go downstairs and give Papi a chance to grab a shower."

In the kitchen, Ava sat with paper and colored pencils while

Em cooked bacon and set to work chopping tomatoes and sweet onions as part of the filling for omelets.

Devin joined them. “Something smells wonderful.” He kissed Em and went over to Ava.

“Hi! What are you drawing?” He bent over to see the picture and then held it up to Em. “A family. *Papi, Mami*, and Ava.”

Emotion clogged Em’s throat. She could only nod before forcing out the word, “Nice.” Everything was happening so fast. Too fast. Devin wouldn’t always have this time at home, helping both Ava and her get used to the idea of being a family. It would take a lot of planning to make things work.

Devin helped himself to a cup of coffee and sat down with Ava. “This morning, I thought the three of us might go shopping. I didn’t know what clothes to buy for Ava, and I want to get her some toys too.”

“Toys?” Ava said, her eyes bright with the promise of them.

Em laughed. “One word she knows very well. It sounds like fun. I’ll look through the things you brought with you and make a list of other clothing she might need. It’s a good time to do it. The stores are having sales.”

“Sounds good. How about I do the toy thing with you and then let you and Ava do the rest?”

“What do you say, Ava? Shall we go shopping?” Em asked, smiling at her.

Ava nodded. “Shopping.”

“After I brought Ava to Miami, Su Lynn helped me get her some clothes. But we bought just enough to get by for the trip here.”

“Okay,” Em said, “we’ll fill in the rest.”

She helped Ava with a bath. “Such a pretty little girl,” Em

murmured as she towel dried her off. Ava might be tiny, but she was perfectly shaped.

"No, not little. I'm six," Ava said, giving Em such a look of disapproval that she laughed.

"Okay, big girl. Let's get you dressed and then we'll go shopping."

Ava's eyes lit. "Shopping."

It didn't take long for them to get ready. Em was as excited as Ava. She'd always dreamed of having a little girl to "dress," and today was an unexpected gift.

Devin wanted to be part of the experience at a toy store and stayed with them while Ava picked out a few of her favorite things. Careful not to overdo it, Em and Devin decided four toys were enough for now. Ava chose a doll, an educational electronic tablet, a unicorn stuffed toy and accompanying book, and a battery-operated dog. Em chose a number of books for her.

When it came time for them to move on, Devin said, "Why don't I meet up with you later? There are several things I have to take care of while you two ladies fuss over clothes."

"Thanks. That way we won't have to hurry. I'll call you when we're done, and maybe you can meet us for lunch."

"Great," said Devin, sounding as relieved as Em felt that he'd decided not to be part of a girls' shopping adventure. He handed her his charge card. "Have fun!"

"Thanks!" Em took Ava's hand. "Okay, girl, like the man says, we're going to have us some fun."

Ava giggled. "Fun."

It turned out that Ava had very definite ideas about what she liked and didn't like. It took a lot of diplomacy on Em's part to negotiate a change in some of the choices Ava made. But, overall, they did well. This girl liked sparkles, and that was that.

After visiting three different stores, both Em and Ava were ready to stop. Em called Devin, and a short while later, the three of them sat in the food court eating a late lunch.

Ava's head bobbed from time to time. As soon as they could, they finished their meals, and then Devin lifted Ava into his arms. "Guess you two really shopped 'til you dropped."

Em laughed. "Ava had a ball. I'm so glad I was a part of it. She now has all she needs and," Em winked at him, "a little bit more. But a lot of these clothes should be suitable for school in the early fall."

"I'll leave that up to you."

As they walked to Devin's car, Em studied him. It seemed so natural to see him with a child in his arms. He was that kind of guy, gentle and caring. She gazed at the diamond on her finger flashing a rainbow of colors in the sunlight and thought of all that had happened in the past year. She'd learned a lot about herself and what she needed to do to grow not only her business, but herself as a person.

They got Ava strapped into a booster seat in the back, climbed into the car, and headed home.

"Did you have a successful morning?" Em asked. Devin had been fairly quiet during lunch making her wonder just what he'd been working on.

"Yes and no," Devin said. "I talked to Ted Stone about coming on board as soon as possible."

"And?"

"And he agrees it would be best."

Her mind spinning, Em clasped her hands. "So much is happening so fast. Do you think we should slow down or hurry up?"

He pulled to a stop in front of Em's condo and turned to her. "How would you feel about getting married right away?

With Ava as part of the household and me a professional in the community, it might be better if we did."

"Not wait until Valentine's Day?" Em knew she sounded alarmed, but couldn't stop herself. Hearing Devin say that made it seem so much more real. How could she make all the plans?

Ava stirred in the backseat.

"Let's talk inside," said Em.

"Sure, we both need to think about it."

Em got out of the car and gazed at Ava, who was staring at her sleepily, clutching the doll they'd purchased earlier. She was adorable.

Em unhooked Ava's seat belt. "Hi. Ready to go inside?"

Ava nodded. "I'm thirsty."

"Okay, we'll get some water inside. Do you want to carry one of our shopping bags?"

Ava's face brightened.

Em handed her one of the smaller shopping bags and watched as Ava proudly carried it to the front door.

"A real shopper, huh?" said Devin, smiling at them both.

Em chuckled. "Watch out! She loves shoes too."

Em helped Ava remove the tags and arrange her new clothes in dresser drawers before Ava was satisfied to play quietly in her bedroom, giving Em and Devin a chance to talk alone.

She fixed glasses of iced tea for them and walked outside with Devin onto the small patio she hoped to enlarge one day.

"A nice spot in the shade," said Devin, sitting down in one of the chairs beside a small table and taking a sip of tea. "Look, Em, I don't want to rush you into anything you might not want ..." he began.

"I understand. But from a practical point, you're right. It would be so much easier if we got married as soon as possible. A Valentine's Day wedding was sort of a silly idea."

Devin took hold of her hand. "No, it wasn't. I promise to do something very special for you on Valentine's Day, regardless of when we're married."

She smiled at him, loving the earnestness in his expression. She thanked her lucky stars she'd found him at the Seashell Cottage He was such a wonderful man. She suddenly straightened in her chair. "How about a wedding at Seashell Cottage?"

Chuckling, Devin shook his head. "Great minds think alike, and all that. One of the things I did this morning was to call the rental agency to inquire about availability of the Seashell Cottage for February. I was told the place is available for the next three weeks."

"You did? Oh, Devin, that would be a wonderful place for us to get married." She pulled out her cell phone. "Let's see ... July 11th is on a Saturday. That would work."

Devin's brow creased with worry. "Are you sure? It takes some women months and months to prepare."

"We'll make this work. Elena and Drew were going to spend the week in New York. I'm sure we can convince them, my parents, and Gran to come to Florida for the wedding." Em beamed at him, excited by the idea. "Being there will be a good way for Ava and us to have the chance to be together without the distractions at home."

"Well, if that's what you want, I'd better call the rental agency now." He got to his feet and pulled Em up into his arms. "Can't wait until everything is official."

"If you're like most men, you probably mean over, not official."

He laughed. "That too. But, seriously, I want it to be

everything you've ever wanted for your wedding."

"I'm sure it will be," said Em, her mind spinning with ideas. She wasn't about to admit it to him or anyone else, but one whimsical day in Florida she'd stopped by a bridal shop and knew exactly what she wanted for a dress. At the time, she thought she was just letting her imagination run away with her. Now, she was glad she had thought to do it.

While Devin called the rental agency, she called her sister. If Elena wouldn't agree to change her plans, she'd be devastated. Her parents and Gran would, she knew, do everything possible to be there.

"Hey, there!" Elena said upon hearing Em's voice. "I was going to call you to see if you had time to do a little after-baby shopping with me."

"If you're talking about a matron of honor dress, I'm in," said Em, unable to keep the bubble of excitement out of her voice.

"Oh, my God! When's the wedding?"

Em giggled. "Next week. Can you change your plans and come to Florida instead of going into the city? I haven't talked to Mom or Gran yet, but I'm sure they'll come."

"Next week? How are you going to get everything done?' Elena said. "It takes a lot of time to plan and pull off a wedding."

"Not if you keep it simple, and that's what Devin and I want. Just a simple ceremony on the beach. But I want you to stand up with me, Elena, like I've always imagined."

"Okay, that's what we'll do. I'm sure Andrew won't mind the switch of places. And the baby is a good little traveler. Oh, you'd better talk to Mom. I'll wait to hear from you, and then we'd better sit down and talk about it. And Em, maybe instead of having an after-baby vacation in New York, Andrew and I can stay at the Salty Key Inn, the place you told me about."

Em was relieved to hear Elena so excited. After she clicked off the call, she quickly called her mother.

"What's going on?" her mother said. "Elena is running around waving her fists in the air and shouting, 'Hooray'!"

Em filled her mother in on the plans. "You and Dad, Gran, and we can stay at Seashell Cottage and give Andrew and Elena a chance to stay at the Salty Key Inn for a little after-baby honeymoon. What do you think?"

"I think it's wonderfully crazy. But, Em, you've always wanted a Valentine wedding. Are you okay with this?"

"Yes, I really am," Em said, more and more pleased with the idea of a July wedding. It wasn't the wedding that counted; it was the man you chose to marry.

CHAPTER TWENTY

Once the idea of a wedding for Em took hold, her family swung into action. Her mother planned a small, private dinner at Gavin's following the wedding; her grandmother and she chose the flowers she wanted for the wedding, and then Gran called a florist in Clearwater and arranged to have them delivered to Seashell Cottage on the morning of her wedding day. Elena and Andrew reserved a room at the Salty Key Inn for the days prior to the wedding and for three days after so they could have their vacation. Her parents agreed to watch Ava while Devin and Em traveled to Naples for a short honeymoon.

The best part for Em was selecting a wedding gown. Elena, her mother, and Gran accompanied Em to one of the nicest bridal stores in the area. What once would have been suitable for a winter wedding was out of the question. Instead of something too formal, Em chose a simple, white sleeveless dress that met her ankles in gentle, silken folds. Em loved it and realized how perfect it was when both her mother and Gran cried when she modeled it for them.

Later, at one of Em's favorite, local, upscale stores, Elena chose a pale-pink, linen sundress that managed to hide the folds of skin she had yet to lose following Lillibet's birth. Her mother opted for a pale blue dress she thought would be ideal for a trip she and Em's father were planning in the late summer. And Gran, looking like a ray of sunshine, modeled a yellow dress with a short jacket.

"We're going to look like a rainbow with all of these colors," said Elena, smiling at Em.

"What about Ava?"

"Yesterday she picked out a purple dress that will be perfect," said Em. "She was upset at not being able to shop with us today, but Devin said he'd make sure they did some fun things together."

"It's amazing how well she's adapting," said Em's mother. "Devin too. I think having him help make the transition has made a big difference for Ava."

"Yes, she's known him for several months before her mother asked Devin to take her," said Em. "I can't imagine having to give a child away."

"So sad," commented Gran.

"Oh, oh," said Elena. She looked down at the wetness on her dress. "I've got to get home to feed Lillibet."

They hurried to Elena's car and headed home.

When they arrived at Em's parents' house, Andrew and Devin were watching a baseball game on television, Ava was coloring on the coffee table in front of them, and Lillibet was laying in Andrew's arms.

"What a peaceful scene! How did you do it?" Elena said.

"Bribery," said Devin. He pointed to the huge box of crayons and stack of activity books next to Ava.

"Pacifiers," Andrew said. "I'm glad you're home because Lillibet is about to have another crying jag."

Elena swept the baby up in her arms. "Poor baby. Mommy's here. Come with me."

Em watched Ava's head jerk up at the word "Mommy". Their eyes met. "How are you, Ava? Did you have fun?"

Ava nodded, but Em saw such a moment of sadness in her eyes that her heart clenched. She went over to Ava and hugged her. "I'm glad you had a good time. I missed you."

Ava lifted her face to Em and studied her until a smile slowly curved her lips.

Em took her hand. "Come sit with me, Grandmother, and Gran."

Ava got to her feet, grabbed a blue crayon and her coloring book, and followed Em into the kitchen.

"We girls will have a treat here," said Em, helping Ava into a chair at the kitchen table. "You can color here. Let's see what you've done."

Ava proudly showed off her colored pages.

Em exclaimed over Ava's neatness. "I think you're going to be an artist, a painter."

"Like *Mami*," said Ava proudly.

Em realized there was a lot she didn't know about Ava's background and vowed to learn all she could so Ava would always have her family history.

The next morning, Em was up early. She had to see to a client's newly built stone wall and the plantings that AAA Landscape were installing. Her other clients were amenable to her being gone for a couple of weeks, and both Bart and Tinker had agreed to handle the store every day while she was gone.

She slipped out of the house while Ava was still asleep. Devin was waking up slowly with a cup of coffee in the kitchen. This early time of day was her favorite. The sky was lit with promise as it brightened from a gray to a pretty blue. Pale pink highlighted the white clouds, adding a welcome, warm tint to them, reflecting the heat of a summer daybreak.

In the stillness, she went to her car and climbed in. She loved her little VW convertible but realized she needed to replace it with either a small truck or a good-sized SUV—something in which she could haul supplies or the garden treasures she selected and picked up for clients. And Ava would be more comfortable in something bigger. She'd make the switch in cars when the late summer sales happened.

She pulled up to her client's home. Mrs. Abigail Madison, a middle-aged woman who knew Em's mother, was one of Em's favorite clients. Originally from Virginia, she was very sure of herself and her vision for an upgrade to the garden behind her house in one of the oldest, most picturesque sections in town. Em had done her best to convince Abigail that a less formal garden would be more compatible with the climate in New York and the rustic nature of the area. As one feature and then another were added, Abigail credited Em with being the most clever, artistic person she'd ever worked with. The compliments were important because Abigail was, to put it politely, a great spreader of news. Gran had become infuriated when Abigail had told everyone that Gran and Bart were dating.

This morning, Em stood by while the crew from AAA Landscaping placed rhododendron and mountain laurel bushes behind the stone wall and above the area designated for perennials, creating varying layers in the space. It made the yard much more interesting.

At the back end of the yard, a grouping of lilacs added springtime color and aroma. On this July day, their leaves provided privacy and texture in varying shades of green in the sunlight. Off to one side, a small stone patio had been laid at the edge of lawn beneath a tall maple tree, providing a spot in the shade. It was an attractive nook perfect for reading, sharing an afternoon glass of iced tea with a friend, or napping on one of the two chaise lounges placed there beside a small table and four chairs. The patio addition had turned out even better than Em had thought. Two of Abigail's neighbors now wanted similar areas installed.

As she stood looking at her notes, Abigail approached her. "I'm pleased you agreed to come today to oversee the work. Getting ready for a wedding takes a lot of time. Is this the young man who accompanied you to the Fourth of July festivities last year?"

"No, this is a man I met earlier this year, one of those magical things when two people click together for all the right reasons."

"Well, I'm delighted for you, my dear. It surely doesn't mean you'll be moving away, does it?"

"No. My fiancé is going to be joining Dr. Stone's practice in town."

"Oh, how lovely. I'm sure your mother is thrilled."

Em couldn't stop the smile that spread across her face. "Thank you. My entire family is pleased." She didn't want to say more, not until after her wedding.

Satisfied things were in order at Abigail's house, Em hurried to the flower shop.

The specials for the Fourth of July holiday were a variety of patriotic floral arrangements of various blooms in red and white accented with blue decorative ribbons, set in blue glass vases, or placed in fabric-lined baskets. Rainbow's End also advertised tiny nosegays of a few flowers tied with ribbons for people to wave as the many bands in the town's annual parade marched by. An ingenious idea of Gran's, it had become a tradition for many in town.

While at the flower shop, Em also put together an arrangement of white lilies, baby's breath, and white freesia for the celebration of Lillibet's christening, which was to take place later that morning. Em's mother had planned a small, catered luncheon for close friends to be held at her house following the ceremony.

After seeing Tinker was set in the shop, Em said goodbye and carried the flowers to the car. She figured she had just enough time to drop them off, return home, get changed, and go to the church.

Her mother caught sight of her in her cut-off jeans and shrieked, “You’re not ready yet? The christening is in a half hour!”

Em plunked the arrangement down and hurried out of the house.

At her condo, she found Devin dressed and ready, standing in the bathroom with Ava, who was wearing a sundress and her new sandals.

Devin gave her a helpless look. “Help! I don’t know anything about doing a girl’s hair.”

“Hold on! I’ll get changed and come back to help you.” Ava’s hair was best tied away from her face in either braids or a pony tail.

Em freshened up, changed into a skirt and a top she especially loved, put on earrings, slid a silver band around her neck, and stood back to examine herself. Her face was flushed with happiness.

Moments later, Em sat with Devin and Ava in a front pew in the small church her family attended, feeling for the first time as if she really was part of her own family. Sandwiched between Devin and her, Ava leaned against Em’s shoulder, silently playing with the curls on her doll’s head. Em wrapped an arm around her and brought her closer.

The service was a sweet tribute to children. Em listened with a new attentiveness about the responsibility of raising a child. She glanced at Devin.

He smiled and sent her a quick wink to let her know he was listening too.

Her lips curved. She'd never felt so connected to another person. Her mother had spoken of friendship and how important it was to a marriage, but before now, she had never known what it meant. But after talking and texting openly with Devin about everything and nothing in the last few months, she felt as if he was truly a special friend. She guessed it wasn't the amount of time involved, but what they put into those moments that had made it possible.

The time came for Em and Devin to rise and stand beside Elena and Andrew and their baby. As godparents to Lillibet, they committed to helping her through life by example and dedication to her.

Em glanced at her sister. Elena's eyes shone with tears as she glanced down at the baby in her arms. she had imagined such a moment for herself. Her gaze turned to Ava. The little girl was focused on them with an intensity Em found touching. She knew that the months ahead might not be easy for them, but gratitude filled her for being given the chance to love Ava as her own.

With the service over, Em hurried to her parents' house. She'd promised her mother she'd make sure the caterers had done their job for their expected guests. She barely had time to check the dining room table before she heard the sound of cars outside. She glanced at the spread: cold, poached salmon; potato salad, a plate of sliced cucumbers, sweet onion and dill; tossed green salad with chilled peas; fresh fruit bowl; and buttery rolls the catering company was famous for. All looked delicious.

Waiting for her parents to arrive, Em took on the duty of welcoming people to their home, some of whom she'd never met. She introduced Devin as her fiancé and Ava as the girl about to become her daughter.

Seeing the surprise on some of the guests' faces, Em almost giggled with delight. After having to endure the role of being dumped, she was loving her new status.

Gran and her parents arrived, and Em was free to mingle with other guests and to see that Ava had lunch. She was sitting with Ava and Devin outside at one of the picnic tables set up in her parents' yard, when Clara and Chip Robertson joined them.

Em introduced them to Devin. "Chip Robertson was my first boyfriend back in grade school. Now, he's vice-president of East Bank. Clara and I went to high school together."

"Nice to meet you, Devin. And who is this?" Clara smiled at Ava.

Ava hid her face in Em's lap and then looked up shyly. "This is Ava, Devin's adopted daughter. Her mother was a patient at Devin's clinic in Costa Rica."

"How lovely. You're in for a lot of fun." Clara turned to Devin. "And you're a doctor? Great! This town needs another doctor."

"I'll be joining Dr. Stone's practice, specializing in pediatrics," Devin said.

Just then a little girl about Ava's age with short blond hair ran over to the table. "Mommy, I have a new friend. Ashley is here with her Mommy." She glanced at Ava and paused. "Who are you?"

Ava glanced at Em.

Em gave her an encouraging pat. "Go ahead and tell her your name."

"I'm Ava," she said shyly.

"And this is Penny," said Clara, smiling at Ava. She turned to her daughter. "Why don't you ask Ava to play with the two of you girls?"

Penny studied Ava and then said, "Okay. Come on, Ava. Let's go."

Ava hesitated.

"It's okay. We're right here," said Em.

Ava grinned and waved goodbye.

Tears stung Em's eyes as she watched Ava and Penny cross the lawn together. They looked so cute together.

"It's sweet to see them like that," said Clara. "I sometimes volunteer at the town library helping during the children's programs there. It's good when I see kids being nice to one another."

"Being a mother to a six-year-old is going to be very new to me," Em admitted. "I appreciate any help you can give me."

"No problem," said Clara. "I'm glad you're back in town and happy that we've become friends again."

"Me too." She and Clara hadn't been especially close in high school, but talking with her now, Em wondered why not. She liked her a lot.

"Is Penny your only child?" Devin asked.

"We have a two-year-old boy and a baby girl at home. We hired a babysitter to stay with them," said Jake.

"Being out of the house like this feels like we're on a date," said Clara, and she and Chip laughed.

Em smiled at their obvious affection, and wondered what it would be like to have three children so close in age.

"Hey, Doc," said Chip, getting to his feet. "Let's go get a beer. I'll introduce you to some of the guys."

After Devin and Chip left the table, Clara beamed at Em. "Looks like our families are going to be friends."

Pleased, Em said, "That makes me happy."

"Absolutely. You're engaged to a hunky guy, about to officially become a mother, and you own a couple of businesses. You're something else, Em." She laughed. "I'm here to take advice from you, not the other way around."

Elena came over and joined them. "What are you two talking about?" she asked as she lowered herself onto the picnic bench beside Em.

"We're going to give each other advice," said Clara. "I'll help her with Ava, and Em will help me with finding things to do outside the home, like running two businesses at once."

Elena laughed. "Sounds good to me."

Em joined in the friendly laughter, wondering if Clara would like working at Rainbow's End someday. She was such a pleasant, easy-going person.

Ava came running over to them and hurtled herself at Em. Crying softly, Ava threw her arms around Em's neck and clung to her.

"Hey, sweetheart, what's the matter?" She looked up as Penny approached her mother.

"What's going on?" Clara asked her.

Em studied Penny's troubled expression.

"I don't like Ashley anymore." Penny glanced at Ava and back to her mother.

"Did Ashley do or say something mean?" Clara asked.

Penny nodded. "She told Ava she can't play with us. She said Ava didn't belong here."

"Ahh, that's it." Clara took hold of Penny's hand. "That wasn't a nice thing to say. It hurt Ava's feelings. Of course, she belongs here. She's a new family friend."

"I tried to tell her." Penny walked over to Ava and tapped her on the shoulder. "Come on. Let's go on the swings again."

"I'll walk you over," said Clara.

"Me, too," said Em. "I don't know Ashley or her mother."

Both girls accompanied them over to the swings, where Ashley was playing by herself. Seeing them approach, Ashley ran over to her mother, who was standing and talking to another woman.

"You girls go on and play," said Clara before turning to the women. "Hi, Jeanne! Hi, Brie. This is Emerson Jordan, Donna and David's daughter, and this is her daughter Ava. Em, this is Jeanne Wethers, who works at the library, and Brie Kendall, Ashley's mother, works at the Anderson Insurance Company. I believe they're in the same book club as your mother."

"It's nice to meet you," said Em.

"Jordan? You're the owner of the flower shop," said Brie. "I sometimes buy things there."

"Thanks. We appreciate your business," said Em automatically. She could swear she'd never seen Brie there.

Jeanne frowned at Ava. "That's your daughter? She speaks Spanish. Is she Mexican?"

"No, she's not," said Em, bristling at Jeanne's condescending manner. "Would it matter if she was?"

"Well, this town is changing so much I can't believe it. When I walk down the street, I hardly recognize anyone anymore with all the foreigners here." An older woman, Jeanne frowned and shook her head.

"Jeanne, I know that you've lived here a long time, but it doesn't mean you can decide who can or cannot choose to live here too. Your mother, bless her, was one of the kindest souls I've ever met. I don't believe she would agree with your thinking." Though Clara's words were said softly, there was no mistaking the anger in her voice.

"Wait a minute," said Brie. "That's not fair. I don't want my daughter playing with just anyone. And until I meet the parents, and she gets approval from me, I want Ashley to stay away from kids like ... well, like some others."

Em swallowed hard. She was so tempted to tell Brie where she could stuff her attitude. Instead, she searched for words. "You know, Brie. I feel the same way. I don't want Ava mixing with children who come from such unaccepting homes. They have so little to offer her."

Brie's face flushed with anger and her mouth opened in surprise when she registered the insult. "Why you ..."

Before Brie could follow-up with that thought, Devin approached them, along with Elena, Andrew, and Chip.

"How's it going, darling?" Devin said to her, and bobbed a greeting to the other ladies.

"You're engaged to him? The new doctor in town?" Brie said, blinking her eyelashes with surprise.

Ava ran over to Devin, "*¡Papi! ¡Papi!*"

He swung her up in his arms. "Are you having fun?"

Ava shook her head. "Not with Ashley. She's not nice. But Penny is my friend."

"I see," said Devin, sweeping his gaze over the two women with disapproval.

"We'd better get home," Chip said to Clara. He gave a little wave to everyone. "See you all tomorrow, no doubt. I'm one of the judges for the parade."

"Have fun," Em said. "The annual parade is one of my favorite things."

Chip and Clara left with Penny.

"C'mon, Em," said Elena, ignoring the other two women. "Let's go see what's happening back at the house."

Em took hold of Ava's hand. "Let's go."

"I want water," said Ava.

They walked back to the house, and Em took her inside to get a glass of water. As they entered the kitchen, Em heard someone say, "It's lovely to see Em so happy. I was getting worried about her finding someone. And to think Devin is going to be a new doctor in town. Maybe now she'll settle down."

Em cleared her throat in warning and entered the kitchen

to find two of her favorite women.

"Oh, Em, we were just talking about you," said Isabel Porter. "We're all happy for you, dear. I had no idea you were dating and to think of Devin becoming part of the community. It's wonderful."

"Yes," said Stacy Greene. "Now you can settle down here." Her glance rested on Ava. "Such a sweet, pretty child."

"Thank you. We're here for a glass of water." She led Ava over to the sink, grabbed a glass and filled it with water. "Here you go, Ava. *Agua*."

Ava smiled up at her. "*Si. Agua*."

Em laughed. "I'll be speaking Spanish in no time."

"She's such a smart little thing," Isabel said. "My granddaughter is another smart girl. The other day she told me she was going to be an astronaut. You know what I said? I told her, 'Go, girl. We're all counting on you.' Such dreams young kids have today."

Gran entered the kitchen. "There you are, Em. I think I've found another customer for you. On his way out, Jake Robertson said we need to dress up the downtown area. I suggested he see you about it."

"It has been looking a bit down lately," Stacy said. "Why don't you talk to Marty Caster?"

Hands on hips, Gran glared at her. "Because my Em does a better job at design than he does. Besides, Em does most of the landscape designs Marty works with."

"Oh, sorry, Julia, I didn't mean to offend you," said Stacy, backing away. "Guess I'd better see if Rich is ready to leave. The afternoon has flown by."

"We've got to go too," said Em, amused by the irritated look that still remained on Gran's face. She kissed Gran goodbye and waved to Isabel before taking Ava's hand and leading her out of the kitchen.

"There you are," said Em's mother. "I want Ava to come with me. It isn't every day I get to introduce not one, but two granddaughters to my friends."

Ava took hold of Em's mother's hand and left. Watching them go, Em decided to find her sister. She'd seen her head upstairs with Lillibet.

She found Elena in her bedroom nursing the baby. Observing them, Em thought of the wonder of childbirth and the bonding of mother and baby.

Elena looked up and saw her. "Hi," she said softly smiling. "How are you, *Mami*?"

Tears blurred Em's vision. She'd waited a long time to hear those words. Now that it was happening, she hoped she was ready for all it meant.

CHAPTER TWENTY-ONE

That night Em and Devin tucked Ava in for the night together. "Sleep tight, sweet girl," Em said softly, kissing her on the cheek.

Ava nodded solemnly and then hugged Devin.

"See you in the morning," Devin said, turning to go.

"Papi? Am I too small?" said Ava, making him stop.

"You're the perfect size, why?" he said facing her.

"A lady said I needed to grow bigger," Ava said. "She called me poor little thing."

Devin looked to Em.

"It's probably one of my mother's friends," she said, wincing. Sometimes, the most well-intentioned of remarks stung. "You don't have to worry about that, Ava. Like Papi says, you're the perfect size and the perfect little girl to us." In truth, she was small for her age, and would, no doubt, put on a little weight in the coming months as she was given regular, healthy meals and settled into a more stable existence. But Em never wanted Ava to think she wasn't exactly right as she was.

Em turned on the new nightlight they'd purchased for the room and hugged Ava. "There now. You're all set. Get lots of sleep. We have an exciting day ahead of us."

"*¿Mami*? Another hug?"

Em's heart filled with love. "As many as you want." She loved them as much as Ava.

Downstairs Em and Devin sat at the kitchen table with

their computers and calendars. It was time to sort out a number of details.

"I like your condo, but realistically we're going to need something different—something with more space inside and out."

Together they made a list of things they were looking for in a house and searched online for housing in the area. When they had no luck finding anything that felt right, she said. "Don't worry. I'll call Barbara Arnold, my real estate agent, and tell her to keep an eye open for anything of interest that might come up. In the meantime, you can bunk here."

"Okay. But let's leave for Florida right away. We'll get set up at Seashell Cottage and wait for your family there. There's a three-day waiting period after getting our marriage license. I've already got the cottage rented so we can move in anytime." Devin clasped her hand in his strong fingers. "Thanks for being so understanding. I can't imagine many women willing to go to such lengths to make things happen so quickly."

She smiled. "You have no idea how happy you've made me."

Devin grabbed hold of her elbow and pulled her up from the chair. "Let's dance."

A giggle of surprise escaped her. "Really? Now?"

"Sure. There's soft jazz playing in the background. That's all we need."

He placed an arm around her and drew her to him. Moving to the beat of the music, he began to sway with her. Em sighed with pleasure. She felt so at home, so safe, so eager for a future with him. "Now, do you remember me from Elena and Andrew's wedding?"

A memory of once dancing like this with Jared evaporated. "It was you," she said softly.

Devin gazed down at her. "I've never forgotten that one dance with you."

"I was such a fool," Em said.

"You were … adorable!" Devin said. "All those flirty glances at your boyfriend."

Em nestled against him, thankful for the way things had turned out. They continued to move to the music until it became obvious that they both wanted a dance of a different kind.

After breakfast the next morning, Em hurried Devin and Ava out of the house. She'd already opened up the top of her VW convertible, packed folding chairs in the backseat leaving a place for Ava, and placed bottles of water in a canvas bag to carry with her.

"I'll park behind the flower shop, and we'll set up the chairs in front for Gran and my parents." Elena and Andrew had opted to skip all the noise and excitement, worried about the effect on Lillibet.

"It's awfully early, Em," Devin complained. "Why the rush?"

"You'll see." She never grew tired of the annual parade that always inspired her.

The curbs along Main Street were already filling with people and chairs when she led Devin and Ava to the front of the store and helped Devin place the three chairs along the curb.

From their places, they could see the reviewing stand set up in the small central park farther down the street. Em strained to see Clara and Jake in the distance and was rewarded with a wave from Clara, who headed their way with Penny in tow.

The sound of horns and other brass instruments being tuned danced in the warm, summery air, a hint of what was to come. Ava hung by Em's side until she saw Penny, and then she ran over to her.

"Hello, there," Clara said smiling. "Beautiful morning for a parade."

"Indeed," said Devin. "I haven't been to a parade since I can remember."

"We may be a small town, but we do the Fourth of July up big," said Clara. She held up the tiny bouquet of flowers from Rainbow's End. "I'm ready for this year's Princess of the Parade."

At his puzzled look, Em explained. "When the young princess goes by, we all wave the flowers at her or toss them into the car she's riding in. A tradition Gran started years ago."

Devin grinned. "I guess the two of you were once the Princess of the Parade, huh?"

Em and Claire looked at one another and grinned. Ellenton was small enough that several young girls were given the honor. It was generally the highlight of their teen years.

"I'll be right back," said Em. "I have to get our flowers from the store."

She unlocked the door, stepped inside, and grabbed six beribboned bunches of flowers she'd made for them earlier.

When she stepped outside again, she noticed the frown on Devin's face.

"What's up?" she quietly asked him.

"The daughter of one of the women I met yesterday was rude to Ava. I don't like it. The mother overheard it, but never reprimanded her. I hope living in Ellenton isn't going to be a problem for us."

"There's prejudice everywhere, Devin. We will have to deal with it the best we can. I don't like it. You don't like it. Our job is to explain other people's prejudices to our daughter, to prepare and show her the good in people," said Em. "Look at how well she and Penny are playing."

"You're right, though it makes me angry to see such treatment."

"I know." She handed him one of the small bunches of flowers. "Here. Thought you'd like to be part of the fun."

He grinned. "How about I toss it at you instead?"

She laughed. "My days of being the princess are long over."

"We'll see about that," he said, and turned as the sound of marching feet grew closer.

Em greeted her parents and Gran and handed them flowers. "Got your seats all saved."

"Good," said Gran. "I'm ready to enjoy the day."

Standing beside Devin, remembering it was just a year ago that Jared had been at her side, Em marveled at all the changes in her life. She'd always been fanciful and a dreamer, but in all those years of being that way, she could never have imagined the fairytale she was living now.

Ava came and stood by her side. Em handed her one of the flowers. "When the princess passes by, you can toss these to her, okay?"

Eyes shining with excitement, Ava nodded.

Small as it was, the town parade had everything one could imagine—three marching bands, a fire engine with siren going softly, several floats—one loaded with Cub Scouts giving out candy—baton twirlers, Girl Scouts marching together, a veterans' group, two clowns handing out coupons to the ice cream store, a group of kids riding bicycles decorated with crepe paper streamers and on and on, one group following another.

Ava was alternately delighted and overwhelmed by everything. But when it came time for the Princess of the

Parade to pass by, Ava tossed her flowers like everyone else into the backseat of the antique, red convertible on loan from the Chevrolet dealer.

"Pretty," gushed Ava at the young teen wearing a fancy blue dress and a tiara in her hair.

Em laughed, certain in her mind that Ava would be the princess one day, betting she'd love wearing a sparkly crown.

After the last group had marched by followed by a number of horseback riders, people picked up their chairs and other belongings and began to move away.

"Well, what did you think?" Gran asked Devin.

"It was nice. Really nice. A slice of Americana."

"I'm glad you liked it. Next year, your medical practice will be tapped for donations. Just saying," said Gran.

Devin returned her smile. "We'll be glad to help."

"I want to be the princess," said Ava to Gran.

"Sweetie, you already are," Gran said. "But to be the Princess of the Parade will take a few years of growing."

Ava nodded solemnly. "Okay."

Amused, Em exchanged glances with Gran and turned to her mother, who was saying goodbye to Clara.

"We'll save you blanket space next to ours for the fireworks," said Clara to Em. "See you then."

"Sounds good," Em replied, grateful for the friendship building between them.

Sitting in the dark, waiting for the fireworks to begin, Em gazed around the crowd. On the whole, people were friendly and kind. A few people like Jeanne and Brie were the exception. She watched Ava playing tag with Penny and some other children and wished she could keep her safe from being hurt. But Em knew how unrealistic that was. She'd thought long and hard about adoption. That would be but one challenge. Ava had appeared to fit in easily, but it would take work on everyone's part to make sure the easy transition would continue.

As soon as fireworks lit the sky, Ava hurried over to Devin and her. Sitting between them, Ava watched the fireworks wide-eyed, and then covered her ears. "It's too loud. I want to go home."

"It won't always be loud," Devin said. "Want to try to stay?"

Ava shook her head. "No. Too loud."

Em and Devin gazed at one another.

"You go ahead. I'll get the blanket and basket of goodies," said Em, doing her best to hide her disappointment.

Clara gave her a sympathetic look. "It takes some kids time to get used to it."

"Yes. I don't want to scare her. See you later."

"Good luck on the wedding," said Clara. "Call me when you get back."

Em gave her an impulsive hug. "Thanks so much! I will."

By the time, Em returned to town, she'd be Mrs. Devin Gerard.

CHAPTER TWENTY-TWO

The next day passed in a blur of activity for Em. She met with Bart and her grandmother regarding the upcoming summer sale, visited all her client projects, and then spent time trying to decide what clothing to take to Florida. She still had most of the items she'd taken there for Valentine's Day, and though Devin had already seen her in a lot of them, she decided they would be best, especially the little black dress he'd loved on her.

As she was packing in her room, a knock sounded at the door. She looked up to find her mother, sister, grandmother, Ava, and Tinker standing in the hallway.

"What's this?" she asked.

"A surprise!" cried Ava, jumping up and down.

"We planned a surprise bridal shower for you," Em's mother said, beaming at her.

"Shopping!" said Ava, holding up a bag overflowing with colorful tissue.

Em laughed with the others.

"She does love to shop," said Em's mother. "It was so much fun. Wait until you see what Ava chose for you."

At the thoughtfulness behind their gesture, Em controlled her emotions. "Shall we go downstairs? I can fix some appetizers, and I'm sure I have a nice bottle of wine."

"Not to worry, sweetheart," said Gran. "We've already taken care of it."

The group migrated to the kitchen where a selection of appetizers was spread out on top of the table. On the kitchen counter, a bottle each of red and white wine were opened and sitting next to wine glasses.

"Andrew and Dad are taking Devin out for dinner. We girls wanted to do something simpler here," said Elena. "Hope you don't mind."

"It's perfect," said Em. "Everything looks yummy."

"Gourmet Delights does a good job of putting events like this together," said Gran.

Em's mother poured wine for everyone but Ava, who was served orange juice. She lifted her glass. "Here's to Em! May you know only happiness with Devin and Ava."

"Yes, here's to becoming Emerson Gerard!" said Tinker. "I'm so happy for you!"

"I can't wait to be in your wedding, sis!" added Elena.

"I'm so happy you've finally met a man worth marrying," said Gran. "He's a good one, all right."

"Thank you all," said Em. "Things are moving along so fast I hadn't even thought of a shower. This is great."

"Well, open your gifts," said Em's mother.

"Me first," Ava said, handing her the bright red bag overflowing with tissue. "It's beautiful, *Mami.*"

Em noticed the grins on the faces of those around them. "I'm sure it is, Ava. Let's see." She pulled the stuffing out of the way and lifted a small package wrapped in black and tied with a broad, silk ribbon in gold. Pretty sure she knew the risqué store it came from, Em told herself to play along.

"Open it," said Ava, dancing around her with excitement.

Em tore off the paper and stared at a bright-red, filmy top with spaghetti straps and lots of crystals around the extra low neckline. "How ... how pretty, Ava. You picked this out all by yourself?"

Struggling to keep her face straight, Elena said, "Ava was with us and couldn't be persuaded to get something else for you. We thought you'd like to see it for yourself."

"There's another part too," Ava said proudly, oblivious of the amusement on the faces of the others in the room.

Em lifted up what she thought were panties and realized it was a skirt if one could call the scrap of material that.

Em's mother smiled at her. "Ava could not be talked into anything else."

"No, I can see that. It's beautiful, Ava, because you chose it."

"I'm betting Devin will like it too," said Tinker in her musical voice.

"I know he will," teased Elena.

Recalling how he'd liked her without any clothes on, Em felt a flush heat her cheeks.

"Let's give her a break, Elena," her mother said. She handed Em another bag. "Open it. I think it will fit perfectly. If it doesn't, I'll exchange it this evening or bring an exchange with me."

Em opened the bag and lifted out a sea-blue bikini.

"There's more inside," prompted her mother.

Em discovered a silky sarong in a print of the same shade of blue. She clutched it to her. "It's great! Thank you. The size should be fine. I'll try it on later and let you know if there's a problem."

"Thanks, I love it," said Em, accepting the box Elena was handing her.

"You'll laugh when you see it," warned Elena.

"Oh? Is it the dress I wanted but didn't buy? The one you told me I had to purchase? That it was totally me?"

Elena chuckled. "You got it. It's so perfect for you."

"Let me see," her mother said, leaning closer as Em opened the box and lifted out a sundress in a light blue that Elena had insisted matched Em's eyes.

"Love the color," said Gran.

"Exactly," said Elena, "and it fits Em like a dream."

Em held the dress up in front of herself and twirled around so everyone could see. She stopped and gave her sister a hug. "Thanks. After we left the store, I was sorry I didn't buy it."

"Here," said Tinker a little shyly. "I thought you might like this for your trip and for here."

When Em saw the white baseball cap embroidered with the words "PLAYS IN DIRT" in green, she laughed. "This is perfect."

Tinker smiled. "I'm happy for you, Em."

"Me, too," she said. "Thanks, everyone."

"Wait! What about me?" said Gran.

"You're doing all the flowers for the wedding," said Em.

"And this," said Gran, handing her a box wrapped in silver and tied with a white satin ribbon.

Em couldn't imagine what it could be, but she gamely opened the gift. Surprised, she lifted out the canvas bag. The size of a purse, it had a zippered pocket that covered one side of the interior, two pockets facing it and two pockets outside.

"It's what the store clerk called a Mom's bag. Casual enough for beach, but usable most anywhere. All the pockets and such are for all the things you'll end up carrying for both Ava and Devin."

Em glanced at Ava and gave her grandmother a big hug. "I love it for so many reasons. Thank you!"

"Okay, let's party. I figure I have another twenty minutes or so before it's time to feed Lillibet."

"Where is she?" asked Em, looking around.

"I've tucked her in the little room off the kitchen."

The image of her struggle with the intruder not too far from the room turned Em's stomach sour. "No," she cried and hurried out of the room.

Elena followed at her heels. "Wait! Where are you going?"

Em kept going until she reached the area and gazed down at Lillibet sleeping peacefully. "I'm sorry," Em said quietly. "This is where I fought the guy off. Every once in a while, something sends my memory back to that time, and I panic."

"Oh, Em, that must have been so scary. I'm sorry. Now, let's move before we wake her. I want to celebrate with you."

Em allowed herself to be led away. Maybe, she thought, it was a good thing she'd be moving out of the condo. That frightening scene would never leave her mind.

All such thoughts disappeared as she relaxed with her family and Tinker. Though there was a difference in age between them, she and Tinker had connected from the beginning, and she loved that her family had included her.

After filling herself with the delicious food and sipping wine, Em said, "I think it's time for Ava to get to bed."

"Oh, my! Yes! I had no idea it was so late," said her mother. "You two go ahead. I'll wrap things up here and put them away."

"Better yet, take them home," said Em. "We'll be gone for three weeks."

"Good idea. We don't leave for another four days."

Em and Ava hugged each person good night. Then she led Ava upstairs. Overtired, Ava made no protest as Em helped her to brush her teeth and put on her nightgown—the one with the princess on it.

She sat on the edge of the bed and brushed the hair away from Ava's face. "I hope you had a good time today."

Ava bobbed her head eagerly. "Shopping and a party."

"Now, it's time to settle down for the night." Em leaned over and kissed Ava's cheek. "Good night. Sleep tight."

Ava's face etched with concern. "Where's *Papi*? I want *Papi!*"

"*Papi* is out with Andrew and Grandpa. He'll be back soon."

"But I want *Papi* now," said Ava, beginning to cry.

"I'll stay right here with you until you fall asleep," said Em. "But I really need the time to pack. See? Your suitcase is over there, ready to go."

Ava propped herself on her elbow and looked over to where the suitcase lay on the carpet.

"We leave tomorrow. That's why I want you to get a good night's sleep. Understand?"

"I want *Papi*," said Ava. "I want my *Mami* too."

Realizing Ava was overtired and overwhelmed by the last few days, Em climbed up onto the bed and lay down beside her. "Okay. Lay your head on your pillow, and I will tell you a story. Okay?"

"I like stories," said Ava, facing her.

"Once upon a time there was a pretty little girl named ..."

"Ava!" she said.

"Okay, a pretty, little girl named Ava who flew all the way from Florida to New York. And while there, she met a special friend of *Papi's* ..."

"Em," said Ava.

"This friend, called Em, had always wanted lots of children, but she didn't have any to call her own. It made her sad."

"You're sad?" said Ava, reaching out and touching Em's cheek with one finger.

"I used to be, but I'm not anymore. You know why?"

Ava shook her head.

"It's because I have you and *Papi* in my life right now. That makes me very happy."

"I want *Papi* here now," said Ava.

"Me, too. But we'll have to wait for him to come home." It was something they'd both have to get used to if Devin kept making his trips to Costa Rica. "I think your baby doll is missing you, like you're missing *Papi.*" Em got up and handed Ava the doll. "Why don't you talk to her while I start packing. I'm right down the hall. Call me, if you need anything. Okay? I'll check on you in a few minutes. I love you, Ava."

"I love you, *Mami,*" said Ava, studying Em's face with such intensity that Em momentarily felt intimidated. "My Dolly loves you too."

Satisfied, Ava rolled over and closed her eyes.

She paused to make sure Ava was settled before going to her room to finish her packing.

She carefully rewrapped the freshly laundered red nightwear Ava had bought for her and tucked it into a pocket inside the suitcase. Elena was right. Devin was going to love it!

Devin came home as Em completed her packing. Because of the circumstances of preparing for the wedding, she had not one but two large suitcases to put on the plane. Clothes at the cottage would be no problem, but a wedding dress and a couple of nice cocktail-type dresses for the honeymoon needed to be packed carefully without crushing them.

"How's it going?" Devin asked her, a relaxed grin on his face.

"Nice time?" she asked.

"Oh yeah. My last big fling before getting tied down, or so they tell me."

She walked over to him in an exaggerated, hip-swinging way. "Oh, yeah? Is that how you think of getting married? Me, tying you up?"

Devin's eyes widened and then he let out a laugh from deep in his belly. "If that's what you want, I'm in."

She chuckled. "What I want to do is go to sleep. But if you hurry, I might be able to stay awake for a few more minutes."

He pulled her to him. "Give me a kiss. I'm afraid I've had more to drink than I usually allow myself. But this is a special occasion. You and me."

"Very special," she easily agreed. "Better get to bed."

"Yes, ma'am." He gave her a silly salute and started to pull his clothes off.

"*¡Papi! ¡Papi!*"

Em and Devin were awakened by Ava's cry as she jumped up on the bed and scrambled across their bodies to lie between them.

Devin groaned and checked the bedside clock. "Guess we'd better get going if we're going to make our flight."

Em had arranged for a transportation service to pick them up and make the drive into the city to Kennedy Airport. Even so, they still had a lot to take care of before leaving. Devin would probably need a second cup of coffee, she thought, studying his haggard face.

"Okay, Ava, let's get you dressed, and then we'll pack the last of your things in your suitcase." Em climbed out of bed and wrapped a lightweight robe around her. At least Ava would be ready in time.

As soon as Ava was dressed and ready to go, Em settled her at the kitchen table with breakfast and started the coffee machine. Racing upstairs, she thought of the few things she had to add to her own suitcase.

Devin was just coming out of the shower as she entered the bathroom. She couldn't help staring at him. He was hot. A sexy smile crossed his face. He reached for her.

She laughed with happiness, twirled out of his grasp, and

blew him a kiss as she entered the shower. She'd wait for the time when they could do it right.

He stared through the glass wall of the shower in a teasing leer then moved away.

Em hurried through her shower and morning rituals, then rushed into the bedroom to dress. She noted the cup of steaming coffee placed on the bureau and gratefully took a sip.

Ava and Devin were laughing over a drawing when she entered the kitchen. Em clutched her hands to her chest, touched by the sight. She was a dreamer who'd fantasized about moments like this.

Devin looked up at her and smiled. "Ava and I are pretty excited about the trip. We were drawing pictures of palm trees."

"I can't wait to get back to Seashell Cottage. It's such a special place."

She made wheat toast with honey and offered slices to the others. At the sound of the doorbell, she quickly turned off the coffee machine and gathered plates. "That must be our limo driver. He's right on time."

As Devin went to the door, Em and Ava used the bathroom. Em locked the front door behind them, realizing when they returned to this condo, they'd officially be a family.

The limo ride into the city was filled with Ava's excitement, listening to her exclaim over everything she saw. It added to Em's anticipation. At the airport, Em took hold of Ava's hand, tightening her grip as they made their way through the crowds. Devin had purchased first class tickets, giving them an opportunity to move through a special line to check in.

When, at last, they got through security and reached their gate, they were among the first to board the plane.

"*¿Mami*?" Ava asked. "Will you take my baby? She's scared."

Em studied Ava seated next to her. Her eyebrows were knit together with worry.

"How about I put the baby doll on my lap and hold your hand in mine?"

Ava's face smoothed with satisfaction. "Yes, I like that."

Em couldn't help wondering about Ava's thoughts. Soon after her mother died, she'd been taken on a flight with Devin, leaving her home and her memories of her mother there behind. How frightening that must have been for a six-year-old. Though she'd been with Devin during the last months of her mother's life, it was a lot for a child to handle. And now Ava had to get accustomed to another new life in New York.

Em squeezed Ava's hand. "I love you, Ava. You're very brave."

Ava beamed at her. "I know."

Em felt her lips curve. Across the aisle of the plane, Devin smiled at them both.

CHAPTER TWENTY-THREE

As she stepped out of the rental car onto the sandy ground outside the Seashell Cottage, Em threw her arms into the salty air and wrapped them around herself as if hugging the beautiful scene before her. Devin came up beside her and put his arm around her. "Lucky thing we met up here," he said. "I can't wait until it's official, and we're married. Who knew I'd fall so quickly for you?"

She smiled up at him. "I think Elena thought you might, which is why she encouraged both of us to come to the cottage."

"Maybe you're right. Whatever the reason, it feels good."

Before she could comment, Ava tugged on Devin's arm. "Let's go swimming."

"Sure. We need to get unpacked first."

"And then I'm going grocery shopping," said Em. "I've already made a list."

"Sounds good. I'm ready to grill up a steak," said Devin, patting his stomach.

She chuckled. She'd forgotten what it was like with a man around. They'd stopped at a fast-food place on the way down the Gulf coast from Tampa, but they needed something better for dinner.

As Em placed her things in the bedroom she'd stayed in before, she looked out at the swaying palm trees and the water beyond and felt the tenseness leave her muscles. There was something about the sun, the sand, and the smell of the water that made her feel relaxed. Or maybe it was the magic of the cottage sitting comfortably at the edge of the wide expanse of white sand that filled her with a sense of peace.

She helped Ava get settled in her room and into her bathing suit and laughed at the sight of Ava prancing around the room in her new, pink, sparkly bathing suit. Brown eyes snapping with excitement, Ava looked like a long-legged puppy galloping for the pure joy of it.

"C'mon, you, let's put some of that energy to use in the pool," said Em. "While I go grocery shopping, you and *Papi* can swim."

Later, Em walked along the beach with Devin and Ava, loving the feel of the sand crystals beneath her feet. Every few steps she stopped to look at a shell Ava held up to her. Em was pleased by Ava's interest in shells. They were such lovely gifts from the sea.

"Tomorrow, before I leave for Miami to check in with my practice, we need to apply for the marriage license. Like I said, there's a three-day waiting period after the issuance of a license unless we take the state pre-marital course."

"That will be perfect. The rest of my family won't be here for another two days. Will your partners in the medical practice understand why you're moving so quickly?"

"They're surprised, but pleased for me. The fact that Su Lynn can take over my practice is very helpful. That's one reason I need to go to Miami. I don't want any misunderstandings between Su Lynn and me. I need her to remain in Miami to take over for me." Devin looked away at the water and then back to her. "She hoped I would change my mind about you." He cupped Em's face and lifted it into the sun before planting his lips on hers. "But I didn't and never will."

"Hey! What are you doing?"

Startled, Em jerked away from Devin and gazed down at Ava. "*Papi* is kissing *Mami*."

"Me too?" Ava held up her arms.

Em lifted her into her arms and gave her a kiss. "There, Miss Ava. Are you okay now?"

Ava nodded, and held out her arms to Devin. "Now *Papi*."

Em and Devin chuckled. Ava was a sweet girl who was needing more and more attention.

On the walk back to the house, Em took her time while the lacy edges of the water washed over her feet and pulled away in a steady rhythm. She heard the gulls crying out as they swooped and dived in the air above her. She laughed at the sandpipers and other shore birds as they marched along the wet sand near the water, leaving imprints of their tiny feet behind.

Devin took hold of one hand; Ava, the other. The three of them faced the rolling waves, lost in the beauty before them. There was something almost mystical about this scene. A lot of the magic lay in the presence of the two people beside her.

"I'm hungry," Ava said, breaking the spell.

"Well, then, let's go get dinner," said Em. "*Papi* is going to grill meat, but we'll give you a little snack to tide you over."

Back at the cottage, working in the kitchen with Devin seemed normal, as if they'd done it for years, not just a few times. Devin poured her a glass of red wine while she gave Ava some cheese and cool, green grapes.

"Let's go outside for a little bit before I grill the steak," Devin said to her. "There's something I want to show you."

Ava followed them out to the porch and sat down on the steps to eat her snack.

Devin sat in a rocking chair next to her. "My mother didn't have many material things in her life, but one thing she loved was a necklace that was given to her by a friend at work." He pulled a small, white cardboard box from his pants pocket. "I thought you might like to wear it for our wedding. It would the 'something old' brides like to wear."

Em's fingers shook as she accepted the box he handed her. She didn't care what the necklace looked like, she knew it was something she'd always treasure.

She lifted the lid of the box and gazed inside. On white tissue paper, a delicate gold chain held a tiny pendant of the sun. Her vision blurred with emotion.

"I love it, Devin. I only wish I could have met your mother. I will wear this with pride. I especially love the idea that she will be part of our wedding."

"Thanks." Devin's eyes were bright with tears. "She would've loved you."

"Tell me about her," she prompted.

Devin sighed. "My mother worked two different jobs to keep us afloat. During the day, she worked as a secretary at an office. At night and on the weekends, she worked for a cleaning service. We never had much, but we got by. When I was fourteen, I had a job after school. All under the table, of course."

"She must have been so proud of you when she knew you wanted to become a doctor."

His expression was sad. "I got good grades, like she expected. And then when I saw what cancer did to her body, I knew for sure medicine is what I needed to do. I ended up in pediatrics after treating young patients in different countries and realizing how good, basic healthcare can make all the difference for a child."

Em took hold of his hand. "I know how much your patients

must like and trust you." She indicated Ava with a nod of her head. "She's just one example of it, I'm sure."

"Yeah, I like them too," Devin said simply.

She loved that he was so modest. She leaned over and kissed him.

"Are you kissing again?" Ava said, breaking them apart with laughter.

"Yes. See the necklace Devin gave me?" Em held it up for Ava to see. "It's very special."

"For me? It's pretty."

"It's for me, but someday, I might let you wear it. Now, give me a kiss."

Smiling, Ava kissed her.

Em hugged her tight. "You know the magical thing about kisses?"

Ava's eyes rounded. "It's magic?"

"Uh, huh. Magic because there are always enough to go around."

Ava nestled closer.

Em nibbled at Ava's neck, covering it with lots of kisses, stopping only when Ava shrieked with laughter.

The next morning, the three of them headed for the Clerk of the Court's office to get the marriage license. It was to be a simple matter—driver's licenses and a fee of $93.50. However, when they arrived, they discovered two other couples ahead of them.

"What's happening?" Devin murmured to Em. "I didn't know so many people were getting married these days."

"July is a nice month for a wedding," said Em, thinking of her own. She held onto Ava's hand as a child ahead of them, shrieked, "No! You can't make me!"

A young mother had a little boy by the arm and was jerking him around. "I told you that you couldn't have any candy right now. Hand it over."

"Noooo!" screamed the little boy. "You can't make me!"

Em glanced at Ava, standing next-to-her, wide-eyed. Ava looked puzzled, then grinned when she heard the mother say, "Aw right, but no more after this."

Em observed Ava's reaction, but decided not to make a lesson of this. Up to this point, Ava had been surprisingly easy to get along with.

After they left the clerk's office with the certificate in hand, Devin turned to Em. "Let's get a rental car for you. I'll drop this one off in Miami and drive my own car back. I want to get to the office, sign some papers, and get back to you as soon as possible."

At the car rental office, they found a SUV for Em, and then Devin took off for Miami.

Em and Ava headed back to the cottage. The thought of a quiet day was tantalizing to Em. She planned to get in shorts and a T-shirt and keep Ava company. She might even convince Ava to take a nap. The last few days and weeks had been busy and emotional ones for each of them.

The day rolled out nicely. Ava was happy to swim and play in the pool, allowing Em to relax while watching her. They had a leisurely lunch together, and then Em suggested they both lie down.

"I don't want to," whined Ava, indicating how much she needed one.

"How about reading on your bed?" Em suggested. From the look of the way Ava's eyes were drooping, Em knew a book would put her to sleep in no time.

Em gathered books and settled Ava on top of the bed with her doll and the books. She leaned down and kissed Ava's cheeks. "Remember, no running around. You stay here and read. I'll be in my room."

"Okay," said Ava.

Em left her and went to her room. She let out a sigh of exhaustion as she climbed onto her bed, punched the pillow to get it comfortable, and lay her head on it. She hadn't realized how busy she'd been physically to get her business up and running, and though Gran's flower shop was running smoothly with Bart and Tinker, it was another thing she had to oversee. Her entire body longed for relief.

She listened for sounds from Ava's room. Hearing none, Em closed her eyes.

Sometime later, Em felt the movement of air around her and opened her eyes to see Ava tiptoe out of the room, carrying something white in her hands. She checked the top of the bureau and sat up quickly when she realized Ava had the box holding the necklace Devin had given her.

"Ava! Wait!" she called, getting up.

Giggling, Ava ran to the front door and opened it.

"Ava! I need that box!" cried Em.

On nimble feet, Ava ran down the porch steps and onto the sand.

Em chased her. "Ava, stop!"

"No!" Ava called back to her, laughing as if this was the best game of tag ever.

Em lengthened her stride. Ava was heading for the water.

"Stop, Ava!"

Ava ran into the water and turned to her with a big grin, failing to see the large, rogue wave heading her way.

One moment Ava was standing waving at her, the next, she was sprawled face down on the sand.

Heart pounding with alarm, Em hurried toward her.

Lifting her head, Ava looked at her and started to cry.

Em picked her up and patted her back. She had scrapes on both her knees and blood on one cheek. It took Em a minute or two to realize the top of the box in Ava's hand was gone, and the gold necklace was missing.

Still holding onto Ava, Em scrambled about, searching for the necklace. The waves continued to rush in and move away again, shifting the sand at her feet, making the task impossible. Tears blurred Em's vision. How could she tell Devin his precious gift was lost?

CHAPTER TWENTY-FOUR

Em sat in the kitchen holding Ava in her lap, staring at the wet, empty box sitting on the table, a reminder of all that had gone wrong. Em's mind whirled with accusation. *It wasn't Ava's fault. I should have placed the box in a secure drawer, should never have fallen asleep.*

Ava turned to her and patted her cheek. "I'm sorry, *Mami*."

"I am too," Em replied, doing her best to rein in her sharp disappointment. It was an accident. An accident that should never have happened. An accident that would hurt Devin.

"Let's have you get changed into a bathing suit so you can take a walk along the beach with me."

"I don't like the water." Ava's lips formed a pout.

Em couldn't blame her. Adhesive bandages covered several scrapes on her legs and on one arm. Her cheek had a good-sized scrape on it too. "I'm sorry you fell, Ava, but it's important for you to get comfortable on the beach again."

Ava jumped off her lap, let the towel drop, and turned to face her, her hands on her hips. "You can't make me!"

Remembering how fascinated Ava had been with the belligerent boy at the Clerk's office that morning, Em laughed. "Not going to work, Ava." She picked up the towel and left the kitchen, smiling when she noticed Ava trailing behind her.

Em knew there would be real challenges with Ava as the newness of the situation wore away. Until then, she was counting on Ava's good nature and desire to please to make each day as pleasant as possible.

###

Out on the sandy beach, Em lifted her face to the sky, allowing the warmth of it on her cheeks to melt some of the angst she was feeling about losing the necklace. She told herself that things could be worse. Ava could have been seriously hurt, even drowned by the unpredictable, large wave that had thrown her down on the sand.

She took hold of Ava's hand and squeezed it. "Shall we look for shells?"

Ava's wide smile lit her face, bringing new light to her dark eyes. "Can I hold the bag?"

"Here you go." Em handed her the net bag experienced shellers used to hold their treasures. "Stay with me."

Em led Ava to the water's edge. On the hard-packed sand next to it, small piles of shells lay in intriguing collections. "Look there. I'm going to search in the water for the necklace."

Em stepped into the water warmed by the sun, its lacy fringe bubbling at her toes. She determined the flow of the water and gauged where it was best for her to look. Seeing no sign of the glitter of gold against the sandy backdrop. it, she gently moved the bottom sand with her toes, sending a cloud of white into the water.

Em continued to look until she heard Ava say, "*¡Mami*, look!"

Ava held up a shell. "See? It's for *Papi*."

"Nice," Em managed to say, wishing it was the necklace. She climbed out of the water wondering what words she could say to Devin to make everything right.

Her cell phone rang. She pulled it from the pocket in her shorts and paused when she saw it was Devin. She clicked on the call. "Hi, Devin! What's up?"

"I just received a disturbing call from my lawyer. It seems that an aunt of Ava's is claiming I stole her from her family. I am to meet her here in Miami tomorrow morning at my lawyer's office."

"But you've already adopted her," gasped Em. Her heart pounded so hard she couldn't catch her breath.

"Yes, but the aunt is claiming that because I went outside of normal channels to adopt her, it doesn't count. I'm pretty sure this is all about money, but I have to be sure Ava will be secure with us."

"Do you want us to come to Miami?" Em asked, feeling sick.

"Definitely not. Ava's mother specifically asked me to take her, told me she couldn't trust anyone else in the family. In all the times I was with Ava's mother helping to care for her, I never met this sister or any other member of the family. Legal notices were posted at the time, but no one came forward."

"Oh, but..." Em stopped, afraid she might burst into tears. She knew from reading about foster care that the courts always preferred children to be with their biological families. Trying not to let Ava see how upset she was, Em paced back and forth on the beach. She'd already opened her heart and her home to the little girl who bound her to Devin. She couldn't let her go, couldn't let someone else tuck her into bed at night, couldn't allow her to be taken away.

Ava came up to her and took hold of her hand, giving her a worried look. "*¿Mami*?"

"Hold on," Em said to Devin. She knelt on the sand and drew Ava to her, hugging her to her chest. "I love you, Ava."

"*Si*," Ava responded, beaming at her. Satisfied, Ava trotted along the beach, dancing on her toes as she lifted her arms to the seagulls circling above her. Standing and observing her, fresh tears filled Em's eyes. Ava was a wonderful child.

"Are you all right?" Devin asked when Em got back to the call.

"I will be," said Em with new determination. "I'm not going to let anyone try to take our little girl away."

"I don't think there's any real danger of that happening," said Devin. "Not with all the legal documents I have, including a signed and notarized statement from Ava's mother. But it's something we have to face so we can settle the matter once and for all."

"If it involves money and it comes to it, I'll help pay whatever it takes," said Em.

Devin chuckled. "That's my girl. But it won't be necessary. As my lawyer told me, we can't allow that to happen. People like Paloma Torres would just keep coming back for more."

"It's an awful thing to use a child to get money," said Em.

"Yes, it is. I'm happy to know she's safe with you,"

Em's stomach curled. He didn't know how careless she'd been with Ava, allowing her to get hurt in the water. It was another thing she dreaded to tell him.

"I've got to go. I'll see you tomorrow," said Devin.

"Good luck with the meeting. Please call me as soon as you can. I'll be waiting to hear from you. Take care, Devin. Love you."

"Love you too," he said quietly, and clicked off the call.

Em held the phone in her hand, staring at the water, wondering how things could get so messed up in such a hurry.

She gazed at Ava bending over to look at a shell. The tan bandages on her dark skin seemed like badges of courage. Em was glad neither Devin nor his lawyer could see Ava now.

That evening, Em and Ava sat on the front porch eating the "picnic supper" Em had hastily put together. The onshore breeze held a bit of coolness that had been missing earlier, and the soft air on her skin felt good to Em. Since Devin's call, she'd been unable to stop the squeezing of her stomach any time she thought of losing Ava.

The sliced chicken sandwiches cut in small squares looked festive on paper plates along with pickles, chips, and assorted fresh fruit.

"Can I have cookies now?" Ava asked hopefully. Her plate was all but empty.

Em smiled. "Yes. You've done a good job." She got up to get the cookies from the kitchen. "I'll be right back."

As Em approached the front porch on her return, she heard soft singing. She stopped and listened. Ava's young, sweet voice filled the air. On tiptoe, Em drew closer. Ava was rocking her baby doll in her arms and singing in Spanish to her. Em clasped a hand to her chest, touched to the core. Here was a little girl who'd known sadness and rupture in her life, singing like an angel to her baby. Em didn't know much about Ava's mother except what Devin could tell her, but she knew in her heart that Ava's mother had been a good woman who'd loved her daughter. Em vowed to do as good a job.

Later, after putting Ava down for the night, Em stepped onto the porch. The glowing orb of the sun was slipping below the horizon. She studied it, looking for the elusive green flash both natives and tourists talked about. Though she'd never seen it, she never got tired of looking for it.

Sitting in a rocking chair on the porch, Em sipped from the glass of red wine she'd poured and gazed out at the water. Somewhere along its edge lay a gold necklace she hoped to find.

When Em felt the tap on her arm, her eyes flashed open. Ava stood smiling at her in the morning light. Em forced her eyes to stay open though they wanted to close with sleep. Her night had been filled with bad dreams about Ava being taken away by an ugly fantastical creature, the memory of which even now sent a shiver down Em's spine. Not a hard dream to figure out.

"Good morning, Ava." Em pulled Ava into bed with her and lay for a moment, contemplating the day. She gazed at the sun shining outside her window and made a wish for Devin to have a good day.

Ava wiggled to get down. Sighing, Em rose and slipped on a pair of shorts and T-shirt, resigned to starting the day.

Time dragged on as Em awaited a call from Devin. She wouldn't be able to rest until she knew everything was fine with the adoption.

When he finally called, she listened intently as he told her that, as he suspected, Paloma Torres was only after money and had no real interest in seeing or hearing from Ava again. "Drugs are definitely playing a part in her life. I can't imagine anyone agreeing to Ava's living with her," said Devin. "It's a shame, but the reason Ava's mother was so set against it. I'm glad her mind was at ease when she passed, knowing I'd take care of her daughter."

"What a relief! You're such a good man, Devin," Em said with feeling.

"And you're a good woman, Emerson Jordan. I'm headed over there now. See you shortly."

"Safe travels." Em hung up excited to see him, worried about his reaction to their battered daughter and the lost necklace.

The sun was lowering in the sky when Em heard the sound of a car entering the driveway. Bracing herself, she went to greet Devin.

He climbed out of the car and stood a moment, gazing around with a satisfied smile.

Ava ran over to him and threw her arms around his legs. "Hi, *Papi*. I have a surprise for you. It's a shell."

"Hi, sweetheart!" Devin took hold of her hands and swung her around in a circle, producing squeals of laughter from her. Devin set Ava down and gave Em a quizzical look. "What happened to her?"

"I fell down in the sand. And I lost the box," said Ava. "Kiss it, *Papi*. Make it better." She held up her arm to him.

He kissed Ava's arm and turned to Em. "Everything all right?"

Em bit her lip and shook her head as Ava raced inside to retrieve the shell. "While I was napping yesterday, Ava took the box holding your mother's necklace and ran away with it, into the water. A huge wave knocked her down, opening the box and ... and the necklace ... is lost in the water." Em's voice wavered.

"I see," Devin said quietly.

Em observed the hurt in his eyes, the slump of his shoulders and knew how upset he was. "I'm so, so sorry. I should've have kept a better eye on her, should have hidden the box away, should have ..."

Devin held up his hand. "Stop! It was an accident. Nobody meant for it to happen."

"But I know how much the necklace meant to you ... and to me. I'm sorry, Devin. I really am."

"Yeah. Me, too," Devin let out a sigh and wrapped his arms around her. "Don't blame yourself, Em. With kids, anything can happen."

"I guess I have a lot to learn about being a mother," said Em, feeling like a complete failure.

"You already are a good one. Look at how easy you've made

it for Ava to transition to your family," said Devin, thumbing the tears from the corners of her eyes.

"I have a feeling that's about to change. She's starting to challenge me." Em told him about Ava's testing bit of defiance.

Devin laughed. "It's just the beginning, sweetheart, but we'll handle it. In Costa Rica, she wasn't given the same freedom to express herself that she has here. I'm sure it's all a matter of time before she asserts herself like other kids her age."

Ava called to them and ran forward, looking like a pink butterfly in the sun dress she'd insisted on wearing. Em observed her with a sense of appreciation for having the chance to have her in her life. Ava was a bright child, full of life, and facing a future of the possibilities they could offer her.

Ava held up one of the shells they'd picked up for Devin. "For you, *Papi*. *Mami* and I found it."

"It's beautiful, Ava," said Devin, squatting to get a good look at it. "And so are you and *Mami*."

When he rose, he smiled at Em. "It's good to be home."

Em accepted the hand he offered her, grateful for his understanding about the necklace. She'd always keep looking for it.

CHAPTER TWENTY-FIVE

The next day, while Devin and Ava stayed at the cottage, Em headed off to Tampa International Airport to pick up her parents and Gran. Elena and Andrew and Lillibet had arrived late last night and were staying at the Salty Key Inn. Em had talked briefly to her sister, but didn't want to interrupt the beginning of the post-baby vacation she and Andrew had planned.

As she drove, she admired the palm trees and tropical green plants and colorful flowers—all part of the landscape lining the highway. Devin had once said he loved living in this kind of setting. It struck her once more how much he loved her to give up the Florida sunshine and move to a northern climate. She promised herself to repay him with that same depth of love. And more children. She felt a smile spread across her face. He'd mentioned children more than once. No wonder he was such a good pediatrician.

Em pulled into the parking garage, left the car, and walked inside the airline terminal. She'd agreed to meet the family in the baggage claim area. She hadn't had a chance to talk to Gran alone, and she was eager to learn more about that test Gran had not wanted her to discuss with anyone else.

A stream of disembarked passengers moved toward her down the escalator leading from the trams on the second floor. Her gaze roamed over the unfamiliar faces and then it stopped at the sight of her grandmother. Gran looked ... well, healthy and happy. The worry about her that had stayed at the back of her mind eased a bit. She waved back at her mother.

Hurrying toward her on sandaled feet, Donna Jordan looked much too young to be the mother-of-the-bride. Her father lengthened his stride at her mother's side.

Sensing their excitement, love filled Em. They'd always been her best supporters. She ran to them.

"Welcome to Florida! I'm so glad you're here!"

"Where's Ava?" Gran said, looking around.

"She's back at the cottage. She wanted to go swimming in the pool with Devin. I think she's planning on showing you a somersault," said Em. "They've been practicing."

"Well, then, we'll be sure to pay attention," said Gran. She took hold of Em's arm and gave it a squeeze as they watched her parents head for one of the baggage belts.

Em studied her. "You all right, Gran?"

"I'll know for sure in a couple of days. But I need you to be quiet about this. Neither your sister nor your mother know anything about the biopsy. I'm pretty sure it's some sort of cyst like always."

Em zeroed in on Gran's face, one hand on her hip. "And if it isn't?"

"Then, my dear, we'll deal with it as gracefully as we can," Gran replied, straightening with a familiar look of determination.

Em swallowed hard. Women fought these worries every day. She just hoped when the result came in, it was a good one for Gran.

After all the luggage was gathered, Em led them to her car. They quickly loaded their things, climbed in, and were on their way.

"Two small beach weddings in the family," Em's father said with a teasing grin. "I like it."

"Me too." Though this wedding wasn't anything like Em had always planned, she loved the idea of being married at the same place where she fell in love.

"It's too bad Devin has no real family to speak of," Em's mother commented. "But after getting to know him through Elena and Andrew and now you, we'll welcome him as our own."

"Devin's friends, Allie and Doug Masters, had to cancel their plans to come to the wedding, so that will mean a lot to him." Em thought of the lost necklace and how that was supposed to represent Devin's mother at the wedding and bit her lip.

At the cottage, Ava ran to greet the family in the pink-flowered bathing suit she'd picked out in Ellenton. "You're here! You're here!" she cried, jumping up and down in her excitement.

"Hi, Ava! Let me give you a hug!" said Em's mother.

Ava allowed a quick hug and then took her hand. "*Abuela*, come see me swim. *Papi* and I can do a trick for you."

Devin appeared in red swim trunks, his body glistening with rivulets of pool water. "Hi, everyone! Welcome! Ava and I have prepared a little show for you after you get settled."

"Now, *Papi*!"

Devin shook his head firmly. "Give them a chance to change their clothes and get something cool to drink."

Ava kicked at the grass with a bare foot but she didn't say anything. "Thanks for understanding, Ava. Do you want to show your grandparents to their room?"

Ava's face brightened. "Okay." She took her grandfather's hand. "Come. I know your room."

Em's mother and Devin followed them.

Em led Gran inside through the front entrance. "And you, Gran, will be sharing Ava's room. I hope that's all right."

"It will be fine for tonight, my dear." A flush of color rose in Gran's cheeks. "Tomorrow, I'm going to move to the Salty Key Inn." Gran winked at her. "Something else your mother and sister don't know."

Em felt her eyebrows leap. "And just what are you doing there?"

Gran's face broke into a wide grin. "Meeting Bart. I decided to close Rainbow's End for the weekend so he could be here with us."

"Oh, my god! The two of you together? That's wonderful, Gran!" Em wrapped her arms around her grandmother and squeezed her with joy. "I knew you had dinner together a time, or two, or three, but I never dreamed ... You always said you didn't need a man ..." Giggling stopped Em's words.

Gran straightened. "Like you, I'm allowed to have a change of heart."

"Oh, Gran, I love you," said Em, hugging her again.

"What's all the excitement?" asked her mother, coming into the living room, followed by Em's father, Devin, and Ava.

She started to laugh and shook her head. "Gran will have to tell you. Not me."

Blushing like a school girl, Gran told them what she'd planned.

Into the shocked quiet that followed, Em's father said, "Mom, you always said you'd never date, never bother to marry. What's going on? I thought you turned down Bart many years ago."

"I did," she said, "but by the time I could tell him I had a change of heart, it was too late."

Em's mother hugged Gran. "Well, this wedding is turning out to be more romantic than I dreamed. Good for you, Julia. I say enjoy every minute you can with him."

Gran bobbed her head. "Well, that's settled then.

Tomorrow, I'll move to the Salty Key Inn. Bart reserved the honeymoon suite for us."

Em and Devin exchanged smiles. Things with Gran and Bart had heated up fast.

"Can you come watch my trick now?" said Ava, breaking into the stunned silence.

That afternoon, Elena and Andrew brought the baby over to visit. The glow on Elena's face amused Em. A getaway was just what her sister needed.

When they heard the news of Bart and Gran joining them at the Salty Key Inn, Elena and Andrew were as surprised and pleased as everyone else.

"It's got to be serious, Gran," said Elena. "You never close the store."

"At my age, it'd better be serious. Neither of us have the time to just fool around." The minute the words left Gran's mouth, her cheeks flamed a bright red. "I didn't mean ... oh, heck. You know what I mean ..."

"Just stop now," warned her son, and everyone laughed.

"Tonight, we're doing a barbeque here for dinner," Em announced. "Tomorrow, I thought we'd all go out for dinner. There are a couple of good bars along the beach with all different kinds of food."

"And Saturday, we have the wedding dinner at Gavin's," said her mother. "I can hardly wait."

"Okay, for now, how about Andrew and I act as bartenders and later, David and I will be the grill masters," said Devin.

Em's father stood and coughed, as he sometimes did before he got emotional. "Devin, son, you can call me Dad, like Andrew does."

Em's eyes filled. She exchanged watery glances with her

mother. She'd already suggested Devin call her Mom, if he felt comfortable with it.

Devin went over to her father and shook his head. "Deal ... Dad."

Ava frowned. "That's not Dad. That's Grandpa."

"To you," Devin said. "But to me, he'll be Dad. Fair enough?"

She studied them both a moment. "Okay, *Papi*."

"A lot to figure out," commented Gran.

"A whole lot more to come, I'm sure," agreed Em.

Later, lying next to Devin, Em felt the heat of his body seep into her, bringing her a sense of deep contentment. He was her man, the father of the child she'd promised to help raise, the friend she'd always needed to steady her.

He turned to her and cupped her face in his capable hands. "Happy?"

"Yes, it's going to be a lovely wedding. I'm so happy my family loves you, Devin. It took my father a while to have Andrew call him Dad, but he's taken to you right away."

"He's a good man. You know, I never had the reason to call anyone Dad before. Now, I can, and it's because of you."

Devin's lips came down on hers, gentle at first and then more demanding, increasing the need in Em to show him how much she cared. She moved closer, fitting her body to his, smiling when he reacted. He was perfect.

At breakfast, Em poured herself a second cup of coffee and took it out to the front porch. The day was unusually hot with summer afternoon storms predicted and cooler weather coming in with the next cold front due that night.

Em's mother came and sat down beside her. "How are you doing?" she asked quietly. "Have you been working on your wedding vows? Devin mentioned an acquaintance of his from Miami is going to marry you."

"Yes. I haven't met him yet, but I understand he's very nice. Apparently, he's done this for another doctor in his practice. I've decided not to get too formal about my vows, just let my heart speak for itself."

"I'm sure that's all you need to do. It's going to be so nice to have you happily settled with Devin, and I adore Ava."

Em shook her head. "I've got a lot to learn. You saw the scrapes on Ava's body. I should have been more careful, more alert."

Em's mother shook her head and placed a hand on Em's. "Motherhood is a difficult job. Don't be too hard on yourself. You're a loving, caring person. That's the most important thing." She gave Em's hand a squeeze. "I still have your dolls from childhood ready to share with children of your own. That's how well you took care of them."

Em grinned. "Ava will love them!"

"See what I mean? You're a natural. Relax and enjoy the ride! It never stops, you know."

"What? Motherhood?"

Em's mother nodded. "You're still and will always be my baby."

They hugged, and then Em rose. "Guess I'd better check to see how the rest of the family is. We've planned a lazy day."

Later, she took advantage of having some time alone on the porch to think about her wedding vows. After writing down a few notes and crossing them out, she decided to do as she'd said and simply speak from the heart.

Devin approached her. "Looks like everyone is busy. Your mother is with Ava and your father is driving Gran to the airport to meet Bart. Want to take a walk on the beach with me?"

"Sure." She looked out the window. "It looks like rain already."

Devin held out his hand, and she took it. Stepping outside, she saw that the gray streaks of early morning had widened and spread across the sky. In the onshore breeze, the fronds of the nearby palm trees whispered a warning of a change in the weather. Em fell into step beside Devin as they headed onto the sand.

"Can you believe my grandmother is actually dating? She and Bart were an item at one time, but I never thought she'd end up dating him."

Devin grinned. "I think it was a big surprise to your father."

"I can't imagine what he's going to say to Bart when he sees him. I hope he doesn't go all protective and scare Bart away."

Devin laughed. "Gran won't let him. I really like your family."

"It's your family now, Dev."

"Yes, I know."

"I'm so sorry about the necklace. I know I've already apologized, but I have to mention it again."

He shrugged. "Accidents happen."

Em lifted his hand to her lips and kissed it. "Love you."

"I know," he replied, sounding for the moment like Ava, bringing a smile to her lips.

The rain that had been promised pounded on the roof of Seashell Cottage with steady, thunderous beats.

"A real tropical rain," declared her father looking out at the beach. Foamy crests atop the waves were in contrast to the deep, gray color the Gulf water had adopted in the storm.

"A good afternoon for naps and family games," said Em's mother, coming to stand beside them.

"Why don't we just do pizza tonight?" Em suggested. "There's a great pizza restaurant in home delivery range."

"Sounds perfect. I'm saving my appetite for Gavin's tomorrow."

The afternoon and evening before her wedding turned out to be a special, low-key, family time. Elena, Andrew, Gran, and Bart joined them for dinner and left early to go back to their hotel.

After Ava had gone to bed, Em sat with Devin and her parents, enjoying a private moment with them.

"So now that you're settled, your mother and I have decided to take some time off and do some traveling. I won't be ready to retire for some time, but I'm going to take more vacation time in the coming years." Her father leaned back against the couch and beamed at her.

"We're going to be downsizing," her mother said. "We don't want the care of a large home anymore. Would you kids be interested in buying the house?"

"But it's your home to Elena and me," protested Em.

"No, Em. It's time for you to make a real family home for yourself," her father reminded her.

Em exchanged questioning looks with Devin. "What do you think, Devin?

"It's a great house in one of the best parts of town," said Devin. "I'm sure we can get it at a bargain price," he said with a straight face.

Em's father laughed. "Not so fast. We've already had an appraisal done on it. Fair market value is what we'll be expecting."

"What will Elena say?" Em knew no matter the price, the house would be a steal. Her parents had taken excellent care of it, making updates on a regular basis.

"I'm sure she'll be pleased for you," Em's mother said.

"We'll discuss it and get back to you," said Devin. "I like the idea."

"Good enough," said Em's father. "You have enough to think of right now."

Talk turned to the wedding and how her father would escort Em to the ceremony site on the beach.

Soon, her mother rose. "Time for this mother-of-the-bride to retire." She beckoned to her husband with a curled finger.

He jumped up from the couch. "Coming, sweetheart." Grinning, he turned to Em and Devin. "This wedding is turning out to be very romantic."

"Eeek! TMI, Dad," said Em, laughing. "Too much information. Go!"

Left alone in the living room, Devin turned to her. "What do you think about the house, Em? I didn't want to say too much without talking to you first."

"I would love to live in that house. I'd want to make changes to wall colors and use our own furniture and all, but it's a great house for Ava and any other children we have."

Devin grinned. "That's what I thought. We'll talk to our real estate agent when we get back from our honeymoon."

"Honeymoon? I can't wait!" Em exclaimed.

"You don't have to," Devin said, pulling her up from the couch into his arms. "Come right this way."

CHAPTER TWENTY-SIX

When Em stepped out the door the next morning, the deep blue of the sky met her gaze. She sighed with relief. The cold front had moved into the area with temperatures in the high seventies. Hibiscus blossoms in nearby bushes were colorful clumps drenched with rain but would open in time for the four o'clock wedding. She felt a little disoriented as she looked around, thinking of the upcoming ceremony. For so many years, she'd imagined her wedding in New York on a brisk, wintery, Valentine's Day. This was so not what she'd planned. Yet, she couldn't wish for a more perfect setting.

She headed toward the beach, wanting time alone. For her, the beauty of the sand, beach, and birds was as calming as a mantra, and today she wanted a few moments to think of all she had to be grateful for. She walked down to the edge of the water and stood a moment staring at the sunshine mirrored on top of the water in sheets of bright light. Enjoying the beauty of it, she drew a deep breath.

"Beautiful, huh?" came a voice behind her.

Em whirled around to face her grandmother. "Gran! What are you doing here?"

"I just heard from the doctor's office."

Em's heart bumped to a stop and then raced ahead. "And?"

"And everything's all right. I have to admit I was scared, too scared to tell anyone. But the mass is benign."

Em threw her arms around Gran. "Wonderful news! It's the best wedding present ever!"

"You'd think at my age I'd be past worrying like this."

She took hold of Gran's hand. "Stand here with me a moment. It's so peaceful."

As they stood together, Em lifted her face to the sun and whispered a silent, "Thank you". She knew Gran wouldn't always be around, but she was grateful for each moment they had together.

As she turned to go back to the cottage, Gran said, "What's this? A shell?" She bent over and picked up something from the sand.

Em stared at the gold necklace in Gran's hand. "Oh my God!"

"What is it?" Gran said.

"It's the necklace Devin gave me! It belonged to his mother. Ava lost it, and now you've found it." Em couldn't stop the tears of joy that filled her eyes. She knew how much it would mean to Devin to have her wear it. She held up a finger to her lips. "We won't tell anyone about it. I want it to be a surprise for him."

"It's a sweet, little, golden sun," said Gran. "So appropriate."

"In so many ways," said Em, swiping her tears away. When she got back to the house, she'd tuck it safely away.

The day that began so quietly turned into one filled with activity. The women set off for a morning of pampering before the preplanned bridal luncheon Elena was hosting. The men had made reservations to play golf and headed out after a quick breakfast.

At the beauty parlor, Em sat with the women in her family, grateful for their presence. Watching Ava get her toes painted, a warm feeling filled her. She'd dreamed of having a little girl of her own, and though Ava didn't look like the mental picture she'd had of her child, she felt doubly blessed because Ava was such an unexpected gift.

Just then, Ava looked up at her and smiled. "Pretty!" She wiggled her toes, showing off the pale purple polish on her toenails.

Em returned the smile. Ava was so adorable.

Elena nursed the baby while sitting in the spa chair getting her nails done. Sighing with satisfaction, she gave Em a thumbs-up. "Best decision ever to pamper ourselves."

Gran held up her hands and wiggled her fingers. "I haven't had such a nice manicure in forever. Working with flowers is hard on your hands."

Rather than have a fancy hair-do, Em decided to leave her hair long and straight. The humid air and the salty breeze would ruin any attempt to do differently, and she liked how Devin often stroked her hair.

After they left the salon, they headed to the Pink Pelican Restaurant on St. Pete Beach for a light lunch. Em paused as she stepped inside. Turquoise linen cloths covered the tables. Light coral napkins sat folded at each place near crystal water goblets and shiny silverware. She loved the tropical feel of the setting.

A hostess met them at the door and led them to a table in a corner where they could have privacy. "I hear we have a bride in the group," the hostess said, smiling at them.

"It's *Mami,*" said Ava. "I'm a bride too."

Em joined in the laughter, though Ava spoke the truth. The wedding was more than Em and Devin marrying. It was all three of them forming a family.

The seafood on the menu was appealing, but Em suddenly felt too excited to eat. To be polite, she ordered only a small salad with shrimp on top.

Her mother gave her a knowing look. "Excited?"

Em bobbed her head. "It may seem silly, but I'm nervous.

I've waited so long for this moment and now that it's here, I wonder how everything is going to work out. It all happened very fast."

Her mother gave her an encouraging smile. "I've seen how you and Devin are together, learned what kind of man he is, and I have no worries about the two of you or the three of you."

"You're right," Em said. "I hope it's everything Devin wants."

"Sweetie, I've seen the way he looks at you. Relax. This is a time to enjoy yourself. Remember when you asked me how I knew it was Dad for me? I told you we were friends first. That's what you and Devin have ... a friendship built on open communication and so much more."

"I've never had a friend like him," admitted Em. "And the so much more is ... so much more!"

Em and her mother laughed.

With the jitters dismissed, Em was suddenly famished and settled down to enjoy the last meal she would have as Emerson Jordan.

After lunch, Em felt as if she'd stepped into a perfect dream as she took a shower and began to get ready for the wedding. She'd declined to have her makeup done professionally, but spent time doing it herself. Wrapped in a terry-cloth robe she padded into the kitchen to check on the flowers Gran had ordered. They'd been delivered earlier.

When she saw the bouquet of delicate orchids and fragrant freesia, tears filled Em's eyes. The bouquet was elegant in its simplicity. Smaller bouquets had been made for Elena, Ava, and her mother, along with a matching boutonnieres for Devin, Andrew, and her father.

Gran came into the kitchen. "How'd I do with the flowers?"

Em wrapped her arms around her. "They're perfect."

"I just got a call from Bart. Devin and the guys are resting at our suite until the wedding. Your father will be here to change soon. He's as excited as I've ever seen him, but then he's always wanted to see his girls happily settled."

"What about you? How's he handling his mother being in the dating scene?"

Gran chuckled. "He's a little more than surprised by how things are turning out between Bart and me, but he's relieved too that he won't have to worry about me so much anymore."

"What are you two talking about," said Em's mother, coming into the kitchen with Ava.

"Your husband," said Em. "Seems like he's not used to his mother dating."

Em's mother shook her head. "Don't worry about him. He gets a little over protective sometimes." She put her arms around her mother-in-law. "I'm happy for you, Julia. You've lived alone for too many years."

"Thanks," her grandmother said. "I never thought I'd say this, but I really love that guy. We missed our chance once; we don't want to miss it again."

"This is such a special occasion for so many reasons," said Em's mother, wrapping her arms around Ava.

"An understatement," said Gran, smiling. "Now let's get ready for my granddaughter's big moment. Devin's friend has already arrived to perform the ceremony and is with the guys at the Salty Key Inn.

"*¡Mami,* you're a princess!" cried Ava, clapping her hands together with glee, staring at Em.

Em studied herself in the mirror scarcely believing how the dress transformed her from Em Jordan, owner of Living

Designs, into Emerson Jordan, bride of the day. Or maybe it was the radiant smile on her face that made such a difference. But at the moment, what she saw was something she liked. Her blond hair swung easily at her shoulders; her blue eyes shown with eagerness. Her sleeveless dress clung to her breasts and waist, then fell to her ankles in silken folds. Her feet would remain bare.

Her mother stood back and gazed at her tearfully. "You're lovely. A beautiful, beaming bride."

The bedroom door opened and Elena and Gran entered dressed for the occasion.

"Oh, Em. I love it!" gushed Elena. "The dress is even prettier than I remembered. You look stunning."

Em's mother handed her a box. "Here are the diamond and pearl earrings I wore to my wedding. I want you to use them today. Elena wore them for her wedding too."

Thanks," Em said. With trembling fingers, she slid them through the lobes of her ears. "Now I have one more thing to add, and then I'll be ready." She went to her bureau and brought out the gold necklace. She leaned over and showed it to Ava.

"Gran found the necklace we lost, Ava. You can help her put it around my neck. I have a feeling that will make you feel better about losing it. This will be our wedding surprise for *Papi.*"

"Okay." Ava handed the necklace to Gran.

Gran hooked it around Em's neck. Nestled against her skin, the tiny glitter of gold seemed to wink at her. "Okay, I'm ready. Where's Dad?"

"Your father is in the hallway, waiting for you."

"Be prepared. He's going to cry," said Elena. She opened the bedroom door and Em stepped into the hallway to see tears filling her father's eyes.

"Gorgeous, honey," he managed, giving her a careful hug. "Don't want to mess you up," he explained. "And this is Josh Franco, Devin's friend who is going to perform the ceremony."

Em's gaze settled on a young, balding man with a friendly smile. He held out his hand. "I'm very happy to meet you. Sorry we didn't have time to meet before now, but I feel I already know you. Devin's been talking about you ever since he got back from his vacation here at Seashell Cottage."

"I've heard good things about you," said Em. "Thank you for being part of our celebration. It means a lot to both of us."

Josh checked his watch. "Guess I'd better get out to the beach. Devin's waiting there for you, along with the guitarist, Andrew, and the baby."

He held out his arm to Em's mother. "I'm to walk you out to the beach. Bart is waiting outside to walk with Gran. Give us all a few minutes to get out there, and then, Elena, you and Ava follow. Then Em and her father. Everyone got it?"

Em took a last look at Ava. Wearing the purple party dress that she'd chosen, Ava looked like a tropical flower. The flouncy skirt of the dress fluttered with her restless movement. Em leaned over and kissed her cheek. "You're the one who looks like a little princess."

Ava pointed one foot in front of her and did a little curtsy, like the princess she wanted to be.

Elena and Em exchanged amused glances. Ava played the part well.

CHAPTER TWENTY-SEVEN

Moving toward the protected spot on the beach where Devin waited for her, Em felt as if she were floating. The scene seemed so right. The smile that crossed his face at the sight of her wavered as emotion took over. He swiped at his eyes and then straightened, his gaze remaining on her.

Em had never felt more connected to another person. Knowing this was just the beginning of a life with him filled her with joy. She quickened her steps, making her father move faster. Laughing softly, he whispered, "Hold on! He's not going anywhere!"

The guitarist continued to play Pachelbel's Canon in D as Em came to Devin's side.

"So beautiful," murmured Devin, kissing her on the cheek and taking hold of her hand. His eyes widened when he saw the necklace.

"You found it?"

"Yes," Em said. "Your mother is here with us now."

His eyes welled with tears. He responded with a nod of acknowledgement.

They stood side by side before Josh as her family formed a loving circle around them.

Josh welcomed the family and then led them through the traditional words of a wedding ceremony. When it came time to exchange rings, Em's father handed Devin the wedding band he and Em had chosen together. Devin signaled to Ava to join him.

She came to his side and together they helped slide the ring onto the proper finger on Em's left hand.

"We promise to love you, protect you, and do everything in our power to make you happy."

"Me, too, *Mami*," said Ava.

Devin gazed into her eyes with such tenderness Em's breath caught. "I've loved you more in the last few months than some people can love in a lifetime," continued Devin. "I want to share all that life has to offer with you, including many more children. You make me a better person and a happy man. I promise to give you all that I have of myself to make you as happy as you make me. I promise you this with all my heart."

When it came time for her to say her vows it was easy for her to speak from the heart. "I, Emerson Jordan, promise you, Devin Gerard, that I will love you always, take care of you when you need it, and support you and your work giving time to others to help them have a better life. I promise that life with you will include time for a dance or two, lots of love, and like the sun shining down on us, will be as warm and wonderful as this moment between us. I swear this in your mother's memory and thank her for giving me such a wonderful man to love."

She slid the ring onto his finger and smiled as he leaned forward to kiss her.

A moment later, Em felt a tap on her hip and stepped back. Ava stared up at her. "*Mami*, are you and *Papi* going to keep kissing?"

"Always," Em said, bringing soft laughter from the others.

Josh said a few more words and then, "I now pronounce you man and wife."

Devin didn't wait. He swept her up in his arms. "Care to dance, Mrs. Gerard?"

"Of course," Em said, taking hold of his hand and moving

with him to the sound of "My Funny Valentine" coming from the guitar.

"Happy Valentine's Day, darling," Devin whispered in her ear.

"And to you, Devin," she said, meaning it with her whole being. This was the best Valentine's Day wedding she could imagine as she danced across the sand with the man who made her heart sing.

Thank you for reading *Change of Heart*. If you enjoyed this book, please help other readers discover it by leaving a review on Amazon, Goodreads, or your favorite site. It's such a nice thing to do.

Enjoy an excerpt from my book, *Coming Home* – A Chandler Hill Inn Book (Book 2 in the Chandler Hill Inn Series.)

CHAPTER ONE

Camilla Chandler walked through the vineyards at Chandler Hill in the Willamette Valley of Oregon toward the grove of trees that meant so much to her. The ashes of her grandmother, Violet "Lettie" Chandler, now resided there along with the ashes of her mother, Autumn, Lettie's husband, Kenton, and Rex Chandler, Lettie's father-in-law and the original owner of the inn and winery that Cami had just inherited.

The gray skies of this cool fall morning held a promise of rain, which suited her mood. The raindrops slated to fall would match the tears she'd somehow managed to hold onto after weeping for days at the loss of her grandmother, a woman beloved not only by Cami, but by all who knew her. For eighteen months of Cami's first two years, Nonnee had raised her, forming an early, loving bond between them. And then, when Cami was only six, Lettie stepped in to take the place of Cami's mother after Autumn was hit and killed by a car while jogging one day.

Cami lifted her face to the sky and watched as a red-tailed hawk circled in the air above her and then glided down to perch on the limbs of a tall white oak, part of the collection of trees that was her destination. As her grandmother had done, Cami sought refuge and answers among the pine and hardwood trees that rose from the earth in a sturdy cluster—sentinels keeping watch over the vines that lined the hillsides like promises of good things to come.

Cami entered the inner circle of the trees and sat on the stone bench that had been placed there long before her birth.

"What a mess," Cami blurted before she could stop herself. Wrapping her arms around herself, she wished she had worn her sweater. The crisp fall cold seeped into her bones as she began to cry. If Nonnee were here, she would hug her and tell her everything would be all right. But at the moment, nothing seemed all right. Especially after receiving the email from Bernard.

Cami rocked in her seat, wishing there was an easy way to get rid of the pain. "Bernard Arnaud is a ... a ... jerk!" Her angry cry filled the air and bounced off the branches and boughs of the trees, making it seem as if their echoes confirmed her opinion of him.

She could hear her grandmother's words in her head. "Take a deep breath, darling, and begin at the beginning."

Following those silent instructions, Cami drew in air, straightened, and spoke aloud. "Nonnee, I thought he loved me. I thought he understood I had to come home to Chandler Hill, that I owed it to my family to be here. After our many months of being together, he called those days ... and nights ... a fun romance. And now, he doesn't want to see me anymore! After I helped to bury you, he told me this in an email ... an email for God's sake!"

Cami fisted her hands as fresh tears rolled down her cheeks. "I feel so ... so ... stupid!"

A sparrow landed on the ground not far from her and peered up at her with dark eyes, like a messenger sent by her grandmother. How she missed her!

Cami bowed her head. As strange as others might think of

it, sitting in the grove, giving up her secrets brought answers. Though all of her Chandler relatives were deceased, they still spoke to her in memories and in stories others shared about them. They were fine people—her mother, grandmother, and the two Chandler men who'd given Nonnee the challenge of making the Chandler Hill Inn and Winery what they were today. Now, it was up to Cami to keep the enterprise healthy and strong. She knew it was an inheritance some people would love to have, but with the breakup with Bernard, it had already cost her dearly. And at twenty-three, Cami wondered how she could ever meet the challenge Nonnee had passed on to her.

The cool breeze blowing through the pines filled the air with whispers. Cami cocked her head to listen. No answers seemed clear but one. Somehow, she'd have to find the courage and strength within her to keep things going. If Nonnee, all five-feet-three inches of her, could do that, then so would she.

Cami stood to leave. Hearing a noise behind her, she turned to see Rafe Lopez walking toward her. Her lips curved, and she lifted a hand in greeting. Her grandfather was a striking man in his early seventies who was struggling with Nonnee's recent death. Cami and her grandfather, Rafe, had always had a close bond, and now that it was just the two of them living in Nonnee's house, they'd grown even closer.

She'd always called him Rafe, even as a child. When it was suggested she call him Grandpa, she'd stamped her toddler foot and said, "No! My Rafe!" He loved it then, and he loved it now.

"Thought I'd find you here," said Rafe. "Get a few things settled in your mind?"

She smiled sadly. "There are no simple answers, are there?"

He shook his head. "Life is anything but simple. May I sit

with you?"

"Sure." She sat and indicated a place for him next to her. "What's up?"

"I just talked to Paloma. She's decided to leave Chandler Hill to live in Arizona with her daughter and her family."

Cami's eyes widened. "But Paloma has been almost as big a part of Chandler Hill as Nonnee."

"Yes, but now that her best friend is gone, and with her new inheritance, Paloma is free to leave." The sadness in his eyes reflected her own. "A lot of things will never be the same."

"I heard that Abby wants to retire by the end of the year." Cami let out a worried sigh. "Sometimes I feel so alone."

Rafe put an arm around her. "You've always got me. But I think it's time for me to move. I'd like to take over the cabin after Paloma is gone. What do you say?"

"You don't want to stay in the house with me?" Cami asked, genuinely surprised.

"Too many memories there. And the cabin is a special place for me. It's where I first spent time with Lettie. Of course, after all the renovations we've done, it's not a simple cabin anymore, but a very nice place for an old man like me."

Cami hugged him. "A very special old man. I'll miss you, but I agree. It's right for you to be on your own without worrying about me." She studied him with tenderness. "But I'll always be there for you, Rafe. A woman couldn't have a better grandfather than you."

He cupped her face in his broad, strong hands. "You'll never know what a gift you are to me, my granddaughter. I never suspected your mother was my child. When I found out, I cried with joy. And now I have you."

Cami had heard this story many times. It was a sweet one. She couldn't help wondering who her own father was. It was something her mother had refused to divulge. But someday, maybe when things were in better shape at the inn, Cami intended to find out. She needed to know.

Some families were complicated, she thought as she got to her feet once more. She held out a hand to her grandfather.

He took it and rose. "Ready to go home?"

"I guess so." *Home was as complex as her family.*

Cami sat in the office within the inn and stared out the window. The room and its history weighed heavily on her shoulders. She'd met with lawyers regarding the transfer of ownership of the inn and vineyards from her grandmother to her, but when she'd asked to see information from the financial advisor, he'd sent her an accounting of Nonnee's investments and requested that the meeting she wanted with him be postponed for two weeks while he dealt with some other issues. Overwhelmed by all the new information thrown at her, Cami had readily agreed.

Now, it was time to decide which of her available funds she'd use for the upgrades to the guest rooms the inn manager, Jonathan Knight, was insisting be done. Jonathan, the young manager Nonnee had hired just before she was diagnosed with cancer, was not one of Cami's friends. He'd all but sniffed his disapproval when Cami told him he would now report to her.

"But you have no experience in the hotel business," he'd protested. "I understand you studied Fine Arts in college. That certainly doesn't qualify you to run an operation like this."

"Nevertheless, I own the entire business," said Cami sweetly, though inwardly she was seething at the insulting tone of his voice.

"Cami? Mr. Evans is here to see you," announced Becca Withers, her assistant, startling her out of her memory of that encounter.

Cami smiled. "Thanks, Becca. Please ask him to come on back." Cami had had a couple of telephone conversations with him. Dirk Evans had sounded very smart, very polished, very cocky. Becca showed Dirk into the office and, standing behind him, waved a discreet hand in front of her face to indicate she thought he was a hottie.

Tall, with sun-streaked brown hair and fine features, he swept into the room and beamed at Cami. Through lenses in black eyeglass frames, his blues eyes surveyed her.

From behind the desk, she rose to shake his hand. "Hello, Dirk. We meet at last."

"My pleasure. Photographs Lettie had of you on her desk don't do you justice."

"Yes, well, have a seat and let's get down to business, shall we?" Cami said briskly. "I want to talk to you about my grandmother's portfolio. We're about to start a renovation project at the inn, and I'm going to need to sell some more stocks."

All confidence seemed to evaporate from him. He sank into a chair and faced her with a look of despair. "We've had some disappointments. One in particular."

A niggling feeling crept through Cami like a python, squeezing her insides. "You're not talking about the Montague Fund, are you? I directed you to sell that two weeks ago."

"Yes, I know. I tried to do that for you and all my clients, but there's a problem. It turns out that the Montague Fund was basically a Ponzi scheme. Most of the money is gone. I'm working on getting back what I can. I've already begun filling out claim papers, but it's going to take time for the Feds to sort through it." He pushed his glasses further up on his nose. "I was given reliable information on the fund, so I'm not sure what went wrong."

Cami's mouth went dry. She gripped the arms of her desk chair so tightly her fingers turned white. "What went wrong? My grandmother was a very conservative woman. I don't believe she would have wanted you to invest her money in something like that. Was she aware of what you'd done? Did she approve?"

"She told me to go ahead and do whatever I could to ensure you'd have enough money to carry on with the inn. The fund promised exceptional returns ..." his voice trailed off.

She narrowed her eyes and studied him. "So Nonnee didn't know?"

He looked at her and then away. "Not exactly."

"I could have you reported and perhaps have your license taken away," said Cami, "but then I guess I'm not the only client of yours who feels that way."

"I did nothing wrong," Dirk countered. "I got the information for the fund from a very reliable source. Believe me, you're not the only person who has been hurt by this."

Cami's lips thinned. "So that makes it all right?"

He shifted in his chair and looked away from her.

"Did everyone in your office suggest their clients invest in this fund?"

He shook his head. "Mr. Berman didn't like it, warned his clients against it."

Cami leaned forward and gave him a steady stare. "I want this entire portfolio transferred to him immediately. Understand?"

"But ..."

"Stay right here. I'm calling him now."

Dirk let out a snort of disgust. "You don't have to do that."

"But I do," she said, with a calmness she had to force.

Cami scrolled through her contact list and tapped in the number. She was immediately put through to Russell Berman.

He listened to her and then said, "I'd be honored to work with Lettie Chandler's funds, and now yours. I suggest going over everything, making sure that the remainder of the money is placed in safe, conservative funds."

"But Mr. Berman, what am I going to do? I need money to pay for the renovation of rooms." Cami felt like crying, but she refused to break down in front of Dirk.

"The market is volatile right now. Hold off on spending any money until I get things sorted out. Then, you and I can talk about funding the renovation of rooms."

"Okay, but the hotel manager isn't going to be happy about it," sighed Cami. As she hung up, she wondered why she felt as betrayed by Dirk as she had been by Bernard.

"Okay, Dirk," said Cami, getting to her feet. "I think we're done here."

He rose and turned to go, then turned back to her. "Maybe we could have dinner sometime."

Hysterical laughter bubbled inside her. *He'd ruined her future and was asking for a date?*

"Really? I don't think so. Goodbye, Dirk."

Later, repeating that conversation to Becca, she said, "Can you believe it?"

"Yes. Have you taken a look at yourself? Thin, but with curves any guy would go for, you're a stunning woman with that strawberry-blond hair and dark eyes. I'd kill for your looks."

Cami wrapped an arm around Becca. "You're adorable. Being short isn't bad, you know."

"And being a little round?" Becca said with an arched eyebrow.

"Cuddly and warm. I've seen the looks Jonathan Knight gives you."

Becca made a face. "Jonathan is in love with himself.

Haven't you noticed?"

The two of them looked at each other and laughed. Tall and broad-shouldered, Jonathan carried himself with confidence. His dark hair, green eyes, and strong features were undeniably attractive. His attitude, not so much.

"For the time being, I've given up on men," said Cami with feeling.

"Not me." Becca grinned. "And you have to admit that Dirk Evans is one hot guy."

"Yeah, but looks aren't everything, Becca." Cami recalled how handsome she'd thought Bernard was. Now, the memory of his face as he leaned down to kiss her made her stomach fill with acid.

Her meeting with Jonathan went no better than her talk with Dirk.

"You can't tell me the renovation program I've planned is kaput," he groused, sitting in the office he'd assigned her. "The timing of it is perfect. Cold winter months are slow at the inn. And if we're going to raise rates, we need to refresh the rooms."

"I don't have any answers yet," Cami said. "But give me time to come up with a plan."

Jonathan's lip curled with derision that matched his tone. "How can we work things out if we don't have the money to do it? It'll take a miracle."

Cami held up a hand to stop him. "I'll get back to you as soon as I can, Jonathan. That's all I can promise right now."

His silence screamed his anger as he stormed out of the office. Cami watched him leave, determined to show him just who she was. A Chandler and a Lopez.

About the Author

Judith Keim enjoyed her childhood and young-adult years in Elmira, New York, and now makes her home in Boise, Idaho, with her husband and their two dachshunds, Winston and Wally, and other members of her family.

While growing up, she was drawn to the idea of writing stories from a young age. Books were always present, being read, ready to go back to the library, or about to be discovered. All in her family shared information from the books in general conversation, giving them a wealth of knowledge and vivid imaginations.

A hybrid author who both has a publisher and self-publishes, Ms. Keim writes heart-warming novels about women who face unexpected challenges, meet them with strength, and find love and happiness along the way. Her best-selling books are based, in part, on many of the places she's lived or visited and on the interesting people she's met, creating believable characters and realistic settings her many loyal readers love. Ms. Keim loves to hear from her readers and appreciates their enthusiasm for her stories.

"I hope you've enjoyed this book. If you have, please help other readers discover it by leaving a review on Amazon, Goodreads, or the site of your choice. And please check out my other books:

The Hartwell Women Series
The Beach House Hotel Series
The Fat Fridays Group
The Salty Key Inn Series
Seashell Cottage Books
Chandler Hill Inn Series
Desert Sage Inn Series

ALL THE BOOKS ARE NOW AVAILABLE IN AUDIO on Audible and iTunes! So fun to have these characters come alive!"

Ms. Keim can be reached at **www.judithkeim.com**

And to like her author page on Facebook and keep up with the news, go to: **https://bit.ly/3acs5Qc**

To receive notices about new books, follow her on Book Bub - **http://bit.ly/2pZBDXq**

And here's a link to where you can sign up for her periodic newsletter! **http://bit.ly/2OQsb7s**

She is also on Twitter @judithkeim, LinkedIn, and Goodreads. Come say hello!

Acknowledgements

I want to thank my readers whose enthusiasm for my books makes all the hours of writing, editing, rewriting, re-editing, and rewriting worth it. You are the reason I keep on keeping on.

On a more practical note, I want to acknowledge my review team members for their input. It means a lot to have your kind of support. And not to be forgotten, I wish also to acknowledge the skill and efforts of my copy and line editor, content editor, book cover designer, and audio narrator and to thank them for their work. Thanks, Peter, Lynn Mapp, Lou Harper and Angela Dawe. You make my books come alive!

Made in United States
North Haven, CT
17 July 2022

21498556R00168